THE LAST SINGER

THE FALCON CHRONICLES BOOK 1

MARJORIE LINDSEY

CONTENTS

The Falcon Chronicles News Signup — v

1. No Way Out — 1
2. Femin Heritage Revealed — 4
3. Intruder From The Sky — 11
4. A Celebration — 16
5. What's In A Dream — 25
6. Unwelcome Journey — 29
7. Hypor City — 36
8. An Old Friend — 45
9. A Terrifying Threat — 57
10. The Recpod — 71
11. Work Break — 81
12. Cave of Secrets — 95
13. A Covert Investigation — 106
14. Rebel Attack — 117
15. The Premier Strikes Back — 130
16. The Betrayal — 141
17. Confinement — 153
18. A New Friend — 167
19. The Tattooed Trio — 178
20. A Deal With The Devil — 185
21. Delio's Deception — 193
22. The Diary Revealed — 202
23. Steepchase Confirmed — 211
24. The Games Begin — 216
25. A Dead Deal — 227
26. Escape From Hypor City — 234
27. The Second Diary — 250

Sign up and reviews 261
Dedication and acknowledgements 263
About the Author 265

THE FALCON CHRONICLES NEWS

Please visit my website (marjorielindsey.com) to sign up for the latest news about special book offers and for details about *THE LOST PROPHECY* - **The Falcon Chronicles Book 2.**

Copyright © 2017 by Marjorie Lindsey

1

NO WAY OUT

I'd never won an argument with my father and deep down I didn't expect to win this one, but I had to try.

"What if—"

Father's hand chopped the air like a guillotine. "Enough. You are eighteen. Tomorrow you must go to Hypor City. It's the law." He pushed away from the kitchen table and placed his empty glass carefully into the sink then glanced my way. "You're shivering, Brynna. Go back to bed."

My thin nightdress offered little protection against the cold kitchen air; bare feet didn't help. I trembled but didn't move, other than chafing my arms with my hands as I watched his movements.

Beyond him, through the window, the sun slanted early morning light across his gaunt cheeks. He winced as the first yellow rays stabbed his red-rimmed eyes. He lifted his hand, rubbed his brow then walked toward the outer door. He stopped to pull on boots and a padded jacket before stuffing a pair of thick gloves into his pocket. Every action slowed by fatigue.

Part of me wanted to let him go. I knew his need to enjoy

a quiet moment with his falcon; it was something we had in common. But time was running out and my future was at stake.

His fingers lifting the door latch acted like a trigger. My teeth chattered as I spoke. "B-but there must be exceptions—special circumstances."

From over his shoulder, he fixed me with an annoyed stare. "Not for us. How would it look if a councilor's daughter was excused from work duty? Be grateful you'll be able to come home to our island on work breaks. Others don't have that privilege."

"But Mother's eyes are getting worse. She'll soon need help." I gnawed at my bottom lip, tasting blood when I bit too hard.

"Your mother is my responsibility. You are considered a citizen of Hypor City and must fulfill your commitment." He opened the door a crack. "That's my final word."

The lock clicked quietly behind him.

It was an untenable argument, but I still hated that I'd lost.

"You won't win against Father." Jarryd, my brother, stepped out from behind a hallway pillar.

How much had he heard? Probably most of it, by the way he shook his head. Normally we had a good relationship but he couldn't understand my resistance to going to Hypor.

"Mind your own business."

"You have to grow up sometime, Bryn." His patronizing tone was unbearable. "Your friend Calia was excited to go. Why aren't you? What are you afraid of anyway?"

His unusually perceptive question ripped at my heart.

What do I fear?

That I won't like my job.

That I won't fit in.

That I'll be found out.

"Nothing you'd understand." I snarled back at him to conceal my hurt, shivering all the while.

He heeled off his slippers and pushed them toward me. "Put these on."

Ignoring his offer, I stalked past him and headed for my bedroom. Changing my nightwear for a warm tunic, tights and boots, I made for the back door. Needing a sympathetic ear, I followed the path to Mother's sanctuary.

2

FEMIN HERITAGE REVEALED

Mother's pride and joy, the old greenhouse, stood in its own garden.

Fifty yards from the house beyond several arrays of solar panels, it was here that I'd first learned to sing surrounded by lush flowering plants, aromatic herbs and plump vegetables. Next to the forest, it was my favorite place to be.

Today I didn't stop in the doorway to smell the lemon thyme and sweet basil that Mother had planted strategically at the entrance. Neither did I stop to admire the plate-sized blue hibiscus nor the ballooning skirts of the golden mallow.

"You're early." Her worsening eyesight had sharpened Mother's already acute hearing.

"I couldn't sleep." I didn't mention my conversation with Father.

"Tea?" She spooned dried leaves into two cups and filled them with hot water.

When she handed me one, I smelled the aroma and smiled at her choice. "Chamomile?"

She draped her shawl around her shoulders and carried

her cup to her favorite corner seat. "I know you're worried about going to Hypor City."

"I'm not like Jarryd, who seems to fit in anywhere." I lifted my cup and blew on the hot fragrant liquid before dropping into the seat beside her. "What if I don't like my job? What if people don't like me? What if someone suspects...?"

"So many what ifs." Mother laughed. "You won't know about your job until you try it. I'm sure you'll make new friends. As for being Femin, there's no reason for anyone to suspect, providing you obey the rules." She hesitated, and then her voice took on a wistful tone. "You can't stay on our island forever. It's time to grow up."

"That's just what Jarryd said, but he doesn't know what it's like to be different."

"*You* know you have a special gift, but others do not. Perhaps one day you can show the world who you are, but for now it must remain our secret."

FOR AS LONG AS I COULD REMEMBER, I'D SPENT MORNINGS IN the greenhouse with Mother. She gave me language lessons and taught me to sing. On my fifteenth birthday, everything altered.

That morning three years ago, coiling my long hair on the back of my neck, I looked into the mirror and got a shock. One of my blue eyes had turned amber.

I tore out of the house and fled along the path to the greenhouse.

"My eyes! Something's wrong with my eyes," I yelled as I entered. "What's happened to my eyes?" I was unable to stop panicked tears.

Mother squinted as she examined my mismatched eyes, then nodded and smiled as her fingers probed the neckline of my tunic and found an outline on my shoulder. "You have the birthmark as well."

I twisted my head and pulled at my shoulder until I saw the tiny raised shape. "Where did that come from? I don't remember seeing it before. It looks like a falcon." I dropped onto a nearby bench. "I don't understand why you're smiling. I look like a freak."

"Don't overreact. Today I can tell you that you are part of a special sisterhood. You are Femin and a healer."

Healer I understood, but it was the first time I'd heard the word Femin.

I wrinkled my nose in confusion. "What's a Femin?"

She sat beside me and took my hands in hers.

"Femin are, or were, singers from my village. Some were able to heal with their voices. The skill of healing appears at random. All Femin sing, but not all singers are healers. The Genetrix—the leader—of the first feminary was a healer. She founded the feminaries as sanctuaries. Femin were preservers of life, able to travel to other lands, cure diseases and provide aid. I am a healer and now so are you—or will be. You have a lot to learn."

"Why can't you heal your eyesight?"

She shook her head. "Only the Genetrix can heal my eyesight."

"You could go there—get healed, couldn't you?"

"When I left the feminary to marry your father, I lost my standing as part of the sisterhood. The Genetrix will no longer acknowledge me as Femin."

"That is so unfair." Injustice flared my temper. "You're still a healer."

"I've learned to live with it, my sweet. Nothing can be

done to change her mind." She smiled absently. "I still have wonderful memories of the feminary as well as a loving family."

"What was it like? Traveling and healing?" It was something I'd yearned for. To see what was beyond our island.

"It was exciting, visiting new cultures and new lands, but oh so long ago. When I settled here with your father, I restricted my visits to neighboring islands. When my eyesight started to weaken I had to stop completely. Now, Old Joe from the village delivers my healing potions by boat when needed locally."

"So it was on your travels that you learned all the languages you've been teaching me." I'd sometimes resented having to be inside on a sunny day, declining nouns or conjugating verbs, but now I understood the value of the lessons. Knowing several languages also meant I was able to qualify for a good job in Hypor City.

"Yes, it was a valuable experience. Perhaps one day you will have an opportunity to see the world as I did."

I liked the idea of belonging to a sisterhood of healers, especially ones that were able to travel. Maybe if I'd known earlier, I wouldn't have felt so lost and different growing up.

"Why didn't you tell me all this before now?" Resentment leaked into my voice.

"It was common practice in my village to wait until a girl became a woman before revealing the responsibility of our heritage. Also, even though you were singing almost before you could speak, I wasn't sure that you would be a healer."

"What about the falcon mark on my shoulder?"

"That's the sign of the healer. I have one too." She pulled up her sleeve and revealed a darkened patch of skin, profiling a falcon.

"That explains why I like falcons." I thought of Circe, my raptor. "But what about my eyes?"

"Wait a moment." She had retrieved a small worn trunk from behind a stack of empty plant pots. Once opened, she flicked through several items, finally removing a crinkled leather pouch. Inside was a blue lens, which she presented to me. "This belonged to your grandmother. She had mismatched eyes as well. Use it to cover your amber eye, then no one will suspect."

"Suspect what? Being Femin doesn't sound like a bad thing. Why do I have to hide my eyes?"

"Be patient, there's more to our story." She sipped her tea before continuing. "Three years ago, the Genetrix at Prima Feminary recalled all Femin. Healers no longer travel and singing outside the feminary is now forbidden. Your unusual eye coloring is a rare Femin trait. It would be easily spotted in Hypor City and reported. The same for your birthmark. Always keep your shoulder covered."

"Why has the Genetrix forbidden singing?"

"Her motive is a mystery. I left the feminary many years ago and only know about the ban on singing because the council on Hypor City agreed to uphold her edict. When you father told me of the decision, I was stunned."

"But we still sing here."

"Yes, but only the four of us know, and Jarryd understands that it can't be mentioned. It's why I asked you not to sing in front of your friends."

"Can I tell Calia about being a healer, maybe just the herbal part?" What would she think about my new abilities?

"No." There was finality in her tone that I didn't often hear. "This is our secret. You must not tell anyone—including Calia."

"Why?" I didn't like having to keep secrets, especially from my best friend.

"The Genetrix is powerful and her reach is long. If she suspects you might be Femin, she could demand your arrest and transport you to Prima Feminary. You might never be released."

My throat tightened. "Could she do that? Wouldn't Father be able to stop her?"

"Things have changed at the feminary and in Hypor City. There's a new Genetrix and a new head of council. I know it's difficult to understand, but we must be cautious and silent."

I was stunned, lost for words. I couldn't take it all in. Overnight, I'd become a different person. A person with dangerous secrets.

"Starting tomorrow, I will teach you specific tonal vibrations. Low ones heal by calming inflammation and negative energy in the body. I'll also show you the plants I use to make the tonics, potions and salves." Her hand dropped softly over mine. "With care, no one will suspect that you are Femin. Over time, you will come to appreciate your wonderful gift."

SINCE THAT CONVERSATION, I'D PUSHED THE WARNINGS FROM conscious thought. Instead, I focused on learning the secrets of tonal healing and the intricacies of herbal preparations. One day I hoped to become a Femin healer and travel to other lands, but for now, I had to face the reality of five years of work duty in Hypor City.

"If I can't sing in Hypor City, I might lose my healing skills." What I'd learned from Mother had become second nature and part of my being. "How can I survive without singing?"

"I'm sure you'll find a way. Femin are strong and resourceful." She touched her fingers to my face.

I pressed her palm to my cheek. "I don't like leaving you alone."

"You mustn't worry about me. As long as I'm on the island, I can see well enough to find my way." She smiled but her eyes no longer sparkled as they once had. "Drink up and let's enjoy our last morning singing together."

"Not our last. I'll be home on work breaks. We can sing together then." More for me than her, I held onto the thought that I'd be able to return to the island. The visits were one of the few privileges of being the child of a councilor and would only be for a couple of days, but gave me something to look forward to.

We sang all our favorite songs well into the afternoon. Our harmonies were sweeter than ever. Eventually, we stopped for refreshments. The silence, usually so noticeable after our vocal sessions, was broken by a strange buzzing. The grating noise rose and fell like a wave.

As Mother listened intently, I searched the sky overhead. Suddenly, she pointed toward the door. Sprinting the length of the greenhouse, I scoured the landscape through the glass, but nothing marred the view of the wildflower field and the forest beyond. The buzzing gradually faded.

"That was bizarre." I walked back to join her. "Have you ever heard anything like that before?"

She hesitated. "No, but I'm sure it's nothing to worry about."

I wasn't convinced.

3

INTRUDER FROM THE SKY

The sun was low in the sky when I left Mother at the greenhouse.

We hadn't discussed the buzzing again, but I decided to mention it to Father and Jarryd. They might know the cause. Perhaps someone from Hypor City was testing a new lander. I'd heard Father commenting that the councilors were always demanding upgrades to their transportation.

I didn't immediately head for home. Instead, I made for the falcons' mews. Thoughts of tomorrow were plaguing me again and seeing the birds always lifted my spirits.

Father's raptor eyed me carefully when I greeted it but didn't move on its perch. I crossed to the opposite cage and pulled on a glove. My falcon edged closer to the wire mesh. With a distinctive white chevron on her black chest, Circe made a striking picture. I opened the cage and thrust in my arm. She quickly hopped on, eager to get flying.

The heavy morning mist had long since burned off, leaving the air fresh and the ground moist. As I walked through the forest, the sun pushed long shadows through the green canopy and across the well-worn path. For the first time in my life, I felt at odds with the lush beauty of my island home. How could the day be so calm and perfect when my life was in turmoil?

I sensed my companion's impatience and lifted my arm as we reached a clearing. Her talons punctured my skin as she thrust from my arm.

"Ouch...Circe!"

Glove off, I sucked the red glob forming on my wrist then looked skyward. It wasn't her fault. She'd done what came naturally to falcons—secured her grip—before splaying the feathers of her powerful wings and thrusting her sleek body skyward. The fault was mine in ignoring the new leather gauntlet my father had given me, instead favoring my old gloves—thin as paper bark in places. Her raking talon had found a weak spot.

Circe's unique white and black markings were visible against the fading sky. She gained altitude but circled overhead, waiting. A quick flick of my fingers sent her off hunting.

As she soared, my heart lifted. I jammed on my glove and leaped onto the nearest boulder, then the next—even higher. The steep climb led to a ridge of granite folds and the place where I brought my joys and my sorrows.

From my favorite perch at the top of the world, the drowning sun sent a fan of color into the sky. A ribbon of light rippled toward me across the gray ocean. Below in the tiny harbor, abandoned fishing boats tugged at their moorings as the men trudged home to moss-covered cottages. On the wharf, two mangy dogs growled and wrangled over a discarded fish head. Lights glowed from the cottage where Calia's family lived. It had been my second home for much of my childhood. I'd miss it, and everything else that felt normal and comforting.

I knew the view by heart, but I wanted—needed—to sear it into my brain. This was my home—until tomorrow. I'd always known the time would come when I'd have to go to Hypor City, but it still felt unexpected, abrupt, and harsh. The thought of spending five years in an enclosed environment, without the sounds of birds, the smell of dewy grass, and the sight of sheltering trees, brought tears to my eyes. Tomorrow everything would change.

I crouched and clutched my jacket tighter as the chilled mountain breeze dropped the temperature. My light clothing offered little protection against the penetrating cold. Any other time I'd have followed the urge to abandon my rocky perch, but not today.

Circe's screech ripped the silence as she swooped into view. Her furious swoops overhead were accompanied by an odd buzzing—unnatural, disturbing, but somehow familiar.

I stood and scanned the sky. Nothing appeared in the gathering dusk. Instinctively, I shut my eyes, allowing my sound sense to follow the buzzing vibration and mentally chart its course. It was approaching. Fast.

I extended my arm and whistled. Within seconds, Circe slowed but didn't land. She continued to circle and let out a fierce squawk.

The buzzing was louder, harsher. It grated in my ears.

A strong instinct to hide sent me scrambling down the steep rocky trail toward the cover of the forest. From the lowest rock, I jumped to the ground and then raced into the trees toward an angled jag of granite. I pushed through a hawthorn hedge but Circe's piercing scream stopped me mid stride. I retraced my steps. Thorns snagged my clothes and hair. I burst into the clearing and searched the sky.

She floated aloft, her talons extended for battle with an unseen foe.

Then I saw it.

A watcher drone.

I remembered Jarryd's description of the ones being built in his lab.

An inverted bowl propped above three vertical legs that attached to a circular ring. Shaped like a lander, solar tiles covered the surface. Three rotors and several antennas protruded from the lower loop. Employed to patrol and protect the city, Jarryd had said. But why was it here? Ninety miles from Hypor?

The drone lost altitude, spun, then hovered a few feet above me. It remained stationary as two protrusions emerged from its underside and swiveled toward me. Circe squealed and attacked. I whistled for her to return to me, but she continued her assault. Unable to anticipate the rotors, her feathers flew in all directions. Eventually, she faltered and veered away but the drone gave chase.

I found a rock to throw but my aim was off. I let out a long, high-pitched yell and stretched my arms helplessly into the air toward it. "Go away! Leave her alone!"

The drone reeled back as if pushed by an unseen force. End over end, it receded into the darkening sky, finally toppling into the ocean.

Circe dived toward me.

I lifted my arm. She landed, restlessly clenching and releasing her talons.

"Are you hurt?" I hummed softly to settle her, then fingered her back and wings, checking for injuries. A few missing feathers but otherwise unharmed.

"Good girl. You must have damaged it." I stroked her breast and sighed while she watched with dark fathomless eyes. "That drone makes me even more leery of going to Hypor City tomorrow."

I jolted when Jarryd's voice rent the air.

"Bryn...na. Bryn...na. Where are you? Dinner's ready." He emerged into the clearing with his usual easy gait. "Hurry up, I'm hungry."

His earlier words still stung, but I couldn't contain my news. "Guess what I saw up there?" I pointed toward the sky. My gesture sent Circe aloft.

"What?" Hands on hips, his head cocked to one side. His mouth held its perpetual grin. "You look like you've just wrestled a bear."

I pulled a thorn from my jacket and brushed back my hair. It wouldn't make much difference, but I felt better. "You missed it. A drone was right here." I pointed to the space above my head. "Like the ones you told me about. You must have heard the buzzing on your way here."

He scanned the sky. "That's impossible. They only have a short range. Besides, they're restricted to the city. Perhaps it was a bird?"

Sometimes brothers were just irritating. This was one of them.

"Birds don't hum when they fly. It was definitely a drone." I crossed my arms trying to appear more imposing. It was silly because Jarryd had four inches on me and his muscled build made my slim body puny in comparison.

He gave me the once over then laughed. "Okay, okay. I believe you." He glanced up as he shrugged. "Let's go. Mother's waiting and I could eat a brick."

As he strode away, I gave the heavens one final glance. No drones, just the moon's full disc commanding the dark sky. An icy cold snaked over my skin. The moon was a threat of a different kind. A harbinger of a nightmare I couldn't escape. I prayed that this moon would pass without incident.

4
A CELEBRATION

Jarryd's longer strides stretched his lead toward home but he eventually slowed allowing me to catch up. "What's got you so quiet? Are you still worried about tomorrow?"

"A little." I didn't mention the full moon and my nightmares.

"You'll soon get used to living on Hypor, I did."

Jarryd had worked as an engineer on Hypor for three years. He came home on work breaks but further travel was restricted. My father rarely spoke about the city and my mother never left our island, so my brother was my only source of off-island information.

He patted my shoulder in brotherly fashion. "Follow the rules and you'll be fine. Your supervisor will watch you for a while to make sure you fit, but after that, it's easy."

I curbed my worries and focused on his words.

"Once you get settled, I'll take you to the recpod. They have a bunch of stuff to do there including rock climbing and an obstacle course. The activities mimic the ones in the games."

Rock climbing was Jarryd's thing, but an obstacle course sounded like fun. "What games?"

"It's called Steepchase. There's a monthly contest—kind of a trial run—and every twelve months there's the final competition. Training is crucial and experience helps. I enter the time trials almost every month. Only those with the best times compete in the final games. The winner of Steepchase can ask for almost any concession, even reduced work duty."

"You mean if you win you can leave Hypor City?" I liked the idea.

"I don't think anyone has left the city. The winners I've heard about opted for promotions and longer work breaks. Besides, Hypor provides for all your needs so there's no reason why anyone would want to leave."

Except if you want freedom, I mumbled to myself.

"What did you say?" he asked.

"I wondered if females are allowed to participate in the games?" I knew that women had restrictions on Hypor. It was another one of my objections to going. Equality was something I'd taken for granted growing up. Some of the city's rules felt oppressive.

Jarryd seemed oblivious to the implications of my question.

"A woman competed in the last two games. She was as big as some of the men. She didn't win, of course. As far as I know, only men have won." Jarryd put his hand on my shoulder. "I've made some good friends while training. You can too."

I hoped that was true. Because Father was a councilor and owned our island, the village children always treated me differently.

Calia was my closest friend, but our relationship

changed when we became teenagers. My desire was to stay on the island until I could fulfill my dream of becoming a healer like Mother had been. Her dream was to leave the island and become someone important in Hypor City. Our relationship remained, but it was strained. However, I missed her when she left for Hypor City three months ago and looked forward to seeing her again.

"Last year's winner was promoted to the Premier's personal guard," Jarryd continued. "He traveled with them to Nuvega." He said the name like it was a precious gem.

"What's Nuvega?"

"A friend told me it's another city, far away and full of excitement—unlike Hypor."

"Another city?" I was puzzled. "I didn't know there was another floating city."

"It's not on water. It's on another island, much larger than ours. Can you believe it?" His eyes widened.

"A city on land?" I mirrored his wonder, envisioning a replica of our island, with forests and rocks, green and lush, unlike the metallic domes of Hypor. "I'd love to see that. Maybe if I win Steepchase I could ask to go."

"Don't get your hopes up. You have to be really skilled to win Steepchase. It's a tough game and participants can get hurt."

The path split. Jarryd continued toward home as I veered right. "Don't be too long."

"I won't." I called to Circe and headed for the mews.

Inside, the falcons nestled into their feathers. Circe continued to watch me as if sensing that this would be our last time together, at least for a while. It was a comfort to know that Father's falcon keeper, Roddy, would care for her but our bond was deeper than bird and keeper. The thought of losing her daily companionship pulled at my heart.

Approaching home, an unlucky chestnut got the brunt of my frustration as I kicked it from the garden path. If only there was a way to remain on the island, with Mother and Circe. But I knew it was impossible. Rules were rules, as Father often said, and taking a job in Hypor City at eighteen was one of them.

My heart took another hit when I reached home.

The windows glowed with a soft yellow light. A familiar hint of mint wafted from the open door. As I entered, Mother placed steaming bowls of vegetables on the table. Despite her failing sight, she sensed my presence. I basked in the love and warmth of her smile. Something else I'd miss.

"Happy birthday, my sweet one." Her hug was warm, her kiss light on my cheek.

"Oh, I forgot. Happy birthday, Bryn." My brother gave me a one-armed hug. "But why only three plates on the table?"

"Father said to say 'Happy Birthday', Brynna. Unfortunately, he had to go back to the city," Mother responded. "Council business."

My father's absence felt like a slap. My face heated in anger.

Eighteenth birthdays were an important rite of passage—an entry into adulthood. It hurt that family and friends had enthusiastically celebrated Jarryd's eighteenth but Father wouldn't be here for mine. He had even made an appearance and given a short speech at Calia's small party before she left for the city three months earlier,

"He's never around lately. He has time for his falcon but not my birthday." I didn't try to disguise the peevish tone in my voice.

Mother calmed my disappointment by rubbing my

shoulders and then guided me to a chair festooned with scarlet ribbons and sprigs of rosemary.

Jarryd joined me at the table. "Too bad he's not here. We hoped to ask if he knew about any drone testing."

"What drones...what do you mean?" A well-masked vibration of fear hummed through Mother's question.

"Bryn saw a drone out near the rock fold, or at least says she did." He missed the dagger look I threw at him as he spooned potatoes into the last empty spot on his plate.

"Are you sure it was a drone?" Mother's face was inscrutable when she turned to me.

"Yes, I *saw* it." I sent my brother another scathing glance, but he remained focused on his food. "And it made the same noise we heard this morning."

"What?" Jarryd stabbed a potato but left it dangling on his fork. "You never told me about that."

I didn't appreciate his annoyance, nor understand it. "No need to get angry. I didn't link the sounds until after we spoke."

Jarryd looked from me to Mother and back to me again. "Where were you this morning when you heard it?"

"In the greenhouse. We couldn't see anything but we heard the buzzing several times," I replied.

Jarryd's brow furrowed. "Is that true, Mother?"

I jumped up. "What's wrong with you? Why would I lie?" I moved to Mother's side, regretting my words when I saw her wringing her hands. She didn't like arguments.

"I'm sorry." Jarryd flashed a dimpled smile. "It's just that I can't understand why drones would be here, so far from Hypor City."

Mother accepted his apology but still seemed shaken. "It's Brynna's birthday. Let's forget about drones and eat." Her worried eyes met my questioning ones.

I was certain she knew more. She shook her head when I started to speak.

Intent on his dinner, my brother missed the exchange. "Is there cake?" Nothing affected his appetite.

I couldn't hide my smirk and gave a piggy snort as I returned to my seat.

He sent me the sibling's 'I'll get you for that' look then laughed.

"There will be cake but only after Brynna finishes her meal." Mother's rule of dinner then dessert was ironclad.

In the silence, my thoughts returned to the drone. I watched Mother walk to the kitchen. Did she know something? What would cause her to look so worried? My concerned gaze lifted to hers when she returned but she was smiling.

"Make a wish." She set the birthday cake on the table in front of me.

I puffed out the flames. There were only three candles but I smiled in appreciation. I knew she'd made them herself from her beehives.

"What did you wish for?" prompted Jarryd as he leaned forward. "You can whisper it to me."

"Not telling," I replied. "It's a secret."

While Jarryd downed a second helping of cake, I opened my birthday gifts.

Father's was a rare printed history of Hypor and the Rising. I knew the stories by heart. I'd seen the videos produced by the council describing the melting of the ice caps and the rising seas.

As the climate warmed, politicians argued interminably about responsibility and strategy, but none could agree. Envisioning an impending tragedy, ten wealthy families formed a consortium and built the floating city of Hypor.

The best minds of the age were invited to contribute their knowledge and skills in preparation for what was to come.

Around the globe, many lost their lives in the watery onslaught as the seas rose. Salt water devastated the land. Later came unexpected earthquakes and tsunamis, killing millions more. It was a time of desolation. Survivors clustered on pockets of higher land. Our small island was all that was left of Father's family's extensive land holdings. As one of the ten founding families of Hypor City ours survived, as did the floating city.

The second gift was from Mother. The package contained three ultramarine-blue, hooded, floor-length jubas, and two pairs of black slippers, all beautifully detailed with Mother's fine needlework. I forced a smile to disguise my disdain. I preferred my usual tunic, tights and boots, but jubas were mandatory dress for women in the city.

After the Rising, the council had a crazy idea about promoting population growth, protecting women, and encouraging them to focus on child rearing and home making. Even now, women were mandated to take jobs that involved home-craft or child care. After completing their work duty, many married, had children and remained on Hypor.

There were few other employment options for women. Fortunately, my talent for languages, Mother's careful tutoring and Father's influence ensured my exemption from traditional women's jobs. I was assigned a position as a translator, but I still had to wear a juba.

"Thank you, Mother." I tried for sincerity. She hadn't made the silly rule about jubas, although I suspected Father's ancestors were probably involved in the decision a hundred years ago.

"Nice dresses." Jarryd's toothy grin confirmed his sarcasm.

I searched my brain for a cutting reply when he pulled a small parcel from his pocket.

"Now don't get all mushy." He placed the wrapped packet on the table beside me. "Happy eighteenth, Bryn."

The string slipped off easily to reveal an intricately carved obsidian miniature depicting a bird. I could tell by the curve of its beak that it was a falcon. The sculpture sat inside a silver ring that swung from a fine chain. I slipped it over my head and pressed it to my chest. Just when I wanted to be mad at him, he'd done something nice and unexpected.

"Oh, Jarryd." I blinked wet eyes.

"Something to remind you of home when you're not here." Emotion welled in his voice but he hid it in a cough.

"Thank you." I jumped up and wound my arms around his neck. "You're the best brother."

"Okay, okay. Just remember that the next time I tease you." He laughed off his embarrassment. "Now, since Father's not here, you and Mother can entertain me." He wasn't musical but loved to hear us sing.

Our harmonies were faultless as Mother and I raised our voices. After years of practice, we understood and anticipated the tones of the other. Our enjoyment continued until Jarryd attempted to join in. His discordant notes tangled the melody. I laughed myself to tears. Jarryd tried to look offended but eventually joined in.

Suddenly, Mother stopped and cocked her head to one side. We went quiet. Then I heard it too. Acute sound sense was something we shared.

"What's up?" Jarryd asked, the hum of the lander too distant for him to detect.

"Father's home." For a moment my irritation at his absence lifted. Maybe he'd remembered. I listened for his footsteps, but he entered his private study directly from an outside door and never appeared.

Mother sighed, sensing my disappointment. "Sorry, Brynna."

"Don't worry, Bryn. We'll ask him about the drone tomorrow, on the way to Hypor," said Jarryd with his usual obtuse understanding. Then his mouth widened in an exaggerated yawn. "I'm for bed."

"Bed for both of you," said Mother. "You have work tomorrow."

Work. The word sent my mind spinning. All my 'what ifs' returned in force, but it was the final one that distracted me the most. What if someone in Hypor City discovered I was Femin?

5
WHAT'S IN A DREAM

Deep in thought, I ambled along the hallway to the doorway of my bedroom.

Harsh streaks of light speared through the open window stabbing the floor. My gaze lifted to the full moon glowering in the sky.

A shudder of anxiety rippled down my back. I dragged the curtains together and blocked the light. Even that small action brought some relief. I undressed, tossing my clothes without care. I donned a nightdress, then crawled into bed, yanking the heavy blanket over my head before curling into a ball. I prayed my sleep would be uneventful and silent, and that my dreams would be kind.

Floating high in a stone cavern. Below me, a circle of women. First humming. Then singing. I feel a rush of delight at the beauty of their harmonies. Two women sit inside a circle. Their faces are unclear, but one appears youthful, the other withered. Through an opening in the rock, moonlight penetrates, bathing the scene in an eerie glow. The singing stops. A central figure lifts her hands. Colors flash wildly. Voices rise, but something is different this time. The singing is intense, almost painful. Building, building to a crescendo. Then the anguish and terror of a solitary scream.

Silent yet piercing.
Imagined yet real.
I want to stop it, but I can't.

I AWOKE TO A PLAINTIVE RIP OF AGONY. IT WRACKED MY senses, stabbed at my temples and pushed terror into my core. I clutched my head and rocked my aching body, waiting for the pain to stop.

I heard a soft humming and forced myself to join in. The healing vibrations lessened the pain. When it finally abated, I opened my eyes. Mother sat at my bedside, as usual her face reflected the anguish she'd also experienced.

"Why is this happening?" I swiped at frustrated tears. "Father and Jarryd don't have these dreams. Why only us?" I was confused and angry—not with her—but at whatever was causing them. "It must be something to do with being Femin."

"I suspect that it might, but I can't understand what it would be. As I explained before, the feminaries were like sanctuaries, dotted on low lying islands scattered across the oceans. The one near my village was a joyous community until we were forced to escape the Rising. Most sanctuaries and my village, were flooded or destroyed by earthquakes. Because of its mountain location, only Prima Feminary survived. Things may have changed since I left and my... the new Genetrix took over." She shook her head. "I don't know what is causing the dreams."

She seldom mentioned the past, which only fueled my curiosity and imagination.

"Are we the only Femin left with—gifts?" I hesitated because concealing my heritage sometimes felt more like a burden.

"No, there are others at Prima Feminary. Older ones, who came from my village. Unfortunately, all singers at the feminary are celibate. To the best of my knowledge, there are no other new singers. I suspect that you are now the youngest and may be the last."

I hadn't expected that. It made my gift even more special, but also made me sad.

"Have you always had nightmares at the time of a full moon?"

She shook her head. "They started more recently."

"Hypor City." I looked at her aghast. "What will I do if it happens on Hypor?"

"Use your voice, discreetly. Low humming works well. I'll also give you some herbs." She stroked her hand across my brow. "They might help."

"What if someone is injured on Hypor? I'd have to respond. That's part of my calling."

"Hypor will have its own medical service." She patted my hand. "Only assist if there is no other option, but be cautious. Remember what could happen if you're caught singing."

"I wish I could just be me, crazy eyes and all." I twisted my face in disgust. "I know, I know." I raised my palms in surrender before she could speak. "It's secret."

"Until the day comes when Femin healers are free again, you must not reveal your heritage." She kissed my brow that now ached for rest. "Sleep well."

I drifted into sleep wondering if one day Prima Feminary might be my sanctuary. Surrounded by others like me, I'd no longer feel like an outsider. I'd be free.

That was my birthday wish.

6

UNWELCOME JOURNEY

The morning sun's golden rays were a reminder of what I'd be missing under the domes of Hypor City.

"You look like hell." Jarryd flicked the back of my head with his finger then took a seat at the breakfast table.

"Thanks a lot." Eyelids barely open and feeling like every blink was gritty torture, I didn't appreciate being reminded of my haggard appearance on the day I had to start my new job.

Mother set a plate of eggs between us. "Your juba fits well."

I didn't answer. More like an encumbrance, it had no pockets, the hood blocked my view and I couldn't walk with normal strides.

"You'll fit right in," my brother teased, dressed in his comfortable gear.

"And you'll get a smack if you don't shut up." My threat was an idle one. I didn't have the energy to swat a bug.

Mother sent me an admonishing look.

"Almost ready?" Father stalked through the dining room

clasping his briefcase. "Meet me at the lander in ten minutes."

A quick peck on Mother's cheek and he was out the door. No 'happy birthday,' not even a smile. I tried not to feel crushed, striving to remember that I was now an adult, but I couldn't prevent a childish pout.

Mother's brow furrowed as she followed his retreat. Her fingers pulled at her bottom lip, a sure sign of concern.

Jarryd noticed the gesture too. "Is everything okay, Mother? Did you mention the drone to Father?"

"Your father's under pressure from the council," she cautioned. "Now isn't the time to badger him with a lot of questions. Soon things will be back to normal." She stacked the empty breakfast dishes. "You'd better hurry and finish eating."

Vague assurances couldn't mask her nervousness. I sensed her fear.

My brother lifted his eyebrows and shrugged. He gulped down a few final mouthfuls, kissed her cheek and left. I took one last bite, grabbed my pack, and hugged her—maybe a little too long.

As we pulled apart, her lower lip quivered. Her fingers touched my face, stroking my slanted brows, then my eyelids and finally my lips. A familiar childhood ritual made more poignant by her failing eyesight.

"I'll miss you, too. Better go. Mustn't keep your father waiting. Don't forget what we discussed last night."

Backing away, I swiped at a persistent tear, then sent her a final wave before hurrying outside.

The sight of the lander parked nearby wasn't unusual but I'd been very young the last time I'd flown to Hypor City. I took a deep breath to calm my nerves. I liked heights. It was water that scared me the most.

I ran to catch Jarryd. Ten feet from the lander, I grabbed the back of his tunic.

"Hey, watch the goods." He grinned and adjusted his clothes.

I lowered my voice, not wanting Father to overhear. "They're hiding something."

"Yes, I got that too."

"Promise me. If you discover anything, you'll let me know."

His expression was serious when he nodded.

Father sat at the controls of the lander with Jarryd beside him and I had the back seat. I felt exhilarated at lift off but was heavy-hearted to see my island home fall away as we headed north toward Hypor City.

Once again, I hoped Father might remember my birthday but he remained silent.

"I saw a drone over the island yesterday afternoon." My tone indicated it was a regular occurrence.

Father's head jerked up. "Impossible." His tone was dismissive but his knuckles whitened as he clenched the controls. "They're short range devices."

"That's what I thought," said Jarryd, "but they heard the same noise in the morning."

"Who are they?"

"Mother and I. We heard a buzzing near the greenhouse but I couldn't locate the source."

After a short silence, Father nodded. "The science lab is probably testing a new model. I'm sure it's nothing more than that but I'll make some inquiries."

"It injured Circe," I persisted, wanting to add weight to the incident.

Father chuckled. "More likely that Circe attacked it and got her feathers ruffled." He knew falcons and guessed the truth.

"She was protecting me. But then it chased her."

"And then what?"

"I tried to scare it away, but Circe may have damaged it. It tumbled end over end, then dropped into the ocean. It was difficult to tell in the dusk, but I think it fell near the line of electric wind generators off Bokk Harbor."

"It was probably a prototype that malfunctioned," said Father.

"But why—"

Father raised his hand. "Let it go, Brynna. I've said I'll look into it. There's no point in speculating when we don't know the facts."

"I'm worried about Mother being alone..." I stopped talking when I saw Father turn to Jarryd and shake his head. I resented the silent condemnation. My brother glanced back with a nod of assurance. At least I had his support.

"Can I take over now?" he asked.

"What?" My life in Jarryd's hands? "What do you mean take over?"

"Don't worry, Bryn. Father's been teaching me to fly for a while." He grasped one side of the dual controls.

When we didn't immediately plunge toward the ocean, I exhaled an exaggerated sigh of relief.

Jarryd chuckled.

"Can I learn someday?" My question was more a test of equality and an urge of competitiveness than real desire. I preferred being on the ground.

Father nodded absently. "In a couple of years." Then

taking my desire to fly as genuine interest, he launched into teaching mode.

I already knew some of it.

The landers, although fast, were only capable of transporting six passengers because of the limitations of the solar batteries. Scientists were hoping to extend the propulsion capability in the near future. He pointed to the dials and indicators, explaining their significance. Then he demonstrated the operation of different levers. When Jarryd interjected technical questions, I tuned out.

I tried to enjoy the view, but the sight of blue ocean in all directions was unnerving. When I was eight, I'd waded out from a beach on our island and my foot had slipped into a hole. I'd cried for help before the water closed over my head. I couldn't swim and the darkness was terrifying. Calia had been nearby chasing Jarryd. He'd heard my cry and scooped me from certain death. I still panic at the thought of that moment and I've never learned to swim.

I forced my eyes to the distant horizon. Faint crescents glimmered in the sun—the steel domes of Hypor City. Two large transporters crept wavelessly toward them, loaded with containers. What was the cargo? Where was it going? I wanted to ask but Father and Jarryd were engrossed in a discussion about solar energy generation. I kept silent knowing that once in Hypor City all my questions would be answered. There was a lot to discover.

Despite my reservations about going to the city, I felt eagerness as we flew closer. I couldn't deny that the newness was exciting. But when I remembered what I'd be losing, my heart plummeted. Five years in Hypor City felt like a life sentence. How would I keep my dreams of being a healer alive?

"We'll be there in five minutes." Father motioned forward. "You can see the city ahead."

I craned my neck for a view over my brother's shoulder. Suddenly the lander tipped forward. The blue of the cold ocean filled the window view. Flashes from my childhood replayed my watery nightmare. Terror froze my lungs. My vision dimmed. Then abruptly we were upright.

"Okay, Bryn?" Jarryd's concerned voice penetrated my panicked fog.

"Fine." I choked back the sour taste of bile and slumped back in my seat. "What happened?"

"Nothing major." Father was in control again. "I'll have the lander serviced and checked once we arrive."

His tone was reassuring, but I still gripped the edge of my seat for the rest of the journey.

The gray domes of Hypor City swelled in size as we approached. They stretched for miles dotting the surface of the ocean. Built on floating platforms, the city resembled a matrix of half-shells discarded on the water, interconnected by long narrow tubes. Spiraling outward were rows of sentinel-like wind generators rising from the ocean. They flanked our flight-path as we neared the landing site.

"It's much bigger than I remember." My last trip to Hypor City was for a Founders' Day celebration. Eleven at the time, my only clear memory was of overwhelming crowd noise. I'd felt disoriented for several days after until Mother had provided a settling tonic.

"There are more than seventy domes," said Jarryd.

"And more to come," added Father. "We're extending the water desalination projects and making room for more solar collectors and greenhouses."

"I'm part of the engineering team working on the new structures." Pride swelled Jarryd's voice.

"And the media lab where you will be working is creating promotional releases, Brynna. You might be involved too," said Father. "How do you feel about that?"

Overwhelmed. Nervous. Excited. "I don't know," was all I could say.

Jarryd took the controls again and dropped the lander precisely inside a numbered red circle on an area skirting the largest dome. Several empty landers were parked nearby.

"What do you think, Bryn?" he asked as he gathered his belongings.

He didn't push for an answer, which was okay because I wasn't sure whether he was asking about his flying or the city. I had mixed opinions on both.

7

HYPOR CITY

From the air, the largest dome had glowed like a jewel in the sunshine, but the fanciful illusion vanished once we landed.

The dreary starkness of the construction materials belied the reflected beauty I'd seen from afar. The shimmer was from solar panels that encompassed the top quarter of the structure.

Riveted sheets of hammered gray metal covered the lower fifty feet of the dome, broken only by two double entryways. The upper portion of the hemisphere, below the reflective panels, was comprised of a dull semi-translucent substance. I squinted into the sunlight, following the vaulted curve skyward hoping for relief from the monotonous presentation, but none appeared.

My excitement deflated, but the sound of pounding feet quickened my pulse.

Two guards ran from the dome. Their uniforms were black with gold trim. One guard sported two red chevrons on his breast pocket. All wore diagonal chest straps, which held several devices that looked like weapons. I started to question Jarryd but was distracted when the men stationed themselves at Father's door and saluted.

"Welcome, Councilor Bokk."

The salute surprised me. I'd never seen my father in his official capacity.

We exited the lander. One guard bent into the vehicle to retrieve any cargo. Father had his case tucked under his arm; Jarryd too carried his bag, only my pack remained. I grabbed it from the man's hands. He retreated and quickly masked his surprise at my reaction. I said nothing, unable to explain that it was my security blanket, full of personal keepsakes and memories of home?

Father glanced at me and shook his head in disapproval, before following Jarryd to a double portal. The doors swooshed open at our approach. I hurried to keep up but my juba forced me to take shorter strides. Once over the threshold, I stopped, wanting to assess my first moments in my new home.

The interior was darker than I expected. The translucent exterior released only thin streams of sunlight, due to a perforated covering inside. The narrow beams created an eerie gloom that permeated the entry. In an attempt to boost my enthusiasm, I glanced behind me, somewhat reassured by the sunshine gleaming on the landers. Maybe things would get better.

Embedded into the upper dome wall, several large fans whirred noisily. Despite the din, Jarryd's booted footsteps echoed as they pounded the hard black floor. Father's steps were quieter. I balanced on my toes as I walked forward. My new slippers made no noise.

Apart from the guards, the only evidence of human occupation was a wall array of ten posters, one considerably larger than the others. I recognized my father's picture second from the left. The other men must be members of the ruling council. The largest frame had to be Premier Delio, the leader of the council.

"Put up your hood, Brynna! Keep up."

I jerked at Father's harsh commanding tone. I hesitated before slipping the juba hood over my head and pushing my long hair in at the sides. Intent on arranging my hood, I accidentally bumped my elbow into his back when he halted beside a guarded entryway.

He went rigid.

I stepped back.

Jarryd put his hand on a glass plate. A light flashed green and he moved forward through an opening in a steel barricade. Father spoke to an official then beckoned me forward. The man positioned my palm on the glass pad. A green light scrolled under my hand.

"From now on, your hand print will be your passport into the city," said Father.

When the machine malfunctioned and my palm had to be rescanned, he started to tap his foot.

"Are you done?" Father asked the guard.

I'd never heard him so impatient with others. He was a different person on Hypor. One I didn't know.

The official nodded but looked embarrassed. "Yes, Councilor Bokk." His salute was crisp as we passed through the barricade into a sterile concourse.

Artificial lighting and dull beige walls sunk my spirits further. I wrinkled my nose at the smell. It hinted at floral but with a chemical edge. Apart from the guards, we were the only people present. Father's cold demeanor offered no reassurance. When Jarryd said 'bye' and walked away, I wanted to call him back and hang on tight.

I fought my growing nervousness with boldness.

"Where is everyone?" I decided I wasn't moving a step further until I'd seen signs of other human life.

"Working. " Father consulted his watch. "It's after ten. No one is allowed in the halls without permission during working hours."

"What if I have to go—?"

His glance condemned my audacity and I shrunk into silent timidity.

Across from us were four double doorways. Off to the right and left, the lobby narrowed into passages that curved with the dome wall. Father pointed to a metal sign and corresponding map. "A hallway runs inside the perimeter and leads to the tubes that are linked to other domes. The administrative offices are here in the main dome, where you will be working."

I had no idea what the other areas would be like. Less barren I hoped. I closed my eyes and thought of the lush forest of home, but the image of colorless walls remained. But there was no point in griping. I had no choice. I was here to stay at least until my first work break, which seemed a hundred years away instead of a month.

"After I drop my case in my office I'll escort you to your workplace."

I hugged my belongings to my chest. Father's coolness was making me edgy. He seemed as remote as our island.

"Don't dawdle, Brynna."

We approached another set of doors. Father pressed a button and they opened. I realized it was a lift.

We shot up silently for several seconds. I focused on the level indicator to take my mind off feeling trapped in the small space. We quickly reached the tenth floor.

When the doors slid open, I followed Father but halted after several steps.

He glanced at me, then continued toward his office. "Close your mouth, Brynna. Wait here. I'll be back in a minute."

My teeth clamped shut but my eyes were popping. Life was definitely better at the top of the dome. The filtered light was warm and bright, highlighting several paintings of Hypor City hanging on the walls.

A soft cream carpet partially covered a multi-colored slate floor. Several deep-cushioned indigo chairs bordered the room. A polished stone table took center stage. Atop it was a glass sculpture of a gyrfalcon—its wings starting to spread, its beak forward, eyes eager. The artist had captured the elegance and majesty of the bird. My glance caressed every glistening curve.

I felt Father's presence beside me.

"Time to go," he said but remained stationary.

"Falcon..." I choked, thinking of Circe and home, so far away.

"Yes." A momentary wistfulness filled his voice. "We must go. Your supervisor is expecting you."

I caught a glimpse of the father I knew. The warmth of his smile was a welcome balm and soothed me as we approached the lift.

When the doors opened, I moved forward but he grasped my arm, pulling me close to his side.

A short, dark-haired man with a florid complexion strutted out of the lift, then turned and bowed toward a striking woman who followed. Five females in purple jubas flanked her.

"Premier Delio." Father acknowledged the head of the Council of Ten with a nod, but he bowed to the woman. "Genetrix."

THE LAST SINGER

Genetrix? The title caught my attention. What was she doing in Hypor City?

Everyone knew Premier Delio's name. Alongside my father's tall frame, he looked insignificant, but he was head of the ruling council. He wore an ornate crimson robe that veiled his portly figure. His thin smile never wavered as his eyes narrowed. His gaze shifted between Father and the woman like an animal trying to decide where to strike. When he glanced at me, I felt an icy shiver baste my shoulders.

The Genetrix was impressive. She was my height and coloring but appeared taller because her mass of dark hair held her hood several inches above her pale face. Her hands were bare, their only distinguishing feature being long fingernails filed to points. The one exception was the small nail of her right hand. It was long but rounded at the end and appeared whiter than the others. Her purple juba was styled as mine but edged in gold. A small pouch hung from a metal chain around her hips. Her only adornment was a necklace with a prominent pendant. A large clear stone surrounded by wavy gold lines that radiated from it.

Were my eyes playing tricks? The stone changed color continuously. First yellow, then orange, red, purple, blue, green then a slight hesitation at white before repeating the colors.

"Brynna!" Father grasped my hand when I didn't immediately respond, then drew me forward. "Genetrix. Premier. This is my daughter, Brynna. This is her first day of work."

When I looked up, three sets of eyes watched me—Father's with annoyance, the Premier's with disdain, the Genetrix's with curiosity. She moved toward me. Instinctively I stepped back, then came to a standstill. It took me a moment to comprehend that I hadn't halted on my own. Something had immobilized my legs.

I panicked when I felt a unusual vibration and detected a high tone. The Genetrix's eyes were fixated on my face. It was coming from her.

The men appeared unaware of what was happening.

I hated being controlled but couldn't break free. Her hold was too strong.

She took my chin and pushed my face toward the light. I dropped my eyes, concerned that she might detect my lens, but her nail points dug into my flesh and my eyes flared open. For several seconds her gaze bore into mine, as if searching for something.

I distracted myself by examining her face, as she was mine.

It was difficult to determine her age. Unusually deep folds surrounded her eye sockets and her skin pulled too taught over her cheekbones. Her pupils were fathomless, disturbingly enigmatic, but something about her mouth was vaguely familiar. It was puzzling. I couldn't make any connection.

She frowned slightly, released my chin, and my legs, and dismissed me with an abrupt turn of her shoulder. Her five acolytes continued to watch me, their heads slightly dipped, their eyes alert. When I moved out of arms reach, they shifted their attention to the men. I sensed they were a protective detail. But why would the Genetrix need guards in Hypor City? Were these women also Femin?

"Is there a meeting I wasn't told about?" Father's voice was icy. His angry vibrations rippled along my skin.

"Not at all, my friend." Premier Delio's words were smooth but I detected an undertone of deception. "I was just about to notify the councilors of the Genetrix's arrival."

Father's gaze shifted to the Genetrix but she gave no indication of the veracity of the Premier's words. Instead, she watched the drama play out between the two men.

Delio continued. "We'll meet in the board room in say...half an hour?"

"Fine, I'll see you then," said Father. "Genetrix." He bowed slightly as she and her entourage followed the Premier.

As they walked away, the premier made a low comment. The only word I heard was 'prophecy'.

I waited until they disappeared into an office then whispered. "I could feel her—"

Father's raised hand stopped further questioning until the doors of the lift closed behind us.

"You mustn't mention anything about the Femin. Never while you're in Hypor City. You know that."

"But why is she here?"

"The council has trade agreements with Prima Feminary, Nuvega and other smaller islands. From time to time, the Genetrix travels here. Sometimes a representative from the council makes trips to broker deals. It's all part of normal business." His smile was reminiscent. "I met your mother on a trade mission to Prima Feminary many years ago."

"Was that before singing was banned?"

Father nodded, cleared his throat and his expression grew serious again. "Which is why you mustn't appear curious about the Genetrix or Femin. You mustn't do anything that will draw attention to yourself."

"I know. Mother explained it all."

"So you understand why your heritage must remain hidden. If revealed, it puts your life and your mother's in danger."

"Why Mother's life?"

"Think Brynna. If it's discovered that you sing and that you are a healer, the Genetrix might attempt to convince the council that because she trained you, your mother is also in violation of the ban."

"No." I shuddered at the thought that I might be responsible for hurting my mother.

"Be careful what you do or say. You never know who might be listening." He patted my shoulder. "I don't want to lose my only daughter."

His warm hand gave little comfort. I'd become an adult but my graduation present felt heavy on my eighteen-year-old heart.

Pride lit his eyes when I squared my shoulders and spoke with more courage than I was feeling. "No one will ever know my secret."

8

AN OLD FRIEND

The lift descended for several seconds before the doors opened.

"This is level six, where you will be working," said Father. "Other floors are off limits unless you are escorted by a supervisor."

"Why?"

"One of the rules." His warning glance squashed my second "Why?".

The harsh overhead lighting made me squint as I peered right then left, eager to see where I'd be spending most of my time. It was another beige hallway, this time interrupted by pale blue doors. Small labels on each door were their only differentiating feature. Red switches alternated along both sides of the corridor.

"What are they for?" I pointed to one as we walked.

"They are for emergencies. A fire, which is unlikely, or flooding. A medical emergency would also qualify. You'll learn the regulations."

Rules for everything. They irritated me like an itch I couldn't reach.

"Here we are." Father opened the door with the sign Media lab.

Inside was brighter than the hallway. People were busy at computer stations clustered throughout the space. Across the room, ignoring the two men attempting to converse with her, Calia leaned one hip against a desk. Her juba looked too large on her short, curvy frame and the hood flopped forward half covering her forehead. Arms crossed, she watched us enter but stared as if we were strangers.

It had been over three months since I'd seen her. I wanted to run and give her a hug but instead gave a discreet wave. A little surprised at her lack of response, I waved again, but she turned her back to me and started talking to her colleagues.

It was then I noticed the bespectacled gaunt individual stooped nearby. His parchment cheeks hollowed as he inhaled. He rubbed his boney hands together, fawning before Father.

"Brynna, this is Supervisor Dench. He'll explain your job and help you get started." Father tapped his watch. "I'm late for a meeting. I hope my daughter will prove herself."

"I'm sure she will be an asset, Councilor Bokk. I am most pleased to have her in my department." His tone was deferential but lacked sincerity.

I swallowed a laugh. The man was what Calia would call a slimy tool, but his deferential posture made him appear harmless. I glanced at her hoping to share the moment, but her attention was on a video screen.

Dench escorted Father to the exit before commanding me to follow him to his office. The respect he'd shown Father didn't extend to me. He settled into a chair behind a metal desk while I stood waiting for an invitation to sit that didn't come. His cheeks expanded and flattened like bellows as his index finger stroked a computer screen.

"So, Brynna Bokk, your file says you have some proficiency with languages. Which ones?"

"Some of the old European languages. German, French, Spanish—"

"And Italian?" He raised his brows, his gaze more intense.

I hesitated. "A little." I felt an impulse to be vague, wondering why his question was so specific.

"A regular little polyglot, aren't you?"

I wasn't sure what he meant, but the sarcasm was clear.

"Yes, well, hmm..." he referred again to his computer screen. "I understand you know Calia. She'll show you around and work with you today, but tomorrow you pull your weight. Come with me."

I followed Dench as he stalked from his office. He called to Calia who rose from her desk and approached. He told her what he wanted and gave her a plastic card then returned to his office. She stuck out her tongue at his receding back and grinned. Her familiar cheekiness made me smile.

"I'm so happy to see you again, Calia. I'm really excited that we're working together."

"Don't look like you're enjoying yourself or Dench will make your life miserable. He's a slimy little tool. Just ignore him and you'll do fine. Come on, I'll show you where we sleep and eat."

We left the media room and took the lift down to the main floor. We followed the hallway around the perimeter of the dome.

"There are lots of domes," said Calia. "Unlike me, I expect you arrived in a lander and saw them from the air, as well as the tubes that connect them. Some tubes are long and have movers or moving walkways, which make the journey quicker. This is us through here." She pointed to an arched entrance.

She went to step on a mover but quickly changed her mind.

"Let's walk. It takes longer." She winked. "I'm not excited about returning to work too soon."

I wanted to ask about her job but got distracted by the view of the water through the clear wall of the tube. "Oh, how beautiful. And the sunshine."

My spirits escalated as I watched the sun sparkle on the water. I looked up expecting to see blue sky but the ceiling material was opaque only the sides of the tube were transparent. In the distance, I could see similar passageways. After the dull beige of the interior, the view was encouraging and comforting. I wanted to linger.

"You'll get used to it. Come on. We have to keep moving or someone will get suspicious."

"Suspicious of what?"

She shrugged. "Anything."

"What do you mean?"

"Nothing. Just be careful. In time you'll understand." An edge of sarcasm cut through her words.

"Calia...?" I grabbed at the sleeve of her juba.

She ignored my hand and nodded forward. Always stubborn, I knew she'd only share if she wanted to.

"This is the nearest foodpod." She pointed to a dining area.

The space was as sterile as the dome entrance. White tables aligned in long rows were flanked by metal chairs. A tall bank of empty racks stood along one beige wall. The faces of the

Council of Ten members adorned another wall, but the frames were larger than those I'd seen before. I was getting used to the floral scent and the constant hum of the large circulating fans.

"Clear out! You're too early." The gruff voice belonged to a grizzled man hobbling toward us. He wore an apron over his clothing and a small cap covered only part of his bald scalp. "Anyway, you shouldn't be here at this time of day without your supervisor."

"Leave us alone, we're not here to eat," said Calia. "She's a new recruit." She tilted her head toward me. "I'm showing her around, and I have a passcard." She flashed the plastic card and turned to walk away.

He grunted, surprising me with a quick wink. I hesitated and had to hurry to catch Calia. When I looked back, he was gone.

"That's Grub, or at least that's what everyone calls him. He thinks he owns the place. I don't know why the council tolerates people like him."

"What do you mean?"

"He's a nasty old cripple with no respect for his betters. He always gives me grief when he sees me. One day he'll get what's coming to him."

I was surprised by the hard edge in her voice and changed the subject. "Can anyone eat here?"

"Yes, but it's mainly the admin workers, like us. The food is brought in on those." She pointed to several trolleys near the racks. "Everyone just helps themselves to what they want."

"How's the food?" I hoped it was more appetizing than the surroundings.

Calia shrugged. "Some like it. You can judge for yourself at lunch."

We crossed the foodpod before veering right toward another tube. This time I noticed an arrow and a sign.

Dormpod.

The entryway split into two open hallways. Signs indicated men to the left, women to the right. There were no doors or other barriers.

"This doesn't look very secure." I'd never slept away from home. I was leery of having strange men next door, and no lock.

"You always were a prude," said Calia. "But you don't have to worry. If you go through the wrong door an alarm goes off and the podmaster arrives in seconds."

"Podmaster?"

"Every pod has a supervisor. They enforce the rules."

Calia stopped in front of half a dozen video screens mounted on the wall to the right of the women's entrance, separated for privacy by vertical partitions. "This is the message area. If you want to contact me, you scroll down to my name, tap the screen and type your message and press send. Your message is locked, waiting for me to retrieve it. No one else can access it, except the podmaster, but even he has to have special permission from the council. To check for messages, just find your name and wave your hand over this pad."

"Is this the only way to make contact?" I was thinking about Father and Jarryd.

"Other than meeting somewhere. Only councilors and upper level employees have personal communication devices. Remember, you're just a grunt now."

As I followed her into the women's dorm, I puzzled over the tone of her last remark.

"You're in with me, four beds to a room." Calia laughed. "I can see by your face that you're freaked out at the idea of sharing, but that's life on Hypor. No more princess treatment here."

My face always betrayed me. I'd have to learn to hide my emotions.

"There's your bed and locker." She indicated an empty bed with a tall narrow closet beside it. "Everything you need is in the big cupboard. Clothes are provided, if necessary." She pulled at my sleeve. "Pretty fancy juba. You won't need to wear one of these." She plucked at her ill-fitting robe.

I immediately decided to pack away my jubas and wear the ones provided. Despite the guilt of rejecting my mother's gift, I decided it was better to blend in. I already felt ill at ease and different. Calia wasn't making things any better.

"It's good to see that even you look plain in a juba." She sniggered and gave me a little shove. "Just joking."

It was a lie. I heard the deception and it hurt. I didn't understand this side of her. She'd been like family. My father had even arranged for her job on Hypor. Why did she resent me?

"The other two are on break." She flopped onto a messy bed and leaned back on her elbows. "One's an artist who also has some council connection, and the other's a girl from the secretarial group on the tenth floor. Have you been up there?"

I nodded.

A forced attitude of boredom accompanied a twist to her lips. "Thought you might, lucky you." Her voice held a bitter undercurrent of jealousy.

My hand went to my churning stomach and I took a step back.

"You okay?" She asked then looked down and examined her fingernails. "May as well get your pack stowed in your locker before we head back. There's not much else to do during the day but work. At night's when the fun begins." Calia's sly grin was familiar, always there when she'd planned something forbidden. However, we were no longer children and I wasn't sure I wanted to know her plans.

"Where's the recpod?" I remembered Jarryd's remarks about the obstacle course.

"It's in a separate dome, beyond the foodpod. Not my thing, but you can check it out yourself after work. We'd better get back. Dench will find some way to punish us if we're too long."

As we retraced our steps, I asked about the other workers in our department.

"Most of them are boring. Carrot and Stick are a pain. They think they're above everyone else."

"Carrot and Stick?"

"That's what I call them. Carrot has orangey hair. Stick is skinny and almost seven feet tall. We give them the information and translations. They're the broadcasters. The ones that get to make the news videos that go out to the rest of the city. The females don't get those jobs, even if you have connections." She opened the door to the media room. "Here we go," she muttered.

My head spun with all the new information I received during the day.

In the early days of the Rising, immigrants flocked to Hypor City from around the planet. The diversity of language still remained. All edicts from the council, approved community notices, and sanctioned articles of interest had to be translated before being transmitted via video. The computers did most of the work though not very efficiently. My job was to ensure that the meaning and nuance of each translation was correct before it went to the broadcasters.

I was slow and lagged behind. Despite Calia's sarcastic remark about trying to please Dench, I worked through lunch to catch up. At six, an automated voice announced day's end. Surprised at the quick passage of time, I joined the line that filed out of the room. Dench followed and locked the door with his passcard. Except for him, everyone turned toward the foodpod.

Calia and I followed the crowd. Carrot and Stick leaned against the wall a few feet along the hallway. They straightened and confronted us, barring our way.

"You." Stick stabbed his bony finger at me. "You only got your job because of your father."

"Nepotism," Carrot sneered.

"You slimy tools." Calia was on them like a spitting cat. "You both have connections to the council. Your uncle and your cousin." She nodded at Carrot and then at Stick. "I'm the only one who got where I am on pure talent."

I knew this was untrue, but appreciated her defense.

"You got a promotion, but not because you're a good translator," said Stick.

"Your talent is what you do on your back." Carrot leered at her.

I expected Calia to be embarrassed or irate; to defend herself against the sexual innuendo. Instead, she laughed.

"You're just jealous because you don't have a chance with me." She tossed her head and grabbed my arm. "Come on, Brynna. What they have might be contagious."

∼

THE FOOD WASN'T AS GOOD AS MOTHER'S.

After dinner, I asked Calia again for directions to the recpod.

"I've got something better in mind," she replied. "Tonight, the Premier's birthday is being celebrated at the marketplace. Everyone will be there. You'll really like it. It will be fun."

After much cajoling, I agreed to accompany her.

Minutes later, we exited the food area and walked through several more domes and tubes. Crowd noise grew steadily louder until it peaked at the entrance of our final destination.

"This is the marketplace," Calia yelled over the deafening hum.

I followed as she wove her way through the mass of people. Colored lights flashed wildly as bodies milled mindlessly among vendors. We moved past displays of simple jewelry, baskets, hair clasps, and small sculptures. An exhibit of intricate black sculptures caught my eye. I paused to take a closer look. When I turned to explain my interest to Calia, she was gone.

"Do you like miniatures?" asked a petite blonde woman behind the stall. She wore onyx earrings shaped like stars. Several ropes of colored beads circled her neck. Her large gray eyes twinkled with welcome.

"Yes, I was given one as a gift. It must take great skill to work the figures so precisely."

"Lots of practice and a good teacher are essential. It's hard on the eyes so you definitely have to love what you do."

I hadn't worked long enough to earn credits so I couldn't consider buying anything. "I'll be back another time," I offered lamely.

She nodded and smiled. "Enjoy the celebration."

Despite the revelry, the atmosphere and the crush of bodies felt oppressive. I joined the flow and quickly found myself at the perimeter. As the throng circled the dome, I knew that I would eventually reach the exit.

Progress was slow and the mass was tight so I was surprised to spot a group of people separated from the rest by a few feet of empty space. Then I noted the cluster of black uniformed men surrounding another in a gold uniform. At his side stood a short woman in a gray juba. When she lifted her head and threw him a coquettish smile, I recognized Calia.

The man circled his arm around her waist and yanked her against him. At the other men's cheers and urgings, he leaned down and kissed Calia. She didn't pull back, but instead flung her arms around his neck and hung onto him in earnest.

Others in the crowd stopped to watch as well. The guards noted our interest and encircled the couple. "Move along." Some of them yelled and waved their arms.

The exit neared and I rushed into the adjoining tube. The noise diminished as I threaded my way back to the dorm. Every step felt heavier than the last. At home, I spent many hours with only Circe for company, never feeling as alone and isolated as I did now.

Calia had changed. Maybe Hypor changes everyone.

Not me. I was determined to find a way to preserve my skills so one day I would be free to be a healer.

THE DAYS THAT FOLLOWED SETTLED INTO A DULL ROUTINE OF work and sleep. Dench controlled the flow of information in the office. I was given only basic government notices that required little skill to translate. The lack of challenge was mind-numbing. In an effort to ease the boredom, I attempted to make friends with other co-workers. All I got was cool disdain that I didn't understand.

Calia seemed preoccupied and never available after work. Even in the dorm, I only got a disinterested answer or a grunt when I tried to converse with her. The two other women often arrived back late. One had a boyfriend. The other was shy and reclusive. We never progressed past hello and a few mundane pleasantries.

Alone, I decided to explore the city as best I could. I visited the marketplace several times, but when I caught sight of Calia with Prince Delio again, I decided to avoid the area. I missed her company, but her priorities weren't mine. I wanted to know more about the recpod and Steepchase.

Eventually, I found the recpod, but a group of guards stood conversing at the entrance. I wanted to go in, but decided to wait for Jarryd, whom I hoped would soon respond to the numerous messages I'd sent him.

On my own in my room, I hummed or sang quietly, trying to keep my vocal skills strong. The exercises helped to soothe my isolation and made me feel closer to Mother. But they also reminded me of the freedom I'd lost.

My future in Hypor City looked dismal.

A week later, I still hadn't heard from Jarryd and considered storming the men's dorm. I stopped at the videos near the women's dorm to check for messages. Expecting another empty screen, I was delighted and relieved to see a missive from Jarryd, until 'URGENT' flashed on the screen.

Meet me tomorrow at noon outside foodpod. Tell no one. JB

9

A TERRIFYING THREAT

It was twelve fifteen when Jarryd finally appeared the next day.

"You're late." I teased, waiting for his answering smile.

It didn't appear. Instead, Jarryd caught my arm and propelled me away from the busy foodpod and back into a connecting tube. "Never mind that. I *know*."

"What are you talking about?" I'd hardly seen him over the past ten days and now he wanted to take up part of my precious lunch hour being mysterious. "What do you know?"

The look he gave me was the one older siblings give to their juniors when they're acting dumb. He glanced over his shoulder before continuing.

"I know what Father and Mother are so worried about." His voice dropped so low even I had trouble hearing it. "Something that'll blow your mind."

"Really? What? Another flood? Earthquakes?" I knew these were possible. They'd occurred in the past.

"Even more serious." Urgency and alarm made his usually warm eyes cold. "The whole planet is in danger."

I was shocked but skeptical. What could be worse than the floods and earthquakes that had occurred during the Rising?

"What kind of danger? How do you know?"

His eyes flicked beyond me and he beckoned to someone. Moments later a blonde woman joined us. It was the artist from the market. I recognized her round gray eyes and onyx earrings. She was cute in a pixie sort of way. The flirty way she glanced at my brother told me that she was smitten.

He smiled as she approached. "Bryn, this is Marta. She's the one who first told me about the threat. Her father's on the council as well." The woman placed her hand on his sleeve and I watched his gaze soften. "Tell Bryn what your father told you."

My mind reeled at the thought that my big brother might be in love. He'd been mine and now I might have to share him with another woman. It was a stupid kind of jealousy but I couldn't help it.

"...when the Genetrix was here a while ago..."

Marta's mention of the Genetrix refocused my attention.

"...she foretold of a disaster. Something to do with the sun, but there was no time or date given."

"That's rather vague." Was this all Marta had? I felt she should do better, but maybe I was being harsh—and a little green.

"That's not all," said Jarryd. "One of the scientists I work with has discovered data predicting a deadly coronal mass ejection."

"What's that?"

"CMEs are huge eruptions of plasma that spew heat and solar radiation from the sun's surface. We're in an eleven-year cycle of sunspots that will hit its zenith around the time of the solar eclipse. Most times they miss the planet but Weyland, my colleague, discovered activity on a specific quadrant of the sun that would put us in line for a direct hit."

I stepped back, stunned by the implications. "But what about our atmosphere? Wouldn't it protect us?"

"Not from a direct hit. In fact, the experts are predicting that our atmosphere would be ripped from the planet."

"No atmosphere, no life," Marta choked out a whisper.

"It must be a mistake." I stared at the two of them, trying to make sense of it all. This couldn't be true. I'd just started my life. I wanted to live to see nineteen at least. "The council must have a plan. What's being done about the threat?"

"My father says there are designs for satellite shields," said Marta. "Premier Delio has also commissioned a fleet of starships to evacuate the planet if necessary."

"And go where? We were told there's been no contact with the Mars colony for ten years, not since the satellites stopped working. We don't even know if anyone is still there." I looked at my brother. "Do we?"

"No." He pushed his fingers through his hair in the same way Father did when he was bewildered.

"So where are we going? Is there anywhere else?" I was as baffled as they were.

He shook his head. "Mars is the only option at this point."

"So basically we're toast or lost in space. What a great choice."

I hadn't meant to be funny, but Jarryd grinned. Nervous tension soon had us all laughing.

"We shouldn't joke," said Marta. "It's a catastrophic situation."

I threw up my hands and shook my head. "What can we do?"

"For the moment we have to keep this to ourselves," said Jarryd. "If it gets out, Marta's father will be in serious trouble, and the council will come down on Weyland for revealing what he found. They don't want people to panic. Who knows what they'd do to us if they learned we'd leaked the information."

I couldn't imagine, but since arriving on Hypor, I'd heard of people banished for lesser reasons. Rumors were that difficult men were sentenced to hard labor in the mines at Haven, on the outskirts of Nuvega. Disobedient women were also transported to somewhere unpleasant. I doubted all the stories were true, but I didn't want to find out first hand.

A bell sounded.

"We have to go. Lunchtime is over." Jarryd looked at me. "We'll meet you tonight at the recpod. Six o'clock. We can talk more then."

MY GUT WAS A HARD KNOT. I COULDN'T EAT.

Dazed, I slumped back against a wall. The news was disturbing and potentially devastating. My mind was a foggy maze, each thought lost as my imagination tussled with the prospects. No future. The end in sight. I'd never felt so scattered or vulnerable.

I didn't notice Calia until she confronted me.

"What's up with you?" She wobbled on tiptoes, her face only inches from mine. "You've been standing here forever with that blank look on your face. Are you on drugs?" Dark eyes bored into my blue ones. "No, of course not. Not *Miss-Prim-and-Proper*. So what's pushed you into fantasy land?"

She must have seen me with my brother, so I couldn't deny it.

"Jarryd and I were catching up. We haven't spoken since I started working."

"What did you talk about? Must have been something important to leave you looking so stunned." Her eyes narrowed to slits. "Come on. Give." She wouldn't let this drop. Tenacity was her middle name.

I couldn't share what I'd learned about the planet so I decided instead to sacrifice a tidbit about my brother's love life. After furtively glancing around, I bent close and whispered. "Promise you won't say anything, but I think Jarryd has a serious girlfriend."

Calia loved gossip and I'd caught her attention. But I'd forgotten she'd once had a crush on Jarryd.

"That bitch, Marta?" Her lips spat the name. "I don't know what he sees in her. Just because her father's on the council. Maybe that's it. Yes, must be. Both from rich families." A sneer marred her red lips.

It felt like betrayal to listen to her vitriol, but it was better than telling her the real topic of my conversation with Jarryd.

"She seemed nice enough to me." My defense was weak.

"Your brother with that no-brain artist? He deserves someone smart. I can't believe you're not angry."

My earlier jealousy melted away. I regretted the sacrifice even though the distraction had worked. "I trust my brother to choose someone who makes him happy no matter what she does." Family loyalty poked at me. "Besides, it's no one else's business but his."

Calia stepped back as if slapped. Uncertainty and confusion reflected in her eyes. I'd never crossed her before.

"Well...you brought it up." Like a viper, she struck out at anyone who challenged her. I'd seen it many times with others on the island.

"You're right. I shouldn't have mentioned it." My admission cooled her annoyance.

"Forget it. Let's get going or we'll be late." She walked ahead but gradually dropped back. Within minutes, she was a chatty magpie, regaling me with Hypor gossip as we approached a lift. Once inside, her finger pushed seven several times. "Let's go up an extra floor."

"What? Why? It's going to make us late. Plus, it's against the rules." I went for the sixth button but she moved her body in front of the panel.

She shook her head. "Don't worry. Dench is at a meeting this afternoon. He won't be back for another hour."

"I don't understand why you want to go to seven. What's up there other than the science labs?" I knew they were there because Jarryd worked on that floor.

"You'll see." Her crafty grin returned. Sensing my withdrawal, she grabbed my hand. "Please come with me. I don't want to go on my own. It's important. Who else can I trust but my best friend?"

Her final plea got to me. A residual childhood loyalty surfaced and I kept silent.

The lift door opened. Calia almost skipped along the empty hallway. It looked the same as our floor. Beige walls and closed doors, then one door opened at the far end. Three men emerged. They walked in formation, one ahead and two behind.

"There he is." Calia's face flushed with excitement. "I

knew he'd come." Her pace slowed to a sashay. She pulled her shoulders back, forcing the chest of her juba forward.

"This is what you dragged me up here for? So you could meet a boy?" My voice rose with indignation. I resented her trickery.

"Quiet." She faced me and whispered, "Not a boy, a man. And, not just any man. He's Prince Delio, the Premier's son. Everyone calls him 'The Little Prince,' but not to his face." She giggled, wet her lips and waved at the approaching trio.

I guessed the front man was Delio's son. I recognized him from the market, the one that had kissed Calia. Short and dark like his father, his chin was high, his eyes hooded and his mouth pouty. Privilege emanated from his haughty demeanor and confident swagger.

Compensating for his lack of stature was my first thought. Not a very nice one considering I didn't know him. Maybe he was different from his father.

The two men following him were dressed like the guards at the lander, except for gold-colored epaulets that edged their shoulders. One was burly, with a misshapen nose that hinted of too many brawls. A permanent sneer warped his lips. The second was broad-shouldered but lean, more athlete than fighter. His expression remained impassive.

As they neared the sign for lab five, the door opened and a gangly man stumbled out. He tripped and fell into Prince and then onto the floor.

"You oaf." Prince fired with rage and his hands curled into fists. The man tried to get up and slipped. The guards finally lifted the offender to his feet and held him.

Prince confronted him. "Do you know who I am?"

The man's head made jerky pivots but he didn't respond. Instead, he struggled frantically. His legs crumpled under him as his eyes rolled back in his head. Like a frightened bird caught in a net, desperate and vulnerable.

I yanked Calia's arm. "We have to get out of here."

"I'm staying." Calia's eyes widened with excitement.

"I'm going—" I retreated then stopped when Prince lifted his arm.

The guards released their captive. Their leader backhanded the man, who collapsed to the floor against the opposite wall. Blood oozed from a gash on his forehead. He whimpered and covered one eye. I felt his agony.

"That's what inferiors get for their impudence. You clumsy fool."

The shorter guard laughed, the other remained silent. Prince spat on the man, then resumed walking.

Compassion and a mournful groan propelled me toward the victim, but the sneering guard barred my way. The threat on his face bullied me to halt. I felt his cruelty from two feet away.

There was no support from Calia, but I guess I hadn't really expected it. She'd found her man. Head nestled on his shoulder she was no longer interested in me. As they moved off down the hall, Prince beckoned the guards.

The nasty one leered at me. Although forbidden to touch a woman in a juba, his shoulder grazed mine in defiance as he passed by. I heard him snicker as he strode away.

I stood rigidly throughout the confrontation but sagged with relief when he'd gone. The injured man had disappeared also. There was no reason to linger. I had no prince to defend me if I was caught.

Turning toward the lift, I froze. The second guard had stayed behind and was now approaching. He walked with purpose but his movements were lithe and without swagger. He was over six feet, like Jarryd, but his hair was coal black.

When he moved closer, I noted his eyes lifted at the corners and were emerald green. A faint white line marked one cheek. Cool and unfathomable were the words that came to mind.

Knots filled my belly. I felt more alarmed by his calm demeanor than by his comrade's obvious aggression. His intentions were unclear. As a mouse awaits a cat's attack, I scrutinized his every motion and expression for signs of hostility. When he halted before me, I thought I'd been stupid not to run. Too close, there was no escape. I was trapped.

A strong urge to sing filled me. A low vibration tingled my vocal chords but died away when our gazes locked. In his eyes, I saw no threat, only compassion. Something unspoken and indefinable lingered between us. Did he feel it too? In the strange silence, my tension slid away. I felt safe.

The swoosh of the lift door attracted his attention and drew his gaze beyond me. He offered a discreet salute then strode to join his detail.

Curious about what had transpired, I watched his retreat —a little too long.

"Brynna Bokk!"

I shuddered and turned at the sound of my name. Dench closed a lab door behind him. Just my bad luck he had business on this floor.

"Why aren't you working? What are you doing up here?" He peered over the rim of his glasses, laboring for air. "Well? Speak up."

Loyalty wouldn't let me incriminate Calia. "I was hoping to see my brother. I needed to tell him something." The explanation sounded false even to my ears.

Dench didn't believe it either. He narrowed his eyes. "Come with me." His tone brooked no argument.

Down the lift and traversing the sixth-floor hallway, I frantically tried to manufacture a believable excuse. In the end, I decided to stick with the original one rather than spin a spiral of lies.

"In my office." He barked, arm straight, finger pointed.

I hurried, but when he didn't follow, I sneaked a peek over my shoulder.

Carrot and Stick stood in a corner of the media lab with Dench. He turned and his face darkened when Calia strolled in wearing a devious smile.

"Calia." For a small man, his voice was deafening. "In my office."

Her face pinched at the command. She didn't acknowledge my presence as she entered Dench's domain. We stood silently side by side before his desk. When he didn't immediately appear, she turned and grasped the front of my juba, forcing me to face her.

"You bitch!" Her eyes were afire as she spoke through gritted teeth. "You told him, didn't you?"

I shook my head. "No." I prepared to defend myself when Dench walked in. She dropped her hands. I smoothed the wrinkled material as he took his seat behind the desk.

"You were both seen on the seventh floor. I've heard Brynna's explanation. I'd like to hear yours, Calia." His voice was quiet but annoyance vibrated every syllable.

"Brynna arranged a secret meeting with a man and begged me to go along—for support—as a friend." Her false concern compounded the fabrication.

My fingers curled into fists. "That's a lie!" Her treachery stunned me. We were supposed to be friends.

The supervisor yawned as if suddenly bored with the circumstances. "Lie upon lie as I expected. You'll both be fined."

I grimaced. Hypor provided necessary items; our compensation for work was small.

Calia groaned in protest.

"Quiet," he barked. "In addition, I'm placing a reprimand in your personnel records. Be warned. A second infraction and you could lose your job, or worse." He flicked his hand. "Go."

My face flamed as we filed out, scrutinized by our co-workers. The younger ones grinned; the others shook their heads in disgust. My biggest concern was Father learning about the infraction. A fine and a warning was a relief, more lenient than I'd expected.

"What are you looking at?" Calia's narrowed eyes spewed venom at the onlookers as she trudged toward her workstation. She avoided me for the rest of the day, even using an intermediary to pass work information between us. She whispered to Carrot, Stick, and others while shooting me hostile glances. Ignoring her seemed to fuel her need to gossip.

For the sake of our friendship, I had overlooked her selfishness and tolerated her nasty barbs. This time, however, her duplicity had permanently soured my feelings. The loss of her friendship was painful but I vowed to keep my distance from now on.

When six o'clock arrived, I was first in line to leave. Dench's condemning stare didn't faze me. I was desperate to escape the stifling atmosphere of gossip and speculation. I needed to see Jarryd.

I hadn't counted on Calia's seething rage. She ran past me, her hood blown back as she rotated her body to confront me.

"Traitor!" The bulging vein on her forehead triggered a

memory. It had always appeared during a tantrum when she didn't get her way.

Her accusation boiled with anger and penetrated the length of the passage. The curious stopped to watch, some started to encircle us. Carrot and Stick sniggered from their ringside position.

Her face was ugly with revenge. "I'll make you pay for this, Bokk." She retreated, shoving her way through the crowd.

Anger at her betrayal festered in my brain, but sadness filled my heart. My childhood friend was gone.

Those gathered sent me curious glances then dispersed. I dropped my head and hurried to the recpod. I had no patience with the slow movers in the tubes today. I ran as fast as my juba would allow.

Tears filled my eyes when I saw Jarryd outside the recpod entrance. I threw my arms around his neck. Strong comforting arms curled around me. For the second time that day, I felt safe.

He led me inside across a hard black floor to a seating area. I sunk onto a couch, surprised at its softness.

"What's happened?"

"Calia..." A sob hitched my breath.

"What's she done now?" His tone held the expectation of a girlish spat.

I wiped my eyes on the sleeve of my juba. I felt ashamed to tell him what had transpired.

"Come on, out with it," he prodded.

"Because of her I've been fined and reprimanded." I lifted my head when Jarryd laughed.

"So have I. Several times for being late to work. That's not worth tears." He brushed one from my cheek.

"That's not all." I gave him a quick rundown about her

lie to cover her own bad behavior. As I spoke I was surprised by the tsunami of fury and hurt that flooded through me again.

"What's upset Brynna?" Marta arrived, sat beside me and flung her arm across my shoulders. Not having a sister, the female closeness felt different, but her smile was warm. She leaned and whispered in my ear. "Ignore your brother. Tell me what happened."

"Sorry, Bryn." Jarryd sat on my other side and rubbed my arm.

Embarrassed and hurt, I repeated what I'd told my brother.

"Everyone knows she's a witch." Marta lifted her hands, curled her fingers and bared her teeth, then grinned.

I responded half-heartedly. "Unfortunately Calia loves to gossip and the story will soon be all over the city. What if Father hears about it?"

"I'm sure he'll believe your version of what happened. You're his daughter." Marta squeezed my shoulder.

"It won't change the reprimand in my file. He won't like that."

Jarryd took my hand. "Not to be unsympathetic, but Father has more important concerns on his mind."

Wrapped up in myself, I'd forgotten the larger issues at stake. "The planet, what about the threat?" Had something happened since lunchtime?

Jarryd shrugged. "Nothing new. It's up to the council. Let's hope they know what they're doing."

Marta nodded her agreement.

I blew out a sigh, feeling drained by the events of the day.

"Right," said Jarryd. "It's time to Bokk."

Marta laughed. I joined her. The phrase was familiar

and meant he had something fun in mind. Energy returned when I saw his blue eyes twinkle. Then the memory of another pair— this time green—surfaced, then faded.

"Come with me, Brynna." She stood with her hand outstretched. "We have to change."

"Where are we going?"

"To introduce you to the elements of Steepchase."

10

THE RECPOD

The soft light and pale green walls in the women's change room made the space inviting.

Except for a few mirrors, the walls were bare. Even posters of the ruling council were absent. Despite the rows of metal benches and dull gray lockers, the atmosphere was welcoming. I even detected the low hum of friendly conversation nearby.

Marta handed me a pile of garments. "They're not very flattering, but they allow for movement."

I stripped off my juba, kicked off my slippers and pitched them into a locker.

"You have a falcon on your shoulder. That's unusual."

"Just a silly birthmark." I'd forgotten to keep it covered. Fortunately, it was only Marta who'd noticed. I quickly pulled on the stretchy black top and leggings.

"I love these clothes." I punched my arms in the air and kicked my feet wide. There wasn't room to do a cartwheel or I'd have tried. I felt free and more at ease than I had anywhere else on Hypor.

She laughed. "And for your feet."

I snatched the red boots from her hand and slipped them on. "Perfect." Inside they were warm and cushioned. Their soft soles gripped the metal bench as I jumped up and ran its length.

She donned the same garb. The fabric clung to her shape. I wouldn't have minded a few more curves of my own.

"You look good." She sighed. "Black suits tall, athletic women. I'd prefer some color, but it could be worse. At least these are cute." She shrugged as she slipped on her boots.

"I'm surprised we don't have to wear jubas. Why is the council so lenient about clothing here?"

"They believe in keeping women—in fact all citizens—strong and healthy. Jubas and exercise don't go together." She plucked at the material. "Heavier garments don't breathe, these do." She threw me a length of ribbon. I followed her lead, pulling my hair back and securing it. "Blonde and dark, we look like salt and pepper." She laughed. "Let's go meet your brother."

We passed through a narrower door into a vast open area. The bright light stung my eyes. I thought we were outside until I looked up and saw the curved dome above us. Despite being enclosed, the semi-transparent roofing made it seem boundless. I was shocked to see grass and real trees, so natural I expected to hear birds singing. The air smelled fresh as well, without the nasty floral chemical smell pumped through the other domes.

The wall behind us was a deep yellow. As runners passed us, I noticed the track was berry red. In the distance, I could see purple, blue, not a speck of boring beige.

"Amazing, isn't it." Jarryd stood beside us wearing similar attire, but his boots were blue.

"What's the chart for?" I pointed to the yellow wall where names and times were listed.

"They're the top competitors from the monthly sprints. The best times are recorded over the year. You have to achieve at least tenth place in order to qualify for Steepchase. These guys have been training for years." He pointed to the top five names.

"Years?" Victory dwindled in my imagination, but I still noted the time of the tenth place competitor. Nothing was impossible.

"Okay. Where shall we start?" My brother deferred to Marta.

"I think the track would be best. Brynna will get to see the different areas as we run."

"Good plan. Okay with you, Bryn? You up for it?"

"Let's go."

I felt as if my feet had wings. But I hadn't had much exercise since arriving on Hypor and I started to lag. Jarryd and Marta slowed to an easier pace that I was able to match. Others on the track shouted encouragement as they overtook us. Their happy laughter was a balm to my spirits. Perhaps my brother was right and I would make some new friends here.

"Here's the climbing zone." Marta pointed skyward.

As the track followed the curve of the dome, a stand of trees on our left gave way to several steep rock-like walls. They extended a hundred feet along the track and almost reached the top of the dome. Black clad figures dotted the vertical surfaces clinging to multicolored handholds. Heights didn't normally bother me, but looking up I wondered how I would feel at the apex of the dome—if I ever got there. *When I got there,* I corrected.

My legs started to ache, but determination kept me going.

"This is the obstacle area for free running," said Jarryd. "I think you'll like this, Bryn."

I could see a variety of box-like structures, much smaller than the rock walls but equally challenging to those attempting to scale them and jump from one to another. People balanced on thin ledges, scrambled across nets, swung between bars and crawled through tight spaces. I was thrilled at the prospect of trying this course. I could already imagine running, jumping—pushing myself to the limit.

"You can't see it from here, but the archery area is on the back side of the rock climbing zone. That's something I really enjoy." Marta spoke easily as she ran. "Perhaps we can go together."

"I'd love that." I could only manage three words without huffing. Disappointed, I was determined to do better next time out.

Marta flicked a quick glance my way. "Let's rest when we get to the waterfall, Jarryd."

I saw her nod toward me followed by my brother's quick scrutiny of my face. I didn't object when they finally stopped. With more practice, I knew I could beat Jarryd. I always had. One day I'd outrun them, but not today.

I took a few deep breaths then gasped when I noticed the surroundings.

"This is the aqua zone. You can practice free diving and distance swimming. You'll need those skills if you want to participate in the games. And there's Hypor Falls." Marta pointed to the far left. A thirty-foot high chute of water plunged into a turquoise pool. As we watched, a diver leaped from the cliff top into the swirling waters at the base of the falls. From there, the pool broadened into a rectangular expanse where others raced in defined lanes.

"Do I have to dive as well?" I'd never learned to swim and didn't relish the idea of jumping into water from any height. "For Steepchase, I mean."

Jarryd twigged to my unease. "It changes every year. You might not need to dive this year, but you definitely have to be able to swim."

I wrinkled my nose at him. He was like a seal in the water and although sympathetic, he couldn't understand why I still feared water.

"I have a friend who helped me speed up my stroke," said Jarryd. "I'm sure he'd teach you to swim if I asked. If you want to compete you'll have to learn."

I heard the challenge in his words and saw his tight grin.

Marta jumped in. "Don't pressure her, Jarryd. Steepchase isn't for everyone. Some of us just like to watch."

I bit my tongue and stifled a retort. I had to remind myself that she was only trying to help. Jarryd and I had always competed, something Marta didn't understand. But this time there was more than just a sibling competition on my mind. Steepchase might be my way out of Hypor City.

"Let's run again. Are you up for it, Jarryd?" I asked.

"More than you," he laughed before speeding off, leaving us trailing behind.

It took several minutes to circle the swimming area. Small huts appeared from time to time. Among the trees, there were a number of grassy sites where people lounged and chatted. It was impossible to believe that those who had designed the other domes had built this place. It was a different world. My kind of different.

Soon, we were back where we started.

"Let's introduce Brynna to Swigs," said Marta.

We ran a few more feet then veered right. When we finally stopped I hunched over, gulping air.

"We're here." She placed her hand on my back.

I looked up at a large red sign with black lettering —*SWIGS*.

A low wall surrounded small tables scattered across a patio. A barrel-like container held a variety of juice bottles cooling in ice. We selected our drinks and chose a vacant table under a tree. It offered the impression of shade, even though there was no direct sunlight.

Nearby, others watched players huddled in concentration over board games, giving encouragement or booing bad moves. Tired runners greeted us as they made their way to an empty seat. The atmosphere was friendly and easy.

"So what do you think, Bryn?" Jarryd took a long swallow of his drink and stretched out his legs.

"I can't believe this is still Hypor City. I wish I'd seen the recpod the first day. I wouldn't have felt so depressed by all the beige."

"I should have brought you here sooner, but I thought you'd be with Calia."

"I'm sorry you've had a rough time with her," said Marta. "The good news is that she doesn't come here. Not the athletic type, I guess."

"She's more interested in men at the moment. Prince Delio for one." It slipped out. I hadn't meant to tell anyone. I didn't want to fall into gossip mode.

My brother leaned his forearms on the table. "How do you know? Did you see them together?"

He didn't gossip so I knew he had other reasons for asking.

I told them the whole story about what had occurred

that afternoon on the seventh floor. I left out the part about the second guard.

"So that's what happened to Weyland." Anger tinged his voice.

"Who's Weyland?"

"He's the colleague I told you about—the one that found the data on the CMEs. He left the office this afternoon but returned a few minutes later with a cut on his eyebrow. I asked him what had happened, but he was too shaken to speak."

Marta shook her head in disbelief. "Why would Prince Delio hit someone like Weyland? He's harmless."

"The son is a bully just like his father. Pick on the weak." Jarryd made a fist. "Maybe next time we meet I'll have a chat with him."

"You mustn't," Marta placed her hands on his fist. "Not now, when the council is so divided. Any further friction might create a rift that nothing will heal."

"What friction?" This was something new I hadn't heard.

Jarryd ignored my question. "Then I'll just have to protect Weyland as best I can." He paused. "Bryn, would you object if I brought him home with us on our monthly break?"

"I wouldn't mind, but you'd better let the parents know."

"Marta, do you want to come as well? It's time you met my mother anyway." He winked at her.

She looked at me for consent. I liked that, so I nodded. My earlier jealousy was gone. We finished our drinks and headed back to the change rooms.

As I started to ask about the friction she'd mentioned, Marta spoke first. "Don't worry about Calia," she said as we slipped on our jubas. "Once she sees she can't push you around, she'll find someone else to pick on or die trying."

I laughed, but I knew that Calia's love of gossip could make my life very uncomfortable.

"We'd better go. Men always complain if they have to wait too long."

Outside, feigning impatience, Jarryd tapped his foot and smiled.

"I'm going to walk Marta back to her dorm. Do you want to come?" Marta's room was in a pod near the marketplace that housed artists and other vendors.

"No thanks. Three's a crowd. I'll see you soon." I delayed a moment and watched them saunter away, hand in hand. To have that connection was something special.

Green eyes flashed across my mind. Perhaps one day it would happen for me.

In no hurry to see Calia, I strolled back to my dorm. I logged into the message screen outside but found no notes, malicious or otherwise. Upon entering our room, I was surprised to discover a new girl occupying Calia's space. Only someone in authority could change room assignments. Someone like Prince Delio.

Relieved that my tormentor was gone from the dorm, I wasn't optimistic about how she'd behave at work. Next morning, however, she wasn't at her usual workstation beside me. She'd wheedled permission to change places with one of the men across the room.

Despite her threats, I hoped that some memory of our past relationship would soften her feelings toward me. Instead, she took every opportunity to undermine me.

"You've made another mistake, Bokk," she'd called in a loud voice just as Dench entered the media lab one day. "I won't continue to cover for you any longer."

"What's this?" Dench responded as expected. "What mistake?" Everyone knew his obsession with accuracy.

This time, her accusation backfired. Carrot and Stick protested that I wasn't the culprit but that Calia had misread a translation. The supervisor confirmed their claim. She got a lecture on sloppiness and had one more reason to hate me.

Surprisingly, my rift with Calia had positive consequences.

Carrot was first to approach me. "Don't let her rattle you."

Others found reasons to linger at my workstation and chat. Within days, I felt accepted and more comfortable than I had previously but I still preferred to spend most of my free time alone at the recpod. There, I could sing softly or hum as I ran without anyone noticing.

One day, I decided to revisit the market to see if Marta was there. Without the crowds I noticed it was inviting and airy, much like the recpod. At one end of the dome, a theater screened documentaries about Hypor City and its achievements. There was another cafe like Swigs and many more stalls selling jewelry and sculpture, paintings and drawings.

I didn't see Marta but was enjoying another artist's display of stone carvings when I looked up and spied Calia and Prince exiting the theater. Chills pricked up my spine. I dropped my head and pulled my hood forward then headed for the exit. I didn't want trouble.

From then on, the recpod became my sanctuary. Not only could I sing quietly as I ran, but day after day, my muscles grew stronger. I climbed faster, jumped farther, and ran longer. I was soon passing others in the speed lane, pushing body and mind to exhaustion.

As my confidence grew, I braved rock climbing. I had a good head for heights but discovered I still needed more strength. I was determined to one day make it all the way to the top of the dome.

Marta promised to give me pointers at the archery range after we returned from work break. I'd made good progress on the obstacle course and my running times were improving consistently, but I had avoided my worst terror.

Swimming was my final obstacle. If I wanted to qualify for Steepchase, I'd have to learn to swim. Jarryd's friend might be willing to help, but did I have the courage to let him?

11

WORK BREAK

Our lander glistened in the sunshine outside Hypor's main dome. Finally we were going home.

Father waited beside our vehicle. The crease between his eyebrows deepened as we approached. His stern gaze focused on me. I knew he'd heard about my reprimand.

Jarryd quickly introduced Marta and Weyland. Father's greeting was curt, especially toward Weyland, who fidgeted continuously. I smiled and kept silent. My father might not be pleased about having company, but I was delighted because I knew that he'd say nothing about my infraction in front of guests.

His dark demeanor didn't diminish the excitement I felt when we touched down on our island. Mother stood near the landing area. Her warm smile vanquished all concerns. I was first out of the lander. After a lengthy hug, I left my brother to introduce his guests and ran to my room.

I threw off my juba. Once in comfortable clothes, I rushed out the back door to the mews. This time I pulled on the new gauntlet. Circe greeted me with a squawk and settled on my arm. I'd been away for almost a month, but she hadn't forgotten me.

I hurried toward the exit, anxious to be alone with my falcon, but Jarryd's form filled the doorway. He knew me too well.

"Bryn. Marta and I need some private time to talk to the parents. Can you show Weyland around?"

Hearing his name, Weyland poked his head from behind my brother. His forlorn appearance tugged at my heart. I remembered that day in the hallway when he lay hurt. He needed a friend and I knew what that felt like.

Though I wanted to be by myself and climb to my perch and sing, courtesy and compassion made refusal impossible. I'd missed my music, but I'd have to wait. Singing in front of Weyland or anyone outside the family was forbidden. Perhaps we could walk through the forest or do some climbing. Then I remembered his clumsiness.

When I smiled, he moved forward and lifted his hand towards Circe.

"Careful, she bites strangers. Even me sometimes," Jarryd warned before turning back to the house.

I held my breath when Circe's intimidating hooked beak opened, but to my surprise, she didn't bite Weyland. Her head swiveled and fathomless black eyes peered at him as his finger stroked her wing feathers.

Weyland was different and this pricked my curiosity. In addition to being smart, he obviously had an affinity with animals. Maybe I'd learn more about him and the threat if I could gain his trust.

I lifted my arm.

As Circe swept skyward, he stood as if awestruck. His gaze followed every swoop.

"Okay, let's go." When he didn't respond, I used his name. "Let's go exploring, Weyland."

This time, he looked at me. The eyes that met mine twinkled with excitement. As we entered the forest, he stopped to examine leaves, veins and stems, stroke and smell the flowers, and brush his fingertips in the rugged grooved bark of old-growth trees. It was like watching a child discover the world. I sensed that he hadn't had much fun in his life.

"Have you always lived in Hypor City, Weyland?"

He shook his head looking puzzled by my question. "No."

"Where is your family?" Perhaps he had relatives. Maybe he wasn't alone.

"Don't know."

He looked sad and didn't elaborate. I decided not to pry.

"Weyland, I'm going to climb the rocks. You can come up or wander through the woods." There was no way of getting lost on our small island. All paths eventually led back home or to the village.

When he didn't answer, I ran to a low boulder and pushed off the ground, landing and jumping easily from one rock to the next. Working out at the recpod was paying off. My feet and balance were sure. I reached the mountain ridge in less than usual time.

I found my spot and sat, dangling my legs over the edge. Weyland plunked down beside me seconds later.

"What? How...?" Was this the same man who had stumbled into Prince?

A bashful expression crossed his face. "I watched where you put your feet and copied how you moved. Focus and control. Mind over body."

"So what else are you hiding?" I sounded snarky and

immediately felt bad when he looked wounded. "Sorry, Weyland. I was surprised that's all."

I tried to make up for my rudeness by telling him the history of the island and the village; how we'd played as kids, making tree forts, pretending to ward off pirates on the beach, collecting discarded crab shells for our curiosity cupboard. He listened intently but said little. Finally, I ceased my commentary and breathed in the silence.

"Your voice," was all he said.

My throat muscles tightened. I'd been humming softly, unconsciously. It was a stupid mistake. "What about my voice?"

"You're a singer." It was a statement, not a question. I felt his eyes on me.

How did he know about singers?

I didn't meet his gaze. I'd never been a good liar. "I don't know what you mean."

"Sing something for me." He made the request as if certain I'd comply.

I wanted to sing, but denial was the only option and I hated lying. I was pondering what to say when he touched my arm.

"I promise not to tell anyone. I'm good at keeping secrets." His voice was solemn and its vibration was true.

I still hesitated. There was too much at stake.

At that moment, Circe descended and perched beside Weyland. He stroked his finger down her breast. She sat quietly, her dark eyes trusting him. Could I trust him too?

Being home and safe, the urge to unleash my voice was stronger than usual.

"Please?"

His soft appeal defeated the last of my resistance. One deep breath and my voice soared through five octaves then

THE LAST SINGER

flowed into an island folk song. Eyes closed, I trembled as the music and tones pulsed through my body. Time lost meaning. The unity of breath and vocal cords intensified the vibrations. Higher, stronger, I pushed beyond, unaware of my surroundings until I felt Weyland slump against me.

"What happened? Are you okay?" Maybe I'd been wrong to trust him. Was he weak in other ways too?

I felt his brow. Instinct overcame shock and I started a low hum.

Circe flapped her wings as if trying to revive him.

He slowly regained consciousness and attempted to stand, but I grabbed his arm and kept him seated.

I felt a little weak myself.

"Your voice." Fear wove through his words. "It hurt me."

"Sorry." I was surprised, but even more curious. "How?"

"The higher notes are brown and black. They hurt." He must have detected my confusion. "I see the colors of your voice. The lower notes are yellow, orange and red. They are warm and comforting. The higher notes are harsh and dark."

Femin use the low notes for healing, so his reactions to those made sense. It was possible that higher vibrations had a different use, but Mother hadn't mentioned them.

"I don't understand." I tried to hide my urgency. "How do you see the colors?"

"I'm a synesthete."

"What's that?" I'd never heard the term. Had he made it up?

"I hear sounds as colors. Special gift I inherited from my mother. Some people think I'm crazy." His quick glance looked for understanding. "You won't tell, will you? Promise?"

"I promise." I raised my hand, binding the oath.

"Your voice is strong. High notes have power. Before I passed out, my body shook like it was coming apart, molecule by molecule." He stared at his splayed hands before clasping them together as if to ensure they were solid.

Shocked and confused by his reaction, I managed to mumble out another 'sorry.' I needed to talk to my mother. There must be an explanation.

"Very interesting feeling." His voice was steadier and curious. "You have a special gift too. We must explore your abilities further. Could be important."

"It's a secret. My singing, I mean." There had been relief in sharing, but now I wished I hadn't. "You have to promise not to tell anyone."

He lifted his hand, confirming his promise. "Trust me, Brynna Bokk. I'm good at keeping secrets."

I scrambled to my feet and hurried down the path. He kept pace, easily following my lead. Overhead, Circe traced our descent and landed on a tree branch when I stopped at the edge of the forest.

The physical exertion calmed my nerves and I laughed when Weyland joined my side. I saw his grin widen as we huffed long breaths.

"This way?" He pointed to a narrow path between two oak trees.

"There's only a derelict windmill and the beach down there." It was the opposite direction to home, and I didn't want to delay. "Not much to see."

"Please, Brynna Bokk." He was Jarryd's age, but the sparkling anticipation in his eyes made him appear younger than his twenty-one years.

I acquiesced and followed. From the grassy slope, I watched him examine shells and stones as he wandered along the beach. He whooped for joy when he discovered a small pink crab under a rock. He waved it high above his head. Its claws clutched the air as he examined it before returning it to its hiding place.

I clapped at his antics then stopped when I detected the buzzing.

"Weyland!" I pointed.

He glanced at me, then at my hand.

"Weyland, run. It's a drone."

It darted toward the beach. Different from the first one I'd seen. It was larger, with more attachments. Several front-mounted objects swiveled and focused on our positions as it approached.

I looked for Circe, but this time she wasn't preparing to attack the intruder. She flew high above. The drone seemed oblivious to her presence. Instead, it honed in on Weyland, who stood motionless.

"Run Weyland." When he didn't move, I sprinted toward him, faltering over the uneven rocks and broken shells.

As the drone sped toward him, he put a hand into his pocket. Seconds later the buzzing stopped. The drone lost altitude, wobbled, then crashed at his feet.

"What happened?" I crunched to a stop beside him. "What did you do?"

Smashed on the rocks, the drone lay in several pieces.

Withdrawing his hand from his trousers, he opened his palm to reveal a small black box. "My invention. A disrupter. Interrupts circuitry." He continued talking as if I was his scientific equal until I held up my hand.

"Won't they know you've destroyed it?" I was concerned about repercussions.

"It shouldn't be here." He pointed to mounts on the

drone. "These lasers are experimental and lethal." His face registered confusion.

I grabbed his arm. "Come on. We have to tell my father." First the drone at the greenhouse, then in the forest clearing, it was no coincidence that a third one had shown up on our island.

"Too dangerous to leave it here." He picked up the parts.

Circe followed as we rushed for home.

AFTER TAKING CIRCE TO THE MEWS, I BOUNDED INTO THE house, Weyland on my heels.

There were no cooking smells or happy chatter. Mother, Jarryd and Marta sat around the dining table speaking in subdued tones.

"We've found another drone."

My brother jumped up from his seat. Weyland moved forward, placing the broken parts on the table.

"Where's Father?" I asked Mother directly. "We have to tell him."

"He had to leave. Marta's father arrived from Hypor twenty minutes ago to pick him up. I don't know when he'll be back."

The little relief that he wouldn't be around to scold me for Dench's reprimand was overshadowed by disappointment that he couldn't provide answers about the drone.

"It's not a watcher," Jarryd confirmed scrutinizing every fragment. "If Weyland hadn't disabled it, the lasers could have hurt someone."

"Killed someone." Weyland's statement pulled all attention to him. Then to the drone.

"This is too much." Marta's wet eyes reflected unspoken fears.

Jarryd embraced her. Mother went to make tea. Weyland examined the drone debris.

"Drones appearing around the island. Council meetings at all hours. What's going on?" I wanted answers.

I caught Jarryd's questioning look at Mother when she returned with tea and sandwiches. I suspected they were keeping something back. I couldn't contain my anger. "No more secrets! This affects all of us."

"Yes, you're right, Bryn," said Jarryd. "I think it's time we discussed what's been happening."

"We know about the threat from the sun. What else is there?"

"Coronal mass ejections," corrected Weyland. "CMEs."

"Yes, I understand they're a deadly threat, but the council has a plan. The shields and the starships? The scientists are working on something, aren't they?" I felt my frustration rising.

"It's not that simple," said Marta. "There's politics involved."

"What does that mean?" I slapped the table in frustration. "For goodness sake, someone tell me the truth. What are you hiding?"

"Your father doesn't trust Premier Delio," said Mother, finally entering the discussion. "He and some of the other members suspect that the Premier is planning to undermine the council's authority, using the solar threat to seize power for himself."

"How can he do that when the council has a plan to thwart the threat?"

"I've been asking around," said Jarryd. "The satellite shielding technology is only in the early stages of development. It needs more research. From what I've been told, Delio isn't doing much to encourage that avenue of defense.

"What about the starships? Is there any hope there?"

"Difficult." Weyland's one word set me off again.

"Apart from the fact that we don't know if our Mars colony exists, why is it difficult?"

"Need special propulsion units."

Jarryd saw me seething and explained. "Hypor City doesn't have the technology to launch large space ships."

"So why is Delio trying to gain power if there's no hope of surviving? It doesn't make sense."

"Delio's made a deal with a man called Tarvek in Nuvega. Rumor is he has developed high-propulsion solar batteries. He's also agreed to build spaceships," said Mother. "Your father is concerned because Delio made the deal without the involvement and approval of the council."

"That's not all." Marta's soft voice hesitated. "The Premier is increasing his personal guard and my father thinks he's trying to build a private military force."

"Your father believes the best route is to channel resources into shield development, but Delio's stalling them saying that Tarvek's ships are the best choice. He's also convinced the majority of the council to back him, except for our fathers and two others." Marta stopped talking and her eyes flicked to my brother.

I was beginning to understand the complexity of the situation. It was far beyond anything I could imagine.

"We don't know if Delio is acting in Hypor's best interest or his own." Jarryd looked at Mother.

Crinkled brows framed her worried eyes. "Your father is attempting to find proof."

"But Delio isn't going to wait while Father investigates." My brother pointed to the broken drone. Even in parts, it looked menacing. "The drones prove that our island is being monitored. They'll know that this one crashed." He scanned our faces. "Prince will be suspicious. We'll have to stay under their radar and hope that they don't realize we're onto them."

"The Little Prince." I scoffed, remembering his nickname. "What does he have to do with this?"

"Designed the drone," said Weyland.

"What?"

"Don't underestimate Prince, Bryn. He's arrogant and ruthless, perhaps more than his father. He's also a brilliant scientist." Jarryd pointed to the broken pieces. "This is very sophisticated technology."

"Father and son plotting together." Marta shuddered as she stood then paced to a window. Returning, she gently placed her hands on Mother's sagging shoulders.

Jarryd picked up one of the laser mounts. "Yes. And I suspect Prince might be the one heading the premier's personal army."

Mother rested her hand on Marta's, their bond already strong. "Your father has demanded that the premier release the details of his deal with Tarvek, without success. He also contacted Prima Feminary but Delio got there first. The Genetrix knows about the threat and the options, but she told your father she'd support the premier."

Was the Genetrix aware of Delio's larger ambitions? What was she hoping to gain from his deal with Tarvek?

Prima Feminary was appearing less like a sanctuary.

"If your father can't produce evidence, no one will believe that Delio has his own agenda until it's too late." Marta slumped into a chair beside me.

"Then we'll just have to get proof." There was no other option that I could see.

"As I said before, they're watching us, so we may have an advantage." Jarryd tapped his nails on the table. It was always annoying but a telltale sign that he was hatching a plan.

After half a minute of clicking I broke. "Stop tapping and tell us how that helps."

Unexpectedly, Jarryd laughed. "It means that if we behave normally, they won't know that we're listening, watching, and digging for proof to help Father."

"What can we do?" I craved action to defeat the hopelessness I'd experienced earlier.

The others chimed in adding their desire to mine.

"I need time to think," said Jarryd. "Tomorrow we'll devise a strategy."

A tense silence followed, broken a few minutes later by Mother's soft voice.

"Now for some good news. Jarryd and Marta have pledged to marry." Her sweet smile accompanied the announcement.

Weyland's hooting and clapping overshadowed my silence.

It took a moment for the news to penetrate. A whirlwind of emotions left me speechless. Tears pricked my lids.

"Bryn?" My brother moved around the table, his eyes full of concern.

"Brynna." Marta circled my neck with her arms. "I'm so happy to have you as my sister."

"Me too," I mumbled into her shoulder but loud enough to be heard.

"That's a relief." Jarryd tugged my hair. "Now it's time to celebrate."

"I'll get the apricot wine." Mother hurried to the kitchen. "No more worry tonight."

I don't know how we forgot about the threat that night, but we did.

Mother's apricot wine might have helped.

But as the icy light of the full moon crawled across my bedroom floor, anxiety flicked at my dulled senses. No longer uneasy about what sleep would bring, there was a more pressing concern—the future of the planet.

The night was blessedly dreamless.

The morning sun, breaking the gap in the curtains, didn't help the headache that pounded over my left eye. Definitely the wine.

I stumbled into the kitchen and rubbed my eyes as I sat hunched at the table.

"Good day for a run." Jarryd pounded my shoulder as he bounded by. "Marta and I are going to get some exercise. How about it?"

I winced. "No thanks. I'm taking Circe out in a while."

"Is Circe your falcon?" Marta appeared in pink workout gear. "I asked Jarryd when I was carving your birthday gift."

"You carved it?" I should have guessed. "It's beautiful. Thank you."

"I enjoyed doing it. Will you introduce me to your bird?"

"When you get back from your exercise, I'll take you to the mews. You can see Father's falcon as well."

They were out the door before I finished the sentence. It was only then I realized that Weyland was still eating. They'd left me to entertain him, again.

I needed to talk to Mother about Weyland's reaction to my singing, but he was a guest. I couldn't leave him on his own.

"Weyland, would you like to go back up the rocks?"

He nodded and gulped down the remainder of his breakfast. Seconds later, he waited at the door like a puppy.

I grinned and pulled on my boots. "We have to get Circe."

"Love her." He beamed. "Beautiful falcon." He almost skipped to the mews.

I released Circe in the clearing. Weyland groaned as she climbed into the air, but appeared happy when she stayed in sight. I ran to the boulders and started to climb. At the top, Weyland was right on my heels. When he saw Circe he passed me to follow her.

She perched on a thin jut of stone that had split from the main boulder.

"Careful, Weyland, there's no path there."

He flattened his body against the rock face. As he neared Circe, she took to the air. My eyes flew up as she soared. When I looked back Weyland had disappeared.

My heart drummed as I squeezed along the slender ledge where I'd last seen him. My back pressed hard against cold granite. I focused my gaze ahead, avoiding the death drop to my left.

What if he'd gone over the edge?

I tortured myself with several scenarios. Relief washed over me when his head popped out further along the path. A fold in the rock concealed his body. He motioned for me to follow.

"Cave. Brynna Bokk. Cave."

12

CAVE OF SECRETS

The dark cavern blinded me.

"Weyland, where are you?" One hand pressed cold stone, I stretched the other ahead.

"Around the bend. No need to fear. The way is clear." His voice echoed in the blackness.

Despite his assurance, I cautiously slid one foot forward and then the other until the stone wall ended. I stopped and waited for my eyes to adjust. I could hear Weyland's shuffle.

The chilly damp air made me shiver. A narrow beam of sunlight streamed from a fissure twenty feet above. Our arrival disturbed layers of soot and dust that now danced in the bright sliver from the ceiling. Gradually I made out shapes and objects. This wasn't just a cave. It was someone's home, or had been.

With ten strides I crossed the room. Along one wall, an oak table was set with one plate and a cup. In the center, hard wax pooled at the base of a half-burned candle. A blackened match lay broken alongside an open wooden box containing several more matches. Left of the table, a fireplace recessed into an alcove. A stack of dry branches and a box of stubby candles sat nearby. I held my hand over the dead ashes and felt an upward draft. A natural chimney.

"I hear water dripping." There must be a catchment nearby. Whoever had lived here would have needed a source of fresh water.

"Books." Weyland's voice brimmed with excitement.

At a glance, I guessed a dozen, piled on either side of the simple bed. They were also crammed into niches chiseled into the stone walls, and leaning precariously along makeshift shelving. A thrill shot through me. I was wrong. There had to be over a hundred books. The cave had suddenly become a treasure chest.

"This is amaz—what are you doing, Weyland?" I squinted, trying to make sense of his actions.

Kneeling beside the bed, eyes closed, his fingertips skimmed the book bindings. "I'm looking for the important ones."

"How can you tell which ones are important?"

"They are the most touched. I feel the body heat—the red."

"This cave has been empty for a long time, how can you still feel heat?"

When he didn't answer, I decided it must be another Weyland thing. I gently drew a book from its niche but the binding disintegrated at my touch. Paper dust floated in the air around me.

I coughed and sneezed. "These are ancient." I searched for another to examine, hopefully in better condition.

Weyland continued his inspection.

I sneezed again as another book fell apart in my fingers. "Have you sensed anything, Weyland?"

"Come, look." He crouched beside the bed. "This one." His palm stroked the book face.

"Bring it over here." I grabbed a few candles from the box near the fireplace and set them on the table. The matches in the box were old but they flared to life when stroked along the stone floor.

"This one is most important." There was reverence in his words as he positioned his find in the candlelight.

Even in better lighting, the impression on the worn cover was difficult to decipher. I was eager to open the book but it was his find.

He reached forward. I held my breath, waiting for my first glance of the wisdom inside.

The page was blank. "It's not a book." I sighed in disappointment.

"No." Weyland gasped when he lifted the second leaf. "A diary."

The word hung between us as we exchanged excited glances.

"It must belong to whoever lived here—and perhaps died here," I whispered.

Unfamiliar script filled that page and the next. There were sketches on some.

I shuddered. "Whose diary could it be?"

Weyland shrugged. "Don't know. Can't read it."

I couldn't either. The language was unlike anything I'd encountered.

"Mother might know. She has a gift for languages."

He turned another page, revealing a larger drawing. The words underneath were unintelligible but the portrait was clear. A female face with mismatched eyes like my own stared back at me.

I stepped back from the table. The cave suddenly felt claustrophobic. I had to get out.

"Find something to wrap around the book." My voice shook with urgency.

Weyland went back to the bed and returned with a length of threadbare purple cloth. My chest tightened as I unfolded it. It was an old juba.

The fabric parted easily and I tore off the hood. I shoved the book inside, then tossed it to Weyland like a hot coal. "You carry it. Let's go."

Circe squawked overhead as I left the cave. I hurried as best I could, given the narrowness of the path, until I'd reached level ground. Weyland pressed close behind me, still holding the bundle.

"What's wrong, Brynna Bokk?" His eyes held concern.

I wiped a sleeve over my sweaty face. I couldn't explain what I'd experienced. "I need to show the book to my mother."

We hiked to the house in silence.

Our arrival coincided with Jarryd and Marta's return from rock climbing. They were rosy-cheeked and laughing but went silent when they saw me.

"Are you okay, Bryn? Did a leech get you on the way home?"

"Don't tease." Marta held out her hand. "Brynna, you're as gray as ash. What happened?"

I ignored her gesture. "I'll explain later. I need to talk to Mother first."

Weyland stooped forward and passed me the wrapped book. "Secret. Promise."

"Thank you." I forced a weak smile then ran to find Mother.

∿

Her humming was a soft balm as I entered the greenhouse. I walked between two rows of flowers, oblivious to the colors and scents, finally stopping within arm's reach of Mother.

"Did you have a good time?" She continued to trim back the rosemary that had become a bush.

"No." My control shattered, a sob escaped.

Clippers clattered to the floor. Mother's arms closed around me. My head fell to her shoulder and I wept.

"Come." She led me to an old couch. I curled up as she covered me with a shawl. I heard her set water to boil for tea. The sounds were comforting as I waited for her return.

"Now." She pressed a fragrant cup of chamomile into my hands before settling beside me. "Tell me what happened today."

After a sip of the hot liquid, I took a ragged breath and fought back tears.

"Slowly, in your own time." She started to hum and I felt my tension ease.

I took another breath, calmer this time and wiped my eyes.

"It's not just today. I guess things have been building up. First, there's Calia who I thought was my friend but now hates me." I briefly told her what had happened. "Not to mention the threat of world destruction. Then Weyland telling me that my singing hurt him, which I don't understand." I glanced up to see her reaction, but her face remained serene. "Now this." I pushed the purple package toward her.

She rubbed the pale cloth between thumb and finger. There was respect in her touch as she gently removed the contents. I sensed that she knew its origin. Her fingers traced the outline on the cover. She pressed the diary between her hands as if absorbing its content.

"Femin." A sad smile followed her whisper. "Long gone. Where did you find this?"

"In a cave at the top of the rock folds. Weyland found it. The place is full of old books. There's a bed, a table and chairs. Who could have lived there?"

"Your grandfather told the story of an old Genetrix whose feminary was flooded during the Rising. Your father's family offered her a cottage near the village, but she preferred to live in solitude in the mountains. The villagers saw her occasionally when they left provisions for her. After the earthquakes, she disappeared, probably trapped in her cave." Mother's eyes were wet. "The last quakes must have uncovered the entrance. This must be her diary."

"But why would there be a picture of me in there?" I flipped over several pages and opened the journal at the drawing. "What does that mean?"

She slowly examined the sketch. "I don't think it's you. Just a face with different colored eyes." She squinted at the strange writing, her fingers floating over each word.

I waited for her to speak, but patience isn't my best quality.

"Can you translate it?"

She tilted her head. "It will take time to decipher her writing."

"What do you think the picture means?"

"It could be a self-portrait, or someone she knew, or perhaps..."

"What?" I anxiously scanned her face. "What were you going to say?"

She shrugged. "I'd only be guessing. I'll work on it and try to have an answer by your next work break. We can talk about it then." She closed the book and placed it beside her, under her shawl.

The diary was out of sight, but I knew what I'd seen inside would haunt me until I had more answers.

"Now tell me about Weyland."

There was no reproach in her voice, but mine was heavy with guilt. "I'm sorry, so sorry. I forgot he was with me. I started humming. He begged me to sing. I wasn't going to but then Circe landed beside him. She trusted him and I felt I could too. After a month without singing, I couldn't stop myself..." I dropped my head and picked at a fingernail, expecting censure.

"What did he say about your voice hurting him?"

I repeated what Weyland had told me. I couldn't remember what he'd called himself, but tried to explain the colors he saw in my different vocal tones. When she didn't speak, I filled the void.

"Again, I'm sorry. I didn't mean to put you in danger."

"Who told you I was in danger?" Mother looked surprised.

"Father said you might be arrested for teaching me to sing if I was found out."

She shook her head. "I'm sorry. That must have terrified you. But except for Weyland, no one else suspects you're a singer, do they?"

"I don't think so, but I was nervous that the Genetrix might suspect somehow. She looked at me strangely when I met her."

I guessed by her surprise that Father neglected to relate my experience. "You met the Genetrix?"

"My first day on Hypor. She used her voice on me."

"She did what?" Mother's mouth tightened and her jaw clenched. "What do you mean?" How?"

I described the high-pitched humming and that I couldn't move my legs. "She held my chin and took the longest time peering into my eyes. Then she let go and went with the Premier."

Mother looked relieved then puzzled. "There were always rumors that the Genetrix had advanced vocal control."

"Do you think it's something to do with what Weyland felt?"

"I've never heard of anyone reacting as Weyland did, but our individual voices were always modulated to the tonal ranges required for healing. Outsiders were never present when we sang together." Mother smiled slightly. "I remember those joyous times. Lifting our harmonies, transporting ourselves into ecstasy."

"That's what I experienced today on the mountain before Weyland slumped against me. It was as if I was in another world. I felt strong and free and my voice was flying."

"Did you say anything to Weyland?"

"No, he only knows what happened to him. I wanted to talk to you first."

"Until we know more about how this occurred I think this should be our secret."

"I wish I could wipe Weyland's mind of the incident."

"I suspect that he isn't the only one who knows you can sing. I'm sure Jarryd has told Marta since she's joining the family. At least they don't know you're a Femin healer, although, Weyland will be curious about today's incident. He's a scientist after all."

"He promised to keep my secret. I promised to keep his, except for you. Do you think what happened to him is important?"

"I'll research my old feminary texts to see what I can learn and we can talk next time you're home. Now we should go. Marta offered to make the midday meal."

We walked home in silence.

"Before we go inside." She took my arm and stopped at the threshold of the kitchen door. "One last thing, about Calia. Do you remember when your gold bangle went missing? The one you inherited from your grandmother?"

"Yes. It reappeared a few days later."

Mother nodded. "Calia took it from your bedroom. She admitted it was yours when her aunt discovered her wearing it. She was forbidden to enter our home again. She's always been jealous. It's something we hoped she'd outgrow."

The revelation wasn't as shocking as it might once have been.

"It's just as well you're no longer friends. Jealousy is destructive."

The condemnation was strong coming from a woman whose nature was always to see the best in people.

"I've learned my lesson where she's concerned. We avoid each other at work. She's out of my life forever." I waved my hands, pushing away her unwanted image, hoping my words were true.

"Good. Let's go and discover what my future daughter-in-law has cooked up."

FATHER DIDN'T RETURN SO WE WERE FIVE AROUND THE dining table. Marta's vegetable soup and homemade bread were delicious and filling but didn't distract me from the broken drone that now lay on the floor by the fireplace. I suspected the others were also pondering it and the threat because no one uttered a word until we'd cleared the table.

We returned to our seats. I waited for Jarryd to speak. His solemn expression made him appear older than his twenty-one years.

"Okay. As I see it, our goal is to collect information." He scanned our faces. "We know we're being watched. There's real danger if we're caught but I don't think we have any option. Father needs to know what Delio is planning. It's not just a council concern. The threat affects all of us."

I leaned forward, eager to help. "What I can do?"

He responded with a nod and a brief smile. "We'll all have a part to play."

There were murmurs of support from the others.

I waved my arm excitedly. "I know. I can search the databases in the media lab for anything that might be linked to Delio, or the CMEs."

"That's a great idea," replied Jarryd. "Marta, your father confides in you, so you're our best source of what's happening with the council. Weyland and I will work on getting into Delio's private computer files. I have friends in various departments that I'm sure will help when they know about the threat. That's the final thing we have to do, to make sure that everyone knows about the CMEs —anonymously."

"How?" Marta nibbled her lip.

"I'm still working on that." Jarryd's nails tapped the table.

Silence held for several minutes.

"You'll find a way." Mother leaned forward and rested her hand on his arm. "What can I do from here?"

"You'll be our link to Father. It's best you keep out of

sight as much as possible when you're alone. They might send more drones."

"Disrupter." Weyland pulled the small black box with a red button from his pocket. "For Mother Bokk."

I'd forgotten his invention. "He used it to kill the drone."

"Not kill," he corrected. "Disrupt circuitry."

"Fantastic." Jarryd examined the box. "Can you make more in case we need them?"

"Easy." Weyland's face bloomed pink with embarrassment as all eyes watched.

My brother's smile hardened into a determined line. "So we continue our usual routines. We'll meet at the recpod in the evenings. Keep everything normal and dig until we find something."

"What do you think will happen when the citizens learn about the CME danger?" Marta's question produced silence. Then Jarryd started to laugh.

"Delio will be up to his neck in problems."

13

A COVERT INVESTIGATION

Leaving Mother and returning to Hypor proved more difficult this time.

The appearance of another drone, this time a lethal one, coupled with the discussion about the Delios had me concerned for her safety and what might come. I'd always viewed my father as an invincible guardian, but his continued absences filled me with doubts about his ability to protect her, especially now.

My brother controlled the lander as we lifted away from the island. Weyland was at his side, Marta and I sat in the rear. Tears blurred my view of the lone small figure waving goodbye.

"Jarryd, what about Mother? With Father away and those drones flying around, she's vulnerable."

"She won't be alone. I've had a word with a few of the villagers. They'll check on her discreetly. And don't forget Roddy. He checks the falcons every day and his cottage is close to the house if anything happens."

"Thanks. That makes me feel better."

Marta squeezed my hand in support. "Delio employs lies and persuasion. He won't gain support using violence."

"I'm more concerned about his son. Prince is a hothead and likes power. I suspect he'll use whatever is necessary to get it." Jarryd looked at Weyland. "But thanks to my brilliant buddy, Mother will have some protection against any drones."

Weyland blushed.

Silence filled the cabin until we neared the city.

"Okay, we're almost at Hypor," said Jarryd. "You all know what to do."

THE LANDING WAS PERFECT. WE MADE LIGHT CONVERSATION as we approached the main entrance, but things had changed. The security force was larger.

Six guards approached. Four held their weapons in readiness while two rummaged through our belongings.

The pod doors didn't open automatically. A guard signaled all clear to someone inside before they slid apart. The empty entrance I remembered was filled with equipment and more eyes watched our movements. I was relieved to see other workers returning from break so we weren't the only ones under scrutiny.

Marta grabbed Jarryd's hand. "Something's happened."

I wanted to hold his other one, but I didn't want to draw attention to our little group.

"Just stay calm. We'll find out what's occurred once we're inside." Jarryd placed his right hand on the palm reader. We did the same and joined the single line into the open concourse.

After a quiet word with Jarryd, Marta left us and followed the hallway to the tubes. We joined the groups waiting for lifts. Uneasy glances and murmurs threaded through those gathered. As the lift doors closed behind us, we exchanged glances. We had a plan.

~

My muscles tightened as I stepped from the lift into the sixth-floor hallway. I walked confidently in case someone was watching, but there were no guards, only workers mounting objects on the ceilings.

I stopped and spoke aloud without realizing. "What are those?"

"They're cameras. So they can keep tabs on us." It was Stick's voice. He stood behind me.

"Why?"

"Delio's paranoid." He chuckled.

"What do you mean?"

"That's right. You've been on work break haven't you?" He continued when I nodded. "Someone's leaked information about a solar threat to the planet. There's graffiti showing up everywhere accusing the council of trying to hide things from us."

I felt light-headed and must have blanched.

"I didn't mean to scare you." Stick appeared nervous. "I'm sure it's all bogus." He opened the door to the media lab. "Better get a drink of water or something."

I smiled and nodded. He hurried to his workstation.

The cold water was refreshing and gave me time to think. Who had released the information about the CMEs and why?

On the positive side, Jarryd and Weyland would be beyond suspicion since they'd been on break. On the downside, graffiti would put added pressure on the ruling council and give the Premier further justification to tighten security and an excuse to add to his private force.

If Delio was deceiving the council and making a bid for absolute power, there was more reason than ever to find the truth.

I returned to my desk just as Calia entered from the hallway. Dench stared at her from his office doorway. She was late, but he said nothing. I'd heard others gossiping about her relationship with Prince Delio. Was that why Dench was silent?

She ignored everyone but managed to draw attention to the flashy bangles on her wrists by fiddling with them as she proceeded to her workstation. She strutted like a peacock, swishing the folds of her blue silk juba. A present from her boyfriend no doubt. Definitely not from the common supply. Would her newfound prosperity appease her jealousy? I had my doubts.

The day's translations were light and I had time to check through the database. There were no obvious items about coronal mass ejections, only a couple about the solar cycle and the upcoming eclipse. I didn't expect it to be easy. Delio wasn't stupid. I had to try another approach. If the Premier was making deals with someone in Nuvega, and possibly the Genetrix, it might be important to track the visits or any talks they may have had. I decided to research the past year.

My efforts were fruitful. Delio had journeyed to Nuvega eight times, three during the last two months. The Genetrix had visited Hypor twice recently as well, not including the day I'd seen her. The visits made headlines and were well documented. I took discreet notes of the times and dates, hoping they'd be useful.

Two minutes before six o'clock, I jumped in my chair when Dench's voice rattled across the room.

"Bokk, in my office. Now."

I felt eyes following me as I approached his domain. Had Calia been telling tales about me again?

"Yes, Sir?" Nervously I clasped my hands behind my back. Nothing good came from an interview with Dench.

"What have you been working on today?" His glasses hung on the end of his nose as he peered over the rims.

"Just translations as usual. Sir."

"Why have you been studying the archives?" His voice penetrated like a spear. My hands got clammy, but he'd given me an idea.

"I thought I'd expand my knowledge of events on Hypor." It wasn't the greatest excuse, but reasonable since I'd arrived only a month ago. "Starting with the year before my arrival."

Since he knew I'd been in the archives he probably also knew the dates I'd been examining. I hoped he couldn't track the length of time I'd lingered on specific news items.

He didn't scoff at my explanation, but his eyes squinted with suspicion.

"Stick to your translations from now on. If you want to know about Hypor City, go to the market and watch the videos. That's all for now, but I'll be monitoring you." He flicked his bony fingers toward the door and I hastily retreated.

It was past six so I tucked my notes up my sleeve and headed for the recpod.

Marta was in the change room. "The boys are waiting for

us at the track. We'll run the course. Later we can eat at Swigs." She nodded toward the ceiling.

Newly mounted cameras were evenly spaced along the wall. I grabbed my track clothes and headed into the washroom. I checked the stall. If there were cameras, they were cleverly concealed.

Despite Marta's reference to 'the boys', I was surprised to see Weyland. He looked like an overgrown insect, all skinny appendages in his black outfit.

We started to run abreast, but Weyland fell in behind me.

"What's going on?" Jarryd laughed when he saw Weyland matching my every stride.

I understood the strange behavior. "He told me it's how he is able to move quickly, by following body movements."

"Mind over matter." Weyland huffed between words. "Brynna Bokk is a good runner."

"Just don't get any ideas, buddy," teased my brother.

Weyland blushed but kept his focus on me.

I was getting used to it.

After track, we conquered the obstacle course. Then the boys left to swim. Marta took me to the archery range. My aim was good and I soon had the knack of it. Marta was a pro.

"Is there archery in the Steepchase?"

"Not with the usual circular targets. But you have to be able to hit a specific mark, sometimes in a tree, or maybe on a beam. It's different every year. You might even have to climb a tree to get close enough to hit your target."

"I love trees." I clapped my hands, which made her laugh.

We practiced for a while, then stowed our bows and arrows and walked to the aquatic zone.

Two men were racing the length of the pool. I recognized Jarryd but was surprised when the other man popped up after winning. It was Weyland.

"Wow, buddy, you're a fish." Jarryd sent a splash of water toward Weyland. "Bryn, I think we have your new swimming coach right here."

I'd been dreading having to learn from a stranger. Somehow, learning from Weyland seemed more comfortable. I trusted him and he knew things about me. I wasn't afraid to show him my vulnerability.

"Will you teach me, Weyland?" I felt momentarily brave.

"Yes, Brynna Bokk. Starting tomorrow."

My stomach clenched at the word. So much for bravado.

"Now that's settled. Let's get changed and meet at Swigs." Jarryd pulled himself from the pool.

On our way to the women's change room, we noticed a crowd gathered outside Swigs.

"What's happened?" Marta was too short to see over the heads.

I stood on my toes to get a better view when a hard shove sent me stumbling. Marta grabbed my arm to keep me upright.

"Outta the way." It was the malicious guard from the seventh floor. He held his weapon horizontally and pushed its hard length against us.

"I'll do crowd control." A second guard appeared, also carrying a weapon. "Get back to the entrance." The men faced off. Green eyes bored into mean ones. It was the second guard from Prince's detail.

I tensed, fearing a physical confrontation, but mean eyes growled and strode away.

Green eyes focused on me. "You and your friends should leave. Now."

His voice was stern, but there was no malice in his gaze. I sensed a connection and didn't feel frightened or threatened. Instead, I felt compelled to smile.

"Yes, Sir." I mocked a salute and watched his lips twitch. "Let's go, Marta." I grabbed her arm and made for the change room.

"Brynna, are you crazy? You could have been arrested," whispered Marta. "He's one of Delio's personal guards, and dangerous. Why did you do that?"

I couldn't tell her that I felt safe with him, that I knew he wasn't dangerous. That he awakened new sensations and feelings in me. How could I explain what I didn't understand?

I motioned to the cameras. "We can't talk here,"

She nodded.

Like a good future sister-in-law, she didn't tell my brother about the incident with the guard, but she did tell him about the ruckus at Swigs.

"Yes, I heard from another swimmer there was a graffiti incident. We need to find someplace else to talk," said Jarryd. "Somewhere we won't be noticed."

"The market," said Marta. "There's a small projection room at the back of the theater. There won't be any screenings today because the video equipment is broken and I doubt there are cameras there."

"How do you know that?"

"An artist friend is the projectionist. I can get the key and we can sneak in through the back door. Most people will be across the market at the café. It'll be dark around the theater."

"Okay, let's go."

The lovebirds paired up. Weyland loped along beside me.

As Marta had predicted, one end was crowded and bright, the other dark and deserted. She slipped away from us and returned moments later with a key. We strolled along into the dimming light until we reached the theater. One by one, we slipped through a narrow alleyway and through the door into the projection room.

"This is great," said Jarryd after checking for closed-circuit cameras. "And private."

"Yes, but unfortunately it's usually used every night until ten." Marta started to speak then shook her head.

"What?" Jarryd prompted.

"I was thinking about an after-hours rendezvous, but it might be dangerous, especially with cameras and extra guards in the market."

"A possibility if we're desperate." Jarryd nodded. "Now let's review what we know. Bryn? Did you discover anything?"

"I went through the archives. There was no mention of any threat so I decided to check Delio's trips to Nuvega over the last year along with the dates of his meetings with the Genetrix." I took out my list and showed the others.

"That's smart thinking. We may be able to link those dates with other events. What about you, Marta? Have you heard anything more from your father?"

"Not a word. But I made contact with my mother. She's in touch with other councilors' wives. There's increased hostility between Delio and your father. Neither side is willing to compromise."

It didn't surprise me that Father would stand firm against Delio, but I feared for his safety. I could see Marta's information had affected Jarryd as well. Silence shrouded us, but not for long.

"Did you discover anything, Jarryd?" I asked.

His blank gaze swept our faces, then he cleared his throat and spoke.

"Weyland did some digging into Delio's files, but they're heavily encrypted. I put out feelers to friends in other departments. The men I spoke with resent the council's secrecy and are determined to find the truth. Whoever released the information about the CMEs did us a big favor."

"Any idea about the informant?" I suspected someone from the sci-lab.

"Haven't heard a whisper," said Jarryd. "Considering the love of gossip in this city, I'm surprised."

"So what's our next move?" Marta asked.

"Oh, I forgot to mention that Dench caught me snooping in the archives and gave me a warning."

"Okay, then you're out for now. So is Weyland since we can't get into Delio's files. All we can do is wait and see what my contacts turn up." Jarryd sensed our disappointment. "I know we were hoping for more, but this may take some time. Perhaps the added pressure of vandalism will force Delio into making mistakes. If he is trying to dupe the council, we still need proof."

We slipped into the alley. Marta secured the door. We parted from her outside the theater. She continued to her dorm as we strolled through the marketplace. Noisy patrons still gathered outside the café. I pulled my hood further forward when I noticed a group of guards.

Jarryd saw them too. "Let's pick up the pace."

We hurried to the dorms in silence. Before we parted, Weyland's reminder added to my worries.

"Swimming tomorrow, Brynna Bokk."

I'd forgotten our agreement. Even with him as my

teacher, the prospect of getting into the water made me cringe.

"I've never been able to conquer my fear." The admission of weakness was difficult.

"Mind over body," said Weyland with a wide, infectious smile.

14

REBEL ATTACK

A high-pitched noise blasted through the dormpod. I buried my head under my pillow anticipating pain until I realized it wasn't a dream. The full moon was almost a month away.

It was a siren.

Seconds later, the door of our room slammed open. Sleepiness and shock pushed everything into slow motion.

"Jubas on and outside. Hurry." The Podmaster's assistant was a tiny uptight woman who rarely opened her pursed lips except to lick them. Then, her thin tongue would flick out like a snake testing for scent.

Two roommates scurried past me as I pulled my juba over my head.

"Can you help me?" It was my shy roommate, Rebecca, who worked on the tenth floor. She struggled with the metal clasps on her leg braces.

I hesitated knowing she was fiercely independent. "What can I do?"

She nodded toward her leg. "One of the clasps is bent."

Together we were able to secure the brace.

"Thanks." She smiled then tested her balance.

"We'd better get outside." I matched her limping progress toward the exit.

The size of the crowd was astonishing. I'd never considered how many people resided in the dormpods. Hundreds spilled into the tube toward the foodpod. I wove through the gathering of sleepy workers, huddled in groups. No one seemed to know why we had been roused from our beds.

Rebecca headed for a group of women. I searched for Jarryd. When I spied Weyland I joined him.

"Any idea what's going on?" I echoed the question most were asking.

"Maybe." He linked his arm with mine. "Come."

We shoved our way through the packed tube toward the foodpod. My steps were restricted to half the length of his because of my juba.

"Where are we going?" I went quiet when I saw my brother. Beyond him, the walls of the beige dining hall were marred with red. Daubs of crimson paint cut through the councilors' portraits and thick, dripping letters spelled
—*LIARS!*

Maintenance workers attempted to obliterate the paint with large mops, but the smears only heightened the impact of the offense.

I froze, shocked at the sight. The violence of the graffiti was beyond my experience. We suspected Delio's treachery, but perhaps someone knew more than we did.

"Let's go before the guards arrive," said Jarryd. "They won't like us seeing this." He herded us back toward the dorm and others around us followed.

"I still don't understand why they pulled us out of bed."

"To search the dorms for evidence," he whispered.

"Evidence of what?" Did I have something in my locker

that was against the rules? My heart beat faster even though I couldn't think of anything.

"Red paint," said Jarryd. "Or someone hiding in the dorm." He must have sensed that my sleepy brain hadn't comprehended. "The paint is fresh. The perpetrators have to be somewhere nearby."

"What about the cameras?"

"They painted them red as well."

"Guards." Weyland pointed.

A double column of the Premier's men parted the tight throng in the tube as they advanced toward the dormpod. I searched for the one I knew, but black helmets concealed their features. I cringed when I saw them carrying clubs and shields. Even the sound of their boots was ominous.

The fear and uncertainty were palpable. Following instructions, we crouched on the floor. Waves of information crisscrossed the crowd; most of it, I suspected, was erroneous. Rumors that they'd found the culprit vied with speculation that the attackers were not Hyporians.

"What do you think, Jarryd?" I spoke softly. "Could it be someone from outside Hypor?"

"There's no way an outsider could enter the main entrance unseen."

His tone made me think he'd given this some thought. "Are there other entrances?"

"Underwater," murmured Weyland. He'd been listening, not asleep, as I'd suspected. His eyes remained closed.

My brother responded quietly. "They'd need the engineering specs of the city. There are ways to get in through access doors to mechanical rooms and solar collection stations. Most domes have emergency escape routes as well. But the underwater routes are difficult to utilize. It would take a highly trained group and extensive planning to infiltrate the city from below."

"Guards again." Weyland scrambled to his feet and the rest of the crowd followed.

Silence prevailed as the armed militia exited our sleeping quarters. There was a collective sigh of relief when they departed the way they'd come. I wasn't the only one who'd felt threatened by their appearance.

"They didn't find anything," Jarryd assured us.

"How do you know?" His confidence puzzled me.

He didn't answer. The crowd condensed and we inched toward the dorms.

Weyland peered over the surrounding heads, craning his head and neck forward before swiveling toward us. He focused on Jarryd. "Searching the men."

My brother's lips formed a rigid streak. Jaw muscles contracted as his eyes narrowed. Our eyes locked. His determined, icy gaze met my questioning concern. Dread tightened my chest. Suddenly I knew the truth. My brother was involved in the revolt to overthrow Premier Delio.

"What can I do?" The words were out before I'd considered the consequences. My mouth was dry, my hands were clammy, and my legs shaky but the instinct to protect my brother was powerful. We were family.

I could see his hesitation.

"I can help." I gritted my teeth and stood straighter, as much to convince myself as him.

"You're my sister and a woman. Too young." His voice in agony, he shook his head.

"Not too young to die." My heart responded, expressing the gravity of what we were all facing. "Let me help."

A surge by the mob pushed him into action. "Okay." His hand brushed mine then held it as he pressed a wadded paper against my palm. "Hide this until you're by yourself, then get rid of it."

I brushed my hand into my hair and dropped the wad into the back of my hood. My brother and I exchanged tense smiles. I didn't know what was on the paper, but I knew I was taking a big risk.

At the front of the line, the Podmaster searched Jarryd then Weyland. I saw Rebecca at the front of the line to the women's entrance and joined the queue. Blood throbbed in my ears. I stumbled slightly.

"Move on, Bokk," hissed the assistant. "Some of us want to sleep."

I went through with no fuss.

Inside, I ignored my roommates and made for the toilets. Locked in a stall, adrenaline shook my hands as I retrieved the paper from my hood. Bleary-eyed, I stared at the note, but couldn't make sense of the strange code. The outer door opened. With the message fixed in my memory, I dropped the paper into the toilet and flushed.

A click accompanied the faltering steps.

"Are you okay, Brynna?" It was Rebecca.

"Yes, just a queasy stomach. Thanks. I'll be fine."

The door opened and closed again.

In the silence, I pondered what the note could mean and what might happen next. When I finally climbed into bed, I predicted a sleepless night, but I was wrong.

∼

"Get up, Brynna. You're going to be late." A roommate shook my shoulder.

I hadn't heard the morning alarm. Disheveled and

unwashed, I missed breakfast but arrived at work in time to hear Calia's remarks.

"You girls could put in a little effort." Her black rimmed eyes were like dark holes against her light powdered skin. "You'll never get anywhere looking the way you do."

Two other workers had entered the media lab with me, but I knew her attack was directed at me. I didn't respond. Besides, if looking like a corpse was the way to get someone like Prince Delio, I'd rather not.

Another woman approached Calia. It was the one Carrot had nicknamed 'Suck up Sue.'

"Your earrings are beautiful," said Sue.

"These old things?" Calia pulled back her hair for a better display.

"Ooh! I love the gold knot and the pearl dangling from it," Sue gushed. "They look old. Are they an heirloom?"

Calia hesitated and glanced my way before responding. "No, a gift." She drifted to her station.

Sue followed her. Carrot imitated a begging puppy.

"Get to work." Dench's screech rivaled the previous night's siren.

Tired and unfocused, I let routine take over. I translated only what was necessary, thankful when the day was over.

That evening, I went to the recpod hoping to see Jarryd and Marta but was disappointed. Weyland wasn't there either, so no swimming lessons. Just as well, I needed sleep more than exercise.

Back in my room, I fell asleep quickly and dreamed of home and my favorite perch with Circe. The dreamscape faded when the siren shrieked and a hand prodded my shoulder.

"Get up, Bokk. Juba on and outside," shouted the Podmaster's assistant.

THE LAST SINGER

"What's going on? Another inspection?" I couldn't believe it was happening again. Concern for Jarryd's safety pushed my pulse into overdrive. I followed Rebecca and the others from our room.

Once outside, I noted that only women were crowded around the entrance. One woman protested loudly at her lack of sleep, others joined in.

"Has there been more graffiti?" I asked one of the dissenters.

"No, another theft."

I released the breath I'd been unconsciously holding. "Have there been many? I've been away on break."

I was surprised I hadn't heard anything at work. According to the rules, theft was a serious offense that often led to the perpetrator being transported to Haven or Prima Feminary, which I'd learned was considered a punishment

"There were two inspections three days ago," answered a woman. "Several items have disappeared from the women's dorm. If you have anything valuable, you'd better lock it up."

I wasn't worried. My most valuable item was the carved necklace that I wore all the time.

A short whistle blast sent us back to our rooms. Our belongings lay in piles on the beds, our closets empty. I threw my possessions back into my cupboard and fell into bed, too tired to care about crumpled sheets.

Next morning, I wasn't the only one late for work. Dench gave us a warning but didn't levy a fine. That night, I skipped the recpod, went straight to the dorm and slept like a newborn.

The morning brought clarity and purpose. I needed to talk to Jarryd about the note he'd given me. I stopped at a screen outside the dorm and sent him a message. If I didn't hear from him during the day, I'd go to the marketplace and find Marta.

On the way to work, I joined the crowd of workers shuffling through the hallways. They walked in twos and threes, engaged in low conversations, going silent as they passed a security camera. I lowered my head and pulled my hood forward when I noticed patches of fresh beige paint dotting several walls. They were reminders that Hypor no longer lived up to its claim as the well-ordered city of the future.

The media lab bustled with activity. Overnight, Premier Delio and the council had issued numerous proclamations that required translation into various languages. Some were assurances of council control with vague references to a threat not yet confirmed. Others were warnings to the vandals, who threatened the peace of Hypor.

The lab grew unusually quiet as the day went on. After a few minutes, I lost interest in the translations until Carrot thrust a paper marked *urgent* under my nose.

"Look at that," he whispered. "We'll be a police state soon."

The ruling council was enhancing what they called safety measures by increasing the contingent of armed guards. My stomach knotted, but I wasn't the only one affected by what the ruling council called essential safety measures. Gasps and exclamations of disbelief sounded around the room as Carrot proceeded to the tell others of the council's actions.

I wondered what my father thought about the graffiti. He was a staunch believer in order and fairness. I suspected he wouldn't like the idea of vandalism any better than Delio, but his response wouldn't be violence. Delio's actions gave evidence of his state of mind. Increased armed guards and extra security pointed to fear.

THE LAST SINGER

The tension in the room lasted most of the day. I looked forward to six o'clock.

My final translation was almost complete when the media lab went black. I stopped and listened in the silence. Seconds later, emergency lights blinked an eerie glow across the surprised faces of my colleagues.

"What's happening?" Suck up Sue gravitated to the supervisor's office.

"Consider yourselves lucky," said Dench. "You get off half an hour early. Everyone out." There was no further explanation. I could hear others discussing the blackout. No one had an answer.

With only a few halos of light in the hall, it was difficult to see who was leaning against the opposite wall.

"Swimming, Brynna Bokk." Weyland moved into a spotlight.

Laughter from a nearby huddle drew my attention. Calia stood with several people from another lab and sent us sneering glances. "I guess that's the best she can do," she said in a loud voice before strolling away with her cronies.

"Brainless and petty." Weyland's comments were succinct.

"And dangerous," I added, thinking of her connection to Prince Delio.

"Recpod," Weyland insisted.

"We can't swim in the dark." The thought terrified me. "But I do need to talk to Jarryd. Maybe he'll be there. Have you spoken with him?"

Weyland shook his head.

A LARGE GATHERING OF UNFAMILIAR FACES CROWDED THE

entrance to the recreation pod, presumably wanting to escape the blackness. Even this late, there would be some natural light inside. Fortunately, the lights powered up and the throng dispersed. Weyland nudged me forward. My excuse to avoid swimming lessons faded with the growing light.

Before approaching the aquatics area, I did a lap around the track, scanning for my brother. There was no sign of him. I fought back fearful thoughts that threatened to overwhelm my common sense. He must be okay. If anything had happened to him, I'd be first to hear about it. Wouldn't I?

There was no sign of Marta either, so I faced the inevitable and donned a swimsuit, then grabbed a pair of goggles. I couldn't take a chance on losing my blue lens.

The suits were similar in style to the women's exercise outfits, but the sleeves and legs were six inches shorter and the fabric was shiny and slick. There was also a matching red swim cap.

The men's suits were blue and didn't flatter Weyland's thin build. He loped toward me.

"In the water, Brynna Bokk." He dove in.

There was no way I was jumping into the pool, even if it was only five feet deep. Then, I noticed him pointing to an access ladder. I eased myself in, keeping one hand firmly clamped to the bottom step. As the water rose up my body, I shut my eyes and hesitated.

"Mind over matter, Brynna Bokk."

I took a deep breath and another step until I touched the floor of the pool. There was comfort in feeling solid ground with my head still above the surface.

"Cup hands, pull one arm behind shoulder then to front into water. Repeat with other arm." Weyland demonstrated the movement. It took several attempts to meet his exacting standards. Next the legs, kicking while holding the side of the pool. These were the easy parts. The difficulty was convincing myself that these motions would keep me afloat.

"Arms, legs, breathe." The intensity of his instruction was fatiguing but successful. By nine o'clock, I had stroked my way across the pool and back several times, without touching the bottom.

"I can't believe it." I wiped the water from my face. "I've conquered my fear." Well not really. I'd definitely progressed, but the idea of swimming in the deep part was still frightening.

"Mind over matter." He beamed. "Tomorrow, more practice, more breathing."

"Didn't I just learn breathing?"

"Hold breath longer, deeper."

I shuddered at the childhood memory of being swallowed by water. "Why would I need that?"

"Steepchase."

I questioned if it was worth going through more agony just to get into a game. The goal seemed trivial in light of what was happening on Hypor. But perhaps that was just a residual fear whispering in my brain.

Weyland pointed to the far side of the pool. "One more time across then we'll go." His voice echoed and I noticed we were alone.

Halfway across the pool, the lights went out.

Glaring emergency lamps shot through the darkness. Uneasy and eager to get out, I stood up and walked toward the lip of the black pool, but I misjudged the direction and stepped into a watery void. All of Weyland's instructions failed to register as I sank deeper. I clawed at the water. In the terrifying darkness, I expelled the final bit of breath I'd been holding. My limbs succumbed to a paralyzing fear.

~

Weyland's bony fingers pushed against my ribcage. "Breathe, Brynna Bokk."

Sour fluid stung my throat. I turned my head as a gagging cough spewed the liquid I'd ingested. A snort forced water through my nasal cavities. They burned when I tried to pull in a breath. It was several minutes before I realized I was lying beside the pool. The main lights were still out. I let exhausted tears flow. I was safe.

"Thank you, Weyland. You saved my life."

"Not me," was his cryptic denial. "We must go, Brynna Bokk."

I attempted to stand but couldn't. He pulled my arm across his shoulder and hoisted me up. We stumbled slowly through white halos of emergency lighting.

"Faster." He took most of my weight on his shoulders in an attempt to hurry.

My brain was still foggy and my footsteps unsure.

"What's causing the lights to go out?"

"Sunspots. First indications of CMEs."

Coronal mass ejections. The threat. It was real.

I'd prayed it wasn't, but the power outages and the certainty in Weyland's voice extinguished any doubt.

"How—"

His hand clamped over my mouth and he dragged me toward a low hedge. "Quiet," he whispered. We crouched, our bodies pressed against spiky branches. "Something happening."

I jerked forward to escape the jutting points that speared my flesh but froze when a dozen shadowy figures crossed our view. They ran in zagging patterns, dodging the halos of light. We remained hidden until they disappeared. Weyland stood, and to my surprise, he pulled me onto his back and ran, keeping in the shadows. I hoped his night vision was better than mine.

He opened the door of the women's change room and pushed me through. "Meet at the entrance. Go."

Inside was silent and dark. I groped my way to my locker, donned my juba found my way to meet Weyland. We approached the recpod entry doors, but they didn't swish open.

"No power." He released a lever above the doors and opened them by hand.

In semi-darkness, we trod silently back to our dorms. The incident at the pool had sapped my energy. I stumbled several times but refused Weyland's help. I didn't like feeling helpless. Listless and worn out, I pushed on but trailed my hand along the walls for support. Nearing the dorm, I grabbed his arm.

"Why did we have to hide? Who were they?" I couldn't see his face in the shadows.

"Can't say, Brynna Bokk." Weyland turned into the men's dorm entrance.

Did he mean that he didn't know, or that he didn't want to tell me? The question nagged at me as I crept into my room.

Two of my roommates were asleep. The third bed, where Rebecca slept was empty, but her leg braces were propped against the end wall. As I drifted into sleep, another question arose that I'd forgotten to ask.

If Weyland hadn't saved me from drowning, who had?

15

THE PREMIER STRIKES BACK

Next morning, the power was restored.

The dorm lights flickered on at seven o'clock. There was no sign of Rebecca, but the braces had slipped to the floor during the night. I leaned them against her bed, trying to decide if I should report her absence. I chose to wait. Privacy was important to her. Also, I didn't want to draw attention to myself.

I sent another message to Jarryd and one to Marta before heading to work. Several of us exited the lift and spied Dench at the media lab door, barring entry. "There's a general assembly announcement. Go down to the fifth."

Unsure of what was happening, I followed the others.

The fifth floor had no internal walls except for those surrounding the lift. Harsh artificial lighting sterilized the setting. Rows of benches paralleled an immense viewing screen. Helmeted sentries were spaced around the perimeter. Their presence was daunting. They directed the women to one end of the room, the men to the other.

The shuffle of feet echoed through the space as hundreds of workers slid onto benches, packed together like frightened marmots in a burrow. I poked my head up trying to spot Jarryd's blond hair among the rows of men, but couldn't see him.

Stale air and hot, heavy breathing contributed to the oppressive atmosphere. Threads of sweat ran under my juba. The woman to my right wiped her face with a sleeve that came away wet.

When everyone settled, I spotted Calia sitting against the dome wall beside Prince Delio. As if holding court, she postured regally on a thin metal chair but fanned her face. Even in her privileged position, she couldn't escape the moist musty air.

There was a collective gasp when the room blackened and the video screen flashed to life. Premier Delio's head filled the display. His earlobes hung like ripe fruit at the sides of his neck. The pendulous discs were half the length of my baby finger. How had I missed noticing them before?

"Good day, citizens of Hypor." His voice boomed. Several people discreetly covered their ears. "Due to extensive vandalism at the recpod last night, it is with great sadness that I must announce further measures to ensure the safety of our populace."

Several groans, some shouts, and hushed whispers followed.

"Silence," yelled Prince from the darkness.

The Premier resumed. His lobes swayed as he gestured, emphasizing his words. "Until the vandals have been arrested, the council will institute a curfew. All citizens without the required authorization will be in their dorms by nine o'clock in the evening."

Protests erupted again, and again Prince yelled for silence.

"After eight o'clock each evening the recpod will be accessible to security personnel only."

Irate shouts of 'dictator' and 'despot' exploded from the men's area. Prince surged from his seat in an attempt to identify who had interrupted the presentation.

The women were silent, but their faces in the screen's reflected light were angry and resentful. Mine was no different. Where was Father in all of this?

The Premier ended the short presentation by assuring the listeners that he and the council were doing everything possible to thwart the vandals and return Hypor to the safe and productive city it had always been.

The screen went dark.

"What are they doing about the solar threat?" The strong, deep voice cracked through the black silence. Light flooded the room and the guards moved toward the men.

"Who said that?" Prince demanded as he strutted through the flank of taller men. "Speak up."

No one answered.

Frustrated, he waved one arm at his minions. "Get them out of here."

Calia scuttled after him as he strode to the lift.

Only the scuffing sound of feet was heard as the fifth floor emptied, but conversations resumed as people flooded from the elevator one floor up. Most whispered, but the tone was clear. People were fuming, bitter. The Premier had inflamed rather than calmed.

"How about you?" Carrot confronted me in the hall with Stick beside him. "Your father is big on the council, what do you know about the solar threat?"

I cringed inwardly. "No more than you." I managed to brush off his question.

A few people joined our group and began to talk but my thoughts were on the previous night. The figures we'd seen at the recpod must have been the vandals. Was Jarryd involved? Was he risking his life? I swallowed hard to displace the fear that clogged my throat.

"Well, I think Delio is hiding something," Stick added his opinion.

Several others voiced their agreement.

"And," said Stick, emboldened by the group's attention, "I think the vandals have the right idea. The council isn't being honest with us."

No one voiced support this time. Instead, the group thinned and drifted into work. I followed Stick into the media lab, but not before noticing that Calia was lurking at the fringes, her eyes narrowed, listening.

Later that day, Stick received a summons to Dench's office. He didn't appear again until the hall door opened and six guards entered.

Helmets masked their faces. Their heavy boots thumped across the floor. I trembled and backed up against the wall. So did everyone else.

"What's going on?" Stick yelled. Two sets of hands grabbed him. He struggled, his heels scraping the floor as he was wrenched from Dench's office and dragged out the door.

Carrot slouched into his chair, white-faced with shock. The silence pulsed with resentment and fear. One of our own was a victim of the Premier's enhanced security.

I glanced at Calia. She didn't hide her smirk as she watched the doors close behind Stick and the guards. She lifted her chin defiantly when she caught my eye. I had no doubt that she had informed against Stick.

Carrot jumped from his seat and smashed his fist onto his desk. "Damn you, Calia. I see you laughing. You'll pay for this," he growled, eyes wide and wild.

Fear flashed over her face but was quickly replaced with contempt. "I don't know what you're talking about."

Fists clenched, he stomped toward her.

"What's going on?" Dench screamed from his office doorway.

Carrot stopped, but the interruption galvanized Calia. She ran from the media lab despite the supervisor's command to halt.

Dench yelled again for an explanation.

"Calia felt sick. With fear," I added under my breath so only Carrot could hear.

His slight smile acknowledged my support. I'd covered for him, and Calia, hoping he'd be safe from her wrath.

After the morning's excitement, the workday seemed long and slow. The only translations were the council's statements confirming the curfew and recpod restrictions. In the afternoon, Dench left for a meeting. I listened as others discussed the vandalism, but the restrictions were their primary concern. Some suggested petitioning the council, but the abruptness of Stick's arrest underscored their trepidation to act. By the time the six o'clock bell rang, an air of frustrated hopelessness had settled in.

"I guess there's nothing any of us can do," said Carrot as the group dispersed.

"There must be something." I couldn't stop myself responding. Although I'd avoided the earlier discussion, I was determined to fight the lethargy that had developed. "We're all scared, but we can't let the council dictate our lives."

Carrot shrugged his shoulders and my resolve intensified.

As I hurried to the recpod, I made some decisions. I'd find a way to contact Father even if I had to invade the executive floor. There must be peaceful ways of getting the restrictions removed. If Jarryd was one of the vandals his life was in danger. But he wasn't the only one. The larger menace threatened the survival of every living thing.

I RACED ACROSS THE RECPOD TRACK TO WHERE JARRYD, MARTA and Weyland were gathered. "Finally. I worried they'd transported you." I realized it was a stupid remark when my brother glared at me.

"Be careful what you say, Bryn. We're being watched, remember? Let's run as we talk."

We did a few laps in silence.

"My father says that they've sentenced a man who works in the media lab." Marta brushed my arm with hers as ran alongside. "He's being transported."

"Stick." I felt nauseated and slowed my pace. Weyland crashed into my back and we both tumbled to the track.

"Sorry," mumbled Weyland, untangling his long legs from mine.

My ankle ached and my knees were sore from ramming the hard track. I forced a hobbling run when several curious guards advanced from their stations along the walls.

"Split up and meet near the swim change rooms." Jarryd and Marta sped off, leaving me limping, with Weyland at my heels. The guards stationed by the track lost interest as we moved away.

Our group of four blended in among the chattering clusters of people gathered in the aquatic area. Only a couple of men glanced our way as we met up. Off-duty guards by the look of their shorn hair.

"I think they're watching." I nodded toward the two nearby.

"Probably, but they'll soon lose interest if there's nothing to see." Jarryd strolled past them.

"They look irritated." Marta's voice was tight.

"It's the extra hours of guard duty. They're not getting much time off," said Jarryd.

"How do you know?" Her surprise mirrored mine.

Jarryd headed to four seats farthest from the pool and other swimmers. He lounged back, stretched out his legs and closed his eyes, but continued to speak.

"I know one of the guards. He was the winner of last year's Steepchase and he became a member of Delio's personal security force. He's from Nuvega. We became running buddies before the games."

I could hear deception in Jarryd's tone. "What else?"

His eyes crinkled to slits as he laughed. "I never could fool you, Bryn."

"What aren't you telling us, Jarryd?" Marta grasped his arm.

"He's one of my contacts and keeps me informed about Delio." His answer appeased his fiancée, but I knew there was something more. He traded my questioning look with one of warning. There was something he didn't want Marta to know.

Sensing his reluctance, I changed the subject. "Have you discovered anything concrete about Delio's plans?"

"Not yet. It's frustrating that the council is still denying any serious threat. With Delio controlling the council's communications, everyone thinks there's nothing to worry about and there's no pressure for him to reveal his solutions. Father is still trying to get proof to persuade the council to question the Premier, but until that happens we have to hope that Delio makes a mistake and somehow exposes his intentions."

"Or that the vandals get their message across."

I told them about Stick and the discussions after he was arrested.

Jarryd nodded. "Despite the graffiti, people only seem concerned about the curfews and cameras. They don't believe the planet's in real danger. Making them take the threat seriously is our...the biggest obstacle."

"Our?" I heard the slip he tried to correct.

"I mean for all of us." He recovered, but it was lame.

I would demand an explanation when we were alone.

Marta looked at the poolside clock "It's too late for a swim. We'd better get changed and back to the dorm before the new curfew. Is there anything else we can do, Jarryd?"

"Not for now. Just keep us informed if your father tells you anything useful. My father isn't responding to my messages. I suspect he's trying to be protective, but it's irritating not to know what he's doing. All we can do is watch and wait for Delio to slip up."

"What if he doesn't?" I hated being the doomsayer.

"He will. As freedoms are eroded, resentment will rise. With a little encouragement, people will become vocal and start protesting. Then he'll really have his hands full. He's a vain and boastful man. One day he'll go too far."

We left for the change rooms. Marta seemed unusually down. I searched for something cheerful to say.

"I'm sure we'll find a way to uncover Delio's plans before anything bad happens."

"I hope so." She hesitated, then quickly donned her juba.

"What's wrong, Marta? Is something else going on?"

"It may be just a coincidence, but three people who work in the market have disappeared. Two were artists. The other was an old janitor at the café. They've been gone over a week."

"Would they have said or done anything that might have gotten them into trouble?"

"No, that's the strange part. They were friendly, but kept to themselves."

"What about the janitor?"

"He was a fatherly type, always kept an eye on things. He just got back to work after a fall. He walked with a cane. Everybody liked him." Marta shook her head. "Maybe I'm being a little paranoid. It's just that I remember Father mentioning that since Delio took power more people have been transported from Hypor City."

"But that's only for offenses, isn't it?"

"Supposedly." Marta shrugged and tried to smile. "It's probably nothing, but those three are so vulnerable."

"How?"

"One of the artists is mute and the other has a shriveled hand. They depend on each other, and I've never known them to be away for so long."

Vulnerable and missing described Rebecca as well. Was there a connection?

Outside the recpod, Jarryd spoke privately with Marta. He frowned as he watched her leave for her dorm. I didn't want to upset him further, but I needed some answers.

As Jarryd, Weyland and I made our way to the dormpod, I decided to confront him.

"What is it that you didn't want Marta to know? Is it

about the note? And what is the secrecy around that guard?" I was breathless by the time I'd finished my list of questions.

Jarryd laughed as if I'd told him a joke. "Smile and keep your voice low. Don't forget the cameras. And move." He strode along the tube toward our dorms.

I fixed my lips into a grin and kept up. "Tell me."

"Okay, but this is between us, no one else, not even Marta. I don't want her to worry."

"I think you underestimate her, but okay." I glanced at Weyland, who looked like he was solving a complex equation in his head.

"It's okay, he knows." My brother grinned at his gawky friend. "I trust him with my life."

Weyland gave a goofy smile.

With more time, I'd appreciate their bond, but we were almost at the dorm. "Okay, great. Best friends. I get it. Now tell me about the guard."

"He's a member of the rebel group." His voice was so low I thought I'd misheard. It was the first time I'd heard the term 'rebel' mentioned.

"He's what?" I stopped walking then started again when a sentry glanced at us.

"The note was from him. We're working together." Steely determination in his voice matched the hard line of his jaw. He was no longer the laughing jokester who had teased me all my life. I saw a warrior, fighting for our future.

Despite having my fears confirmed, I was relieved to see Jarryd strong and purposeful.

Anticipation pulsed through my body. I wanted to do my part.

"What can I do?"

"I'm not sure. Just be patient for now." He nodded congenially to the two men posted at the entrance of the dorm as he entered the men's side.

Patience wasn't my strong suit. I was determined to find a way to help.

"Swimming tomorrow, Brynna Bokk," called Weyland as he followed my brother.

16

THE BETRAYAL

My imagination swirled as I climbed into bed.

I was part of the rebel force, saving the world with Circe on my arm and a sword in my hand. The thoughts of thwarting Delio were exciting and scary. He was a powerful opponent but in my dreams he was easily conquered. I was on the verge of vanquishing him when an ear-splitting alarm bell sounded. This time I knew what it was.

Three of us pulled on jubas. The fourth bed was still empty. Rebecca's braces had disappeared. Marta's concerns about missing colleagues flashed into my mind but were pushed aside as the Podmaster's assistant hurried us out the exit.

Again, only the women filtered out of the dorm. Suspicions were high and the women glanced nervously at one another. There was whispering about another theft.

An hour later, the guards left the area and we were told to return to our rooms. Tired and grumbling, I shuffled back inside, hoping this would be the last of the late night inspections.

The next morning, I awoke to a roommate shaking my shoulder.

"Have you seen my earrings?" she asked.

"No," I mumbled, snuggling back into my bedcovers. But with two women noisily rummaging through their belongings, sleep was impossible. I sat up and pulled my blanket around me. "What do they look like?"

"They're old. A knot of gold with a pearl hanging down. My grandmother gave them to me." She was almost in tears. "I don't know what I'll do if I can't find them. They're a family heirloom."

Her description formed an image in my brain. A gold knot and a dangling pearl. I'd seen something like that, but where? Then I remembered Calia had worn similar earrings a few days ago.

"I'll have to look later." The distraught woman shrugged. "We'd better get moving or we'll all be late."

"I forgot to tell you, Brynna." The other roommate stopped near my bed. "One of your friends was here yesterday. I hope you got her note."

I hadn't seen one. "What did she look like?"

"Petite, dark hair. She had a wrist full of gold bracelets and an expensive juba. Does she sound familiar?"

"Yes, thanks." There was no mistaking the description of Calia. Did her appearance have anything to do with the missing earrings? Had she taken up thieving again? It was too much of a coincidence. What Mother told me about Calia stealing my bracelet made me surer than ever that she was the thief.

I spent the morning trying to decide what to do. Once the lost earrings were reported, Calia would have to hide them. She'd never be able to wear them because of their distinctive design. Apart from catching her with them, the only way to convict her would be if two of us were to testify that we saw her with the earrings. They probably wouldn't believe a single voice, especially since Calia and I had reprimands on our files about a shared incident of misconduct. I'd have to rely on Suck up Sue to tell the truth.

While Calia was across the lab, I approached Sue. I didn't know her well but hoped that she would feel the injustice of Calia's act and agree to support me and my roommate. I explained the situation, confirming with her the description of the earrings. She agreed to think about it and let me know the next day if she'd back me up. I left the media lab that evening feeling uneasy about Sue's hesitation to support me. I hoped that her sense of right would prevail.

At the recpod, Weyland waited by the swimming pool. He was alone near the shallow end. I skirted the group of guards that mingled around the deep end.

"Warm up, Brynna Bokk." He motioned toward the pool. "Practice swim like yesterday."

I fixed my goggles. My old nerves returned as I descended the ladder into the pool, but after swimming several widths, I regained my confidence. He then directed me to the deep end of the pool. A taut rope dropped from an overhanging metal arm into the water.

"Next lesson. Hold your breath. Use the rope to descend. First time, stay down thirty seconds. Each time increasing. Building lung power."

"Are you positive this is necessary for Steepchase?" I gave him a doubtful glare as he handed me a timer.

"Yes, positive." He answered solemnly. "First practice deep breathing."

I spent half an hour breathing deeply and holding my breath, one hand on the side of the pool. I progressed, but under water was another matter.

"Now down." Weyland pointed to the rope.

"Okay." After several deep breaths, I moved away from the poolside and grabbed the rope. Hand over hand, I pulled my body down until I was fully submerged. When I looked up, I could see Weyland's hazy outline looking down at me. When the timer reached thirty, I surfaced.

"Good," said Weyland." Now deeper. Put this around your waist."

"What is it?" I reached for the belt. My arm slapped to the water with the unexpected weight.

"Keep you submerged."

I wasn't sure I liked the idea of being weighted down in ten feet of water. I felt twinges of fear, but curbed them when I remembered the rope. I'd have a safety line.

I strapped on the belt. This time my descent was easier and quicker. Through the goggles, my eyes focused on the timer, hoping the seconds would go quickly. As I acclimated to the feeling of being fully submerged, I sat on the bottom of the pool and started to enjoy seeing my time progress. The dark outlines of other swimmers moved around me.

I mastered thirty seconds, then one minute quite easily. Perhaps being a singer helped with breath control.

The final test was two minutes. I sat on the bottom of the pool checking the timer. At two minutes, I lifted my arms above my head in silent celebration. I pushed against the bottom and pulled on the rope when someone grabbed my ankle.

All I could see was a dark outline.

Panicked, I kicked my other leg as hard as possible trying to strike the offender but then that ankle was shackled as well. My lungs begged for air. The surface seemed miles away. Instinctively I started to hum and was suddenly free.

Hand over hand I pulled frantically up the rope, kicking and twisting to reach the surface. My open mouth sucked in air and water. Spluttering and coughing, I stroked to the poolside and clutched the edge. "Help!"

Weyland grabbed my arm and pulled me from the water. "What happened, Brynna Bokk?"

"Someone grabbed my ankles. They were holding me down. I think they were trying to drown me." I looked along the length of the pool.

At the far end, two men emerged from the water; one was thick and stout, the other tall and dark. Their angry voices reverberated across the water then the shorter one laughed and walked away. The tall one looked back at me. Too far away to see his face, but the way he moved was familiar.

I felt confused. "Who was that? Why would someone do that?"

"Do what?" My brother appeared accompanied by Marta.

I told them what had happened and pointed to the group of guards.

"I'll speak to my contact," said Jarryd. "He won't let it happen again, even if it was meant as a joke."

"Some joke. Whoever did it is a psycho." Marta shivered in horror.

Jarryd rested his hand on his friend's shoulder. "Weyland, I think we should forget swimming lessons for now."

"No argument from me." I was relieved. "I've had enough of aquatic misadventures."

"What do you mean? Did something else happen?"

I told them about the night I floundered in deep water when the power was out. The night someone had pulled me to safety. The same night we'd seen the shadowy figures and the recpod had been vandalized.

"Weyland didn't tell me about that part? Did you tell anyone else what you saw?" Jarryd asked.

"Of course not." I felt my spunk returning. "Do you think I'm crazy?"

Jarryd grinned. Marta giggled.

"Smart, Brynna Bokk," said Weyland.

I didn't feel particularly smart. Fear rather than any conscious thought had kept me silent. I didn't want to admit to seeing the people in the shadows, especially since I was sure they were rebels.

"It's almost eight. We'd better go." Marta linked her arm with mine. "You'll feel better tomorrow."

After a restless night, my sleepy brain debated if lunch might be a good time to approach Sue. When I reached the media lab, shouts penetrated the walls. I opened the door into chaos. Angry glares flashed toward me, then away.

Blood red words splayed across one wall.

Herbert Pilchard has been transported to Haven. You may be next.

It took me a moment to make the connection. It was Stick. He was Herbert Pilchard.

Carrot jumped onto a table and started to rant against the injustice, vowing to do something drastic. Others voiced their support, but all went silent when Dench entered the lab. Halfway to his office, he spotted the graffiti. His gaze dropped and his hand shook as he pushed his glasses up his nose. There was none of his usual callousness when he spoke.

"Quiet. Back to work or you'll end up like your friend." There was no threat, only a warning.

Carrot leaped from the table and joined the men as they shuffled to their stations, still whispering among themselves.

The women were huddled in one corner of the room and it was only when they dispersed that I saw Sue. Dressed in a new juba with several gold wrist bangles, I was immediately suspicious. I figured she'd warned Calia and been rewarded with new clothing and jewelry. The thief would have lots of time to hide my heartbroken roommate's earrings.

Calia didn't show up during the morning. Dench seemed oblivious to her absence or decided not to notice it. After his earlier warning, was he fearful of confronting someone so closely connected to the Delio family? We were all surprised when he gave us extra time off at lunch.

The halls were quiet when our group returned from eating. I was at the back of the pack but heard shocked exclamations from those ahead.

"What's going on? Why are they here again?"

My heart started to pound when I saw armed men standing with Dench.

Carrot's chalky face was the first one I saw when I entered the lab. Others looked down or away, not wanting to be part of what might come.

Then I saw Calia. She stood near her desk, between two burly guards.

"There she is." Her finger pointed at me. "The earrings were in her locker. She's the thief."

I heard gasps of surprise. Events unfolded in flashes. Calia's taunting expression. Sue's sly smile. The horrified faces of my colleagues. The pressure on my arms as the guards took hold. The stark hallway, one tube, then another and another until I lost count. Finally, thrust into a thinly lit room.

The air was dank and foul. I recoiled at the odor of rotting fish, but a hand pushed hard on my back. My foot caught in the hem of my robe and I toppled to my knees. The door clanged shut. A lock clicked. Booted feet clattered then faded.

"Brynna?"

I thought I was dreaming when I heard my name. From the shadows, beyond the circle of faint light, a figure emerged.

"Brynna?" An arm linked with mine and pulled me upright. It was Stick.

"St...Herbert? Are you okay?" I wiped my wet hands down my juba then squinted to see him in the dim light. His clothes were wrinkled and soiled, but there were no signs of physical abuse. "We thought you'd been sent to the mines at Haven."

"Impossible. Whoever said that is fear mongering. I have connections on the council. They can't send me away." He seemed confident and almost cheerful. "But why are you here?"

"Calia accused me of stealing. I'm more certain than ever that she's the one behind all the thefts from our dorm."

"Greedy liar. But don't worry. Your father will get you released." He pulled a metal chair from a dark corner and waved me to sit.

I perched on the chair and looked around. "Where are we?"

"We're in a storage room in one of the water purification domes but I expect to be out of here very soon. You probably will too."

"I'm not so sure." His offensive statements had been bravado at best, whereas the authorities had found physical evidence of my alleged crime. "Stealing is more serious than a subversive speech."

"Not to Delio." Stick leaned against the wall beside me. "When I got here yesterday, there was a woman being held because she refused to take a job in the children's nursery. She eventually worked in the kitchens, but couldn't keep up because of a back problem. A waste really, because she was super smart—knew all about solar batteries, sunspots and other science stuff. This morning, she was shipped off to Prima Feminary. Can you believe it?"

My vision of the feminary had become tainted. I could no longer discard as fiction stories of women being sent to Prima Feminary. Less a sanctuary, it was spoken of in the same dreaded tones as Haven.

"My cousin told me that more people have been transported since Delio became Premier than during the whole history of Hypor City. It makes you wonder what he's up to."

I remembered Marta's concerns about people disappearing. Rebecca hadn't returned either. More recently, Grub had vanished from the foodpod.

"It's a good thing we have family on the council." Stick repeatedly kicked one heel against the stone wall. "Privilege has its benefits as they say." His laugh faded but the kicking continued.

"Did that woman say anything about the threat from the sun?"

Stick looked momentarily puzzled. "Oh, the one who was here? Yes, she believed it was real. That's why I've decided to try to find out more when I get back. Perhaps you could help me. We could work together, secretly." His eyes widened like an eager young boy with a mystery to solve.

"Sure." I agreed. Who was I to break his balloon of optimism? Besides, part of me hoped he was right and we would get released.

Later that night four guards took Stick. I lay curled in a corner.

"See you soon, Brynna." His cheery tone sounded forced as he left the cell.

The guard closing the door growled, "He's for the boat."

I prayed for his safety but was certain I'd never see Stick again. I felt his loss. We were only colleagues but his presence had made the cell less oppressive. While I clung to the memory of his optimism, doubts arose as the night progressed. Would Father be able to help me or was I destined for the docks to be shipped across the water to Prima Feminary?

The darkness amplified every tiny sound. My mind writhed with fear, causing me to clench and twitch uncontrollably. My acute hearing had become my foe and I covered my ears in an attempt to silence it.

I surrendered to tears, allowing them to exhaust my overwhelming emotions. Tired and hungry, I unconsciously started to hum. It was an old folk song and the melody was soothing. I felt stronger, braver. In defiance, I sat up and sang louder, not caring who heard me. No one did, no one cared. I lay back down and sang myself to sleep.

A booted foot nudged my thigh, thrusting harder until I groaned.

"Get up. You've got a visitor."

I saw a man outlined in the doorway but couldn't see his face.

"Leave me with my daughter."

The familiar voice acted like a balm. I jumped up, ran toward the doorway and threw my arms around Father's neck. I didn't care that my juba was dirty and reeked of fish. His solid presence brought comfort. I was a child again needing his support. I didn't want to leave the safety of his embrace.

"Steady, Brynna." He held me at arm's length. "I need to ask you some questions."

His tone puzzled me. It was clinical when I needed compassion.

"I didn't do it. I didn't take the earrings. It was Calia. She's the thief." I blurted my defense and moved so that his face was visible in the dim light. I needed to see his eyes.

"I believe you, but they found the earrings in your locker. And one of your co-workers says she saw you wearing them."

"That's a lie!"

"Unfortunately the council has voted." A sigh shuttered from his chest. "They found you guilty, but not unanimously."

Blood drained from my head. I felt faint. "What will they do to me?" Prima Feminary loomed dark in my imagination.

"Fortunately, I'm not without some influence and your roommates all vouched for you, even the one whose earrings were stolen. As a result, your sentence has been reduced to three months labor in the laundry."

"Can I see Mother and Jarryd before I go?"

He held up his hand to halt further questions. "In addition, during that time you will have no contact with your friends and family."

His words knifed my chest.

No Jarryd, no Mother, no Marta, no Weyland, no Father.

"No—" I pushed at his arms as he reached for me. "They can't do this. I'm innocent."

"I'm sorry." His shoulders sagged. "I did what I could."

I wanted to rant at him and the injustice, but Father's tired face crumpled my resistance. He'd aged ten years.

"I'm so sorry, Bryn." Anguish choked his voice. His eyes were wet.

This time I reached for him. Our arms encircled one another. I felt the beating of his heart as he held me, and mine answered.

"I know Calia is a troublemaker. I'm sorry you've been caught in her web. I love you and I believe in you."

His simple words acted like an injection of courage. "I love you, Father. Give my love to Mother and Jarryd. Tell them I'll see them soon. Take care of Circe." I forced some of Stick's optimism into my voice. "It's only three months."

A guard entered. "The premier is waiting, Councilor Bokk."

Father's kiss was light on my cheek. We stood apart and I watched him once again become a leader: back straight, face stern, attitude confident. However, as he moved into the hallway's brighter light and glanced back, his gaze reflected apprehension.

I took two steps forward and whispered, "Don't worry, I'll be okay."

There was hope in his faltering smile, and pride.

The rigid guard saluted as Father walked past, head high. His steps died away.

I repeated the words for me this time.

"I'll be okay."

17

CONFINEMENT

The metal cell door banged shut.

Confined and alone again, I slumped into the chair and took a deep breath barely, noticing the rank odor. Thanks to Father, I wouldn't be transported. I preferred three months physical labor in the laundry to the uncertainty of Prima Feminary. The hardest part would be the isolation from family and friends.

I waited for guards to appear. Several times, I heard muffled noises outside, but no key rattled the lock. My stomach growled. My lips were dry and cracked. Thoughts of thirst and starvation churned through my mind. A vivid imagination was sometimes a curse. I forced my brain into another direction.

Mind over matter.

Weyland's favorite words surfaced, reminding me of the day on the island. Had Mother found an explanation for his reactions to my singing? Would the diary from the cave explain the portrait I'd seen?

I gasped as the door hammered back against the adjoining wall and light flooded into the cell.

"Out." A beefy outline filled the doorway.

I stood and stumbled into the light, following one guard as another fell into position behind me. My arrival had been a blur so I glanced around as I walked, curious about my location.

Apart from the guards' booted steps, the only sound was the low hum of machinery. Large pipes snaked through the dome, twisting and turning before disappearing into towering holding tanks. Workers monitored numerous gauges on the monolithic structures. No one looked up as we passed.

Nearing an exit, the first guard veered toward a cupboard and extracted two waterproof capes. They settled them around their shoulders and pushed me forward. When one opened the door, a horizontal spray of water slapped my face, drenched my juba and blew my hood down my back. Gasping for breath, I struggled to reposition the soaked material, stretching the hood forward to shield my eyes.

I was on a dock, outside the dome.

The lashing storm made progress difficult. Head down, my view was restricted to my feet as I picked my way unsteadily along the heaving wharf. Water crashed on either side, each wave threatened to sweep me into the cold sea. I held my footing but cringed when the ground beneath me swayed.

My mouth went dry when I saw the boat. I wanted to run, but the two guards flanking me made it impossible. I stoically accepted my fate. Father's efforts had been in vain. A trip by water meant Prima Feminary. Like Stick, I was being transported.

The waiting vessel was unlike the long Hypor transports I'd seen from the air. It was a small fishing dory like the ones from home, equipped with nets and outriggers. It thrashed against its fenders, snapping the tie lines like whips.

My slippers were sodden and useless on the slippery dock. As the guards urged me into the boat, I grasped the edge of the wheelhouse and lifted the hem of my juba to step down. When my foot landed on a coiled rope, I started to fall forward toward the metal anchor. I windmilled my arms for balance but continued to fall. I cried out with relief when two strong hands gripped my waist.

"Thank you." My words were lost in a howl of wind.

He dragged me forward. "Watch your head," he yelled in a gruff, but familiar voice.

I ducked as I entered the cabin then clutched the arm of a portside bench and sat, hunched and trembling.

"Thank you." I glanced up but only saw the back of my rescuer's grizzled hair as he stood at the opening of the cabin. The guards stayed out on the deck, huddled under their rain slicks, despite the steady downpour.

"Where're we heading?" The old man called out to them.

I held my breath anticipating the guards' response.

"The laundry."

I closed my eyes and exhaled. I was wrong. I wasn't being transported after all. Three months in the laundry suddenly felt like a reprieve.

FREE OF ITS MOORING, THE BOAT PLUNGED WILDLY AS IT ventured into the choppy waves. White caps sloshed onto the deck. I raised my feet onto the bench and hugged my knees, but my tense body quaked with the cold.

The seaman stood at the helm, his hands gripping the wheel. He muttered as he fought the gusty wind and thrashing crests. I'd never been good on boats and started to feel my stomach roil. My feet hit the floor. I lurched toward an open hatch, hoping a few deep breaths might help, but a sudden plunge increased my anguish. When I started to heave, the old man thrust a rusty bucket at my chest. Sick and miserable, I collapsed to the floor.

I closed my eyes and forced thoughts of home. The pungent air of the ancient forest. The heady delight when Circe soared elegantly overhead. The soft sweet melody Mother sang as she tended her greenhouse blooms. I tried to hum along, but my throat was raw. Hot tears warmed my cheeks as my body heaved again.

My eyes stayed closed until the pitching stopped too many agonizing minutes later. In the lee of a city dome, the gale had subsided and the sea was calmer. I swiped a sodden sleeve over my wet cheeks and mouth.

"I'll be okay," I spoke aloud, but the seaman seemed not to notice.

I felt better and looked out a cabin window, curious about the laundry. Clean clothes were something I'd taken for granted. I'd never considered where they came from.

The laundry dome's structure was similar to others, except the top third was transparent. Along with the usual fans, giant vents at the peak belched continuous clouds of steam. As we neared, the boatman steered the craft into a wide channel cut into the side of the dome. The diminished light made it difficult to see, but above a steady hum of machinery I heard voices. Women's voices.

The vessel veered right. At the far end of the docking area, the engine rumbled to a stop as the boat nudged a cement landing.

"Get the lines," the old man commanded the guards. Then he approached me and shoved a small oil-skin wrapped parcel into my hand. I looked up into a familiar face.

"From your mother," whispered old Joe Campbell, one of the village fishermen from home. "Hurry, hide it somewhere. They're returning." He stood so he blocked the guards' view.

There was no time to ask questions. I pushed the package under my hair at the back of my sodden hood. From its size and shape, I knew it was the diary.

"Take care, Lassie." He gave my shoulder a gentle squeeze that I didn't want to end.

The connection to home brought tears. I choked out a thank you for his warm gesture. As the guards neared, he returned to the wheel.

"Out." One guard flicked his thumb at me.

I stood, but the hem of my juba caught the ragged edge of the metal seat.

"Hurry, we haven't got all day. If I have to come and get you, you'll be sorry." The second man fumbled under his rain cape and produced a document and a small leather bag.

Fabric ripped as I freed my juba. I climbed onto the landing and hastened after the guards.

I heard women talking again. Then a man's voice yelled for quiet.

Across an expanse of water, another landing ran parallel to ours. A metal barge, piled high with clothing, clanged against it. The women ferried armloads of garments from the massive pile into the dome. An obese man stood nearby, surveying their progress for several moments before switching his gaze to us. He crossed his arms and waited for us to reach him.

The document and the bag changed hands. The guards

lingered only moments. After saluting the fat man they returned to the boat.

The recipient of the salute ignored the guards and scanned the information. I took note of his heeled boots that boosted him to my height. His corpulence was evident under a knee-length tunic, heavily stained with patches of sweat. Oily strands of hair curled on his brow. He pushed them back with a pudgy hand and looked up.

"Prisoner 6572?" His accent was difficult to decipher, but I detected a hint of an old Mediterranean language.

"So...Councilor Bokk's daughter." There was no warmth in the man's thin-lipped smile. "Such shame on your father and your family." His eyes roved over me. Despite efforts to loosen the wet material, my grimy robe clung tight. His inspection left me feeling dirtier than before. As much as I hated the juba, my nondescript garb was a welcome if ineffective shield against his lascivious gaze.

I suppressed a shudder and waited for his next words. He looked at the paper again. It was then that I noticed his long earlobes. They were an unusual feature I'd seen before.

Other things started to add up. Short stature, dark hair, swarthy complexion. Except for the paunch that threatened to burst the seams of his tunic, he was a double for Premier Delio. There was one other difference. Whereas the Premier's eyes showed cunning, this man's eyes radiated cruelty.

Three months felt increasingly like a life sentence.

I'll be okay was my silent mantra.

"I am Podmaster D." His lips twitched in an attempt to grin. Tilting his head back, he took a full breath that widened his nostrils and curled his upper lip. "There'll be no privileged treatment here despite your parentage. You'll work as long and hard as the other detainees and have to earn any concessions."

I hated to imagine what a woman would have to do to gain privileges from this man.

"At the end of three months, there will be a review. Then, depending on your behavior, your sentence will be extended or you may be released. The decision will be mine." His narrowed gaze searched my face.

The last statement terrified me but I forced a neutral expression. I was sure this man would prey on weakness.

"Ruby." The man beckoned to someone behind me. A thickset woman strolled toward us. Her dress was unlike anything I'd seen elsewhere on Hypor. Clearly, the rules were different here

She wore skintight leather leggings tucked into knee-high boots and a deep-necked tunic pulled taut across her ample bust. Her bare arms were muscled and covered with tattooed sleeves. Inked designs ringed her thick neck and plunged into her cleavage. An army of studs made her ears more metal than flesh. Several hoops adorned her bottom lip and nose.

Red stubble topped her head. In one hand, she held a cigar; the other was hooked on her hip, exposing long fingernails. Pointed and red, except for the smallest whose rounded tip smeared a patch of white powder on her leg as she walked. When she came within reach, the Podmaster put his arm behind her, pulled her forward and rubbed his fleshy torso against hers. Several inches taller, she laughed and caressed his head as he buried his face in her cleavage.

Their intimacy sickened me, but I didn't turn away. I needed to understand the dynamics of this place and she was important to him.

"Do you have my package, lover?" Her dull eyes focused

on me, her raspy voice emphasized the endearment as if issuing a warning.

"Yes, but I'll keep it and we can enjoy ourselves later. I think you've had enough for now."

Her lips thinned and her hands curled into claws, then she shrugged and instead took two steps toward me.

"A new prisoner?" She circled me as if assessing an opponent. "I hope she works out better than the last one. She's skinny as a drowned rat."

"She's a celebrity," he sneered. "Councilor Bokk's daughter. She's all yours." He slapped Ruby's backside before strutting away.

"Well then," she mocked with a slight bow. "We'll have to give her the best treatment." She blew a mouthful of fetid smoke in my face. "Follow me, your highness."

As we neared the entrance to the laundry, the stench from the barge forced me to hold my nose and blink repeatedly. Ruby, as well as the group of workers, showed little awareness of the rank odor that permeated the docking area. The women gave me curious glances as I followed Ruby. Just as curious about them, I slowed and turned to watch them hauling clothes. It was a mistake.

A booted foot shoved me from behind. I stumbled, landing face down, scraping my cheek on the cold sodden floor. I scrambled to my feet and adjusted my hood to check for the hidden package. I started a low hum to ease the pain in my back and shoulder but stopped when I noticed the women were circling Ruby and me. All activity had halted.

Physical violence opposed everything I'd learned from my mother. I was a healer, but I couldn't stop the anger that flamed my tense muscles. My instinct to strike back was strong until I realized that's what Ruby wanted—a fight.

She threw her cigar to the floor, clenched her fists and

THE LAST SINGER

folded her arms under her ample breasts. Like a brawler, eager to attack, tensed in readiness, but waiting for their opponent to make the first move. "Afraid?" She sneered.

"No. Just cold." It was the truth, and besides, I didn't need another physical confrontation that I was sure I'd lose.

Several women snickered until a look from Ruby sent them scurrying back to work.

She tilted her head as if considering whether to accept my response, then relaxed her stance. She pulled another cigar from her cleavage and lit it.

"Quick on your feet." She exhaled a stream of smoke. "You'll need to be, in here."

She turned on one heel and swaggered into the dome.

Relief came with the realization that I'd been lucky. At least today.

THE SOUND OF MACHINERY INTENSIFIED AS I FOLLOWED RUBY inside. The steady hum of the overhead drying equipment, combined with the thud of the washing vats, made communication difficult. I was conscious of many moving parts and wanted to watch the operation but didn't relish another boot.

The area reeked of chemicals and disinfectant. My nose dripped with moisture. It was like breathing through a wet rag, but for the first time in hours, I was warm.

Across the dome, we entered a half-moon shaped chamber. *The Bunker* had been scratched on the door. Metal berths lined the straight wall. Thin mattresses and pillows lay neatly on each bunk. The curved wall of the pod contained open shelves with piles of clothing and numbered hooks. No lockers for personal items was a concern. Where would I hide the diary?

Two long tables, worn and bare, bisected the area. Closest to the door, a dozen chairs clustered around a video screen. At the far end, I could see the bathroom area.

I jerked when the door slammed behind me. Ruby stood barring the exit, her flexed arms crossed over her chest.

"I'm in charge here. Whatever I tell you to do—you do it. Do you understand?"

I nodded.

"You have ten minutes to shower, change, and then work. Get what you need from there." She pointed to the shelves. "Move," she yelled when I hesitated.

A hot shower sounded like heaven. I grabbed one item from each stack: towel, underwear, a pair of loose trousers and a short-sleeved tunic. There were no hoods on the tunics. I'd noticed that some women wore a headscarf while others wore nothing. I grabbed two scarves, deciding to use one for my hair, at least for a while. I'd use the second to tie my bundle to my leg. Socks and boots I'd get after my shower.

"One more thing." Ruby walked to where I stood with my arms piled with clothing. "The podmaster is mine."

My first assignment was unloading the barge. I joined the line of women circling to and from the dock. The work was monotonous. The women chatted quietly as they worked, but ignored me. I wasn't expecting to make friends here. There was no Calia to pave my way—or undermine me. I was on my own.

After a couple of hours, the barge was empty. Ruby reassigned everyone. I found myself in another line carrying wet clothes from the washing area to the dryers.

Despite workouts at the recpod, my biceps and shoulders ached. The heavy armfuls pulled every muscle. I watched the others and copied them, shifting my loads from one hip to another, hoping to relieve the pain.

I pushed my body through the next hour. I'd almost given up hope of a break when the line stopped. Grateful for a halt, I rubbed my neck and rolled my shoulders. Other workers dumped their loads and rushed to the opposite end of the pod near the sewing area. I didn't follow but stepped onto a low stool to see over the heads of those clustered across the room.

A tight circle of jeering women enclosed two others. One was small and slender. The other, tattooed like Ruby, sleeves, neck and even head, was a bull of a woman. The smaller one, already bloodied, cringed against the crowd who pushed her inward. As the bully pulled back her fist waiting for the next strike, I imagined the impact on her victim.

"Stop," I cried, but my voice couldn't penetrate the loud mechanical throb of machinery and the spectators' shouts. I leaped from the stool and ran, but reached the crowd too late.

Silence fell like a curtain. I realized that the final hammering blow had landed.

As I pushed forward, the women parted. Emotionless faces drifted past me. The tight circle dispersed revealing a battered, bloody body. There was no attempt by anyone to help the woman.

Not knowing if the woman was even alive, I rushed to her side. I felt a weak pulse. I couldn't tend her wounds without herbs. All I had was my voice. I hummed several notes hoping the machine noise would cover the sound. The rule against singing and the risk of being caught fought my instinct to help.

Damn the rules. They probably couldn't hear me above the clamor of the laundry.

I chose the tones with care, remembering all I'd learned from my mother. Placing my hands gently on the woman's torso, I sang softly and felt the vibrations quivering through her body. Her arms, legs, then head. I was so focused on my task that I didn't immediately notice another worker kneeling across from me, holding one of the victim's broken hands. Her long black hair fell in a thick braid over her shoulder.

When she looked up, I was surprised to see emerald eyes moistened with tears. "Thank you," she mouthed the words as I continued to chant healing tones.

"What's going on here?"

Out of the corner of my eye, I spied high black boots two feet away, but I defied the urge to jump to my feet.

"What are you saying?" Ruby demanded, not realizing that I was singing.

The beaten woman's pulse returned to normal so I stopped and stood, as did the kneeling woman. Her expression turned icy as she faced the podmaster's girlfriend.

The bully pushed past another tattooed friend to Ruby's side. "She interfered in my business." She pointed at me. "I demand satisfaction—according to the rules."

Ruby swiped her little finger into a leather pouch that hung around her waist. The digit came out white. She lifted the rounded fingernail to her nose and sniffed, filling her nostril with powder. Her eyes drifted shut. When they opened, they were wild and glassy.

Mother had told me about the addictive nature of some

substances. Whatever drug Ruby was taking wouldn't bode well for me. Submit or show strength. Either way, I'd probably lose. I decided to go on the offense. "She beat this poor woman almost to death. Surely she should be punished." I was on unfamiliar ground. The rules might be different here, but we were still in Hypor.

"She's interfered with my rights." The tattooed offender stabbed a stubby finger toward me. "She has to forfeit. I demand battle."

I didn't understand what rights she was referring to. "I demand to speak to the podmaster. This is ludicrous. Hypor City is a civilized society," I ranted. "The laws must still be obeyed, even in the laundry."

The tattooed entourage laughed, others shifted nervously. Ruby even grinned but it quickly became a scowl.

"What did I tell you?" She jabbed a pointed nail into my shoulder. "I'm in charge. Therefore, I make the rules. Right?" She scanned the faces around her but most avoided her gaze.

I stayed silent, waiting.

"Your rights will be upheld." Ruby nodded to the challenger. "Bokk interrupted the fight. The dispute between you and Bokk will be settled. Now."

My opponent sneered and lifted her clenched right hand.

I knew I'd never survive even one blow from that massive fist. Dazed at the prospect ahead, I didn't notice the workers once again circling, defining the battleground.

A small hand slipped into mine. I looked down into green eyes. As the hand pulled away, I felt a sharp prick. My fingers curled around a small knife. The comfort of having a weapon didn't diminish the horror of wielding it against another person.

"What's going on here? Why aren't you working?"

All eyes turned as the questions boomed across the laundry. It was the only time I'd ever be grateful to hear the podmaster's voice.

My fingers were pried open and the knife removed. A quick smile and green eyes were gone.

"Where's Ruby?" He pushed the women apart.

"Here, Lover." She wiped her nose and sidled toward him. "I'm settling an argument."

"I don't care. Get them back to work. Now!"

"Get back to work," Ruby growled, then followed him to his office. As the workers dispersed, the tattooed woman and her friends blocked my way.

I stood breathless, frozen, waiting for them to attack.

Instead, they brushed by me.

One of them shoved my shoulder and snarled. "This isn't over."

18

A NEW FRIEND

Several hours later, nightfall darkened the overhead skylights.

The machines stopped. Silence fell over the laundry like a shroud. The rhythmic slosh of water subsided. The throbbing whine of the dryers dwindled. There was no chatter, just the scuff of boots as weary women abandoned their duties. On the perimeter wall, the half dozen lanterns brushed light across bowed heads as we filed toward the bunker. I joined the line of shuffling feet, wary of the darkness.

I felt less vulnerable as I entered the brightly lit bunker, but remained cautious. The tight quarters would make avoiding the tattooed trio difficult.

"Don't worry, they don't sleep here." The small woman who had slipped me the knife spoke behind me. "They have their own room near Pig's. I'm Leika. Thanks for helping my friend."

It was oddly formal the way she held out her hand, but I shook it without hesitation.

"I'm Brynna. Who's the pig? Ruby?"

"The podmaster. Likes us to call him Podmaster D, but we prefer to call him Pig. Come and eat."

Leika and I joined a line. From a wall dispenser, we each took a loaded food tray. My stomach rumbled at the prospect of a good meal. At least I wouldn't starve.

We sat at one of the tables. Others lay on their beds or perched on benches that fronted the video screen. From time to time, the women glanced up at the clock. What were they waiting for?

Two women joined our table. It took a moment before I realized they were twins. The only difference was their hair color. One had teal blue hair, the other lemon yellow.

We ate in silence for a few moments, but I had so many questions. "Why aren't there any guards here?"

"There's no need because there's no way to escape unless you fancy a swim in the frigid ocean. Besides, Ruby's always around," said Leika

"Tell me about her. Does she work for the podmaster?" I spoke quietly, but the twins heard me and snorted in unison.

"You might call it work." Blue sniffed then returned to eating.

Leika grinned. "He uses Ruby for sex, but she's a prisoner like the rest of us. She's been here for three years. I don't think he'll ever let her leave."

"Is she in charge?"

"Only when Pig isn't around. He keeps her happy by giving her power over us."

"And drugs," said Yellow.

"And Steepchase," added Blue.

"She won't be much good if she's high," said Leika. "She came second last year. I don't think she has a hope in the upcoming games."

"How can she participate if she's a prisoner?" I asked.

"Pig is connected," said Leika. "He has power."

"To the premier," I answered.

Her eyes widened. "Yes, how did you know?"

"There's a strong family resemblance and the droopy earlobes are the clincher."

The others grinned.

"I've heard the Delios have similar appetites as well," said Blue. "Particularly sexual."

"Yeah, that's something you'll have to watch out for. Pig has wandering hands." Leika's lips curled in disgust. "When he walks through the laundry, it's best to get out of his way."

"Beware of Ruby as well." Yellow thrust out her fist. "She punishes those that Delio favors. She's a nasty piece of work and even more so when she's jealous."

As if on cue, the three stood and took their trays to a wall receptacle. I did the same and joined them in the video area just as the screen flashed live. I was surprised when the nightly broadcast started. I hadn't expected this privilege.

I gasped when Carrot's face filled the monitor. His lips moved but I couldn't hear his words, only the echo of Stick's voice as we parted. *See you soon, Brynna.*

"What's wrong? You're sweating." Leika's eyes roamed my face. "Are you sick?"

"No, just surprised." And relieved that Carrot hadn't been punished for his outburst. The camera panned right and another man came into view. "I used to work with the one on the left."

The other presenter, tall and skinny like Stick, started to speak. I focused on his words when the women around me clapped and cheered.

"...perpetrators of these wanton acts of vandalism have yet to be apprehended. The council is taking every step to locate the

rebels who are a serious threat to our government. The increasing hostile actions will not go unpunished."

"Boooooo! Boooooo!"

"Hyporians are encouraged to report any incidents of rebel activity. Bonuses will be awarded for information leading to the arrest of these criminals. Until then, citizens must comply with all curfews. We thank you for your cooperation."

More boos followed.

Details about new curfews and restrictions continued, but nothing about the threat from CMEs. I wanted to ask Leika if she knew about the danger but decided to wait until I knew her better. A bigger priority was to learn what I could about the laundry.

When the screen went dark, the women dispersed to their bunks or hunched around the tables playing cards. I was surprised that my new friends stayed with me and then realized they also had questions.

"So what did you do to get put in here?" Leika asked.

"I was wrongly accused of theft—by the thief." It sounded ludicrous even to my ears and I understood why the others laughed. "What about you three?"

"We're here because we wouldn't follow orders and become domestic slaves," said Leika.

"What do you mean?"

"They're scientists." Leika pointed to Blue. "She's a hydrologist." Then to Yellow. "She's a physicist. I'm just stubborn."

"Wow, I'm impressed and surprised that you weren't transported out of Hypor City. I heard that people who didn't conform were sent away."

"The laundry was short of workers, so we hear. I guess we were lucky," said Leika.

"What about you? Where did you work?" Blue asked.

"I work—or worked—in the media lab. I guess you could say I have an ability with languages."

"So what's happening on the outside?" Yellow asked. "We only get the stuff the council feeds us."

I hesitated. Premier Delio could have spies even in the laundry. "I heard there's a threat from the sun, but Delio seems more concerned with the rebels."

"That's about all we know as well," the twins added in unison. The lights flickered.

"Time for bed." Blue yawned. Yellow did the same.

The twins left but Leika lingered.

"Besides languages, what else are you good at?" she asked.

"Well, I used to think I might be good at the Steepchase events, but having seen Ruby I'm not so sure. I don't think I'd be able to compete with her. Especially since I can't train at the recpod anymore."

She leaned toward me and spoke quietly. "And you're a singer."

Nerves skittered down my spine. "What?"

"I overheard you when you helped my friend." She shrugged and pushed back into her chair. "Don't worry, I won't tell anyone. Besides, I don't think they'd care here."

She might be right, but I wasn't so certain. I didn't want Pig to find an excuse to extend my sentence or ship me off to Prima Feminary.

"Where did you learn to sing? The elders of my people told stories of singers and their ability to heal, but I thought they died out long ago."

I was curious about Leika's background and her knowledge of singers, but I didn't know her well enough yet to share my secret.

I was saved from answering when the door slammed open. Ruby stood in the doorway, glassy-eyed, arms crossed.

"Lights out in two," she bellowed, then banged the door closed.

Leika grabbed a metal wedge and jammed it under the door.

"To keep Pig out," she explained. "He likes to roam at night."

"Doesn't he object?"

"Yes, but Ruby doesn't."

It would also keep out the tattooed threat.

"You're there," she indicated a lower bunk before climbing onto the one above me.

I quickly made up the bed before grabbing a nightshirt from a shelf. After the lights went out, I slipped off my boots, undressed and hid the parcel under my pillow. A faint glow from the bathroom doorway made me determined to investigate that location sometime during the night. Perhaps there would be enough light to read the diary.

HEAVY POUNDING PULLED ME FROM A DREAM OF HOME. My smile died as I remembered where I was. Fatigue had pushed my body into deep slumber. I'd missed the opportunity to investigate what Mother had discovered in translating the diary. There would be no time this morning either, I realized as Leika yanked the wedge from under the door.

"Hurry—or you'll go hungry," she called over her shoulder, already dressed and heading for the food dispenser.

I threw off my blanket and pulled on my uniform, eager to get breakfast. As I straightened my bedclothes, I enclosed the diary in a headscarf, ran to the bathroom and lashed the book to my lower leg before donning my knee-high boots.

Most women had finished eating by the time I started. I downed the mash, swallowing the last grainy mouthful when the door whipped open. I rushed my tray to the waste receptacle and joined the waiting group as Ruby entered.

"You'd better put that out of sight." Leika pointed to my necklace, which I'd forgotten to conceal under my tunic. "Or someone will take it."

I closed my hand around the black stone and felt my only reminder of home cold against my chest. "Thanks." Her friendly gesture increased my trust that I'd gained a friend.

"The barge is in early, so everyone out to the docks for unloading," shouted Ruby.

"Good," said Leika. "At least we'll get some fresh air out there."

Initially, the cold sea air was a shock and blanketed my bare arms with goose bumps. But by the third load of heavy laundry, I was sweating and realized the truth in Leika's comment.

The soiled clothing was damp and rank. The briny air helped to dispel the stench that wafted from the massive pile, but even our small loads reeked of stale body odor. After carrying the first load in front of me, I tried to escape the smell by shifting my load to my hip.

"Move! No stopping." Pig's voice shot at me from the office window that overlooked the dock.

I glanced up. It was a mistake. He immediately recognized me.

"Stop, Bokk."

When I halted, other workers skirted around me. They

continued on their path as if avoiding an inanimate obstacle. I assumed they were eager to avoid Pig's attention.

"Come to my office." His voice was normal, but I detected an undertone of malice.

At the washing station, I dropped my load. As I backtracked to Pig's office, Ruby's entourage gathered nearby. I expected a confrontation, but all I heard was a long hiss as I passed them.

His office door was open. Pig smiled and beckoned me in, then circled behind me. I turned as the sound of the laundry diminished and a latch clicked into place. His eyes were greedy, his smile lascivious. I glanced at the open window. Could I survive the jump?

As if reading my mind, he laughed and closed the window, then approached me. I stepped back until the edge of his desk pressed my thighs.

"I dreamt of you last night, Brynna Bokk." His hot breath flicked my face as his corpulent stomach pressed against my body.

I twisted and pushed against him, smothered by his bulk. He grabbed my wrists in one hand, trapping them behind my back. I cringed and hollowed my chest as the other clawed hand reached for my breast.

Unable to move my body, I spiked my head forward, latched onto his earlobe and bit down hard. He screamed in pain. Blood flowed down his neck. He seized my throat. I gasped for air as black spots darkened my vision.

The door clanged as my awareness slipped away.

Raised voices breached my oblivion as I lay on the floor. A hard kick to my spine set me rolling into a ball and groaning.

"Get up," Ruby commanded.

Despite the pain, I uncurled and struggled to my feet.

"What did I tell you, you whore." The color of her face matched her name. Anger tensed every muscle.

Another "get out" was followed by a two-handed shove that propelled me from the office. My arms flailed as I struggled to stay upright. I grabbed the doorframe and glanced back.

"Out!" Ruby glared at the cluster of women, who had stopped to watch, then strode to the door and slammed it shut.

"Are you okay?" Leika pulled my arm across her shoulders as I started to collapse.

"I've never been so relieved to hear Ruby's voice." I rubbed my throat and blinked to check that my lens was still in place, then felt for the diary. It was still secure.

From behind closed door, the voices grew louder. Ruby berated Pig for his interest in me. He shot back that drugs were taking their toll on her looks. The heated exchange continued for several minutes. Suddenly all went silent. The door banged open and Ruby strode out.

"You won't win Steepchase if you keep taking those drugs." Pig's cutting blow stopped her short.

Ruby's face contorted with red fury when she spied me watching. I expected a response, but she turned on her heel and stalked away.

The spectators scattered.

Leika dragged me away but I didn't need any urging to leave.

"She'll want revenge. You'll have to watch your back."

The next couple of hours passed quickly. The pain eased, but I knew I'd have bruises on my neck and back. As I worked, I hummed to soothe my aches.

"They're planning something," Leika paused by my side and tilted her head toward the exit to the dock.

A shiver of fear snaked down my spine when I noticed the bully and her friends conversing as they shot menacing glances my way.

"They probably won't try anything until you're alone, so make sure that doesn't happen."

I was working on the laundry line with five other women and felt safe enough. I hummed quietly, keeping pace with the rhythm of the work until a loud snap followed a grinding crunch and the washers stopped. Water sloshed over the sides of the vats and seeped across the floor. Everyone stopped working.

Within minutes, an old man arrived. He carried tools and I assumed he was there to fix the machines. Ruby challenged him. At his quiet response, she laughed then waved him on.

Gray-haired, he walked with a stoop, his tools clanged in a sling that hung from his shoulder. I watched him shuffle toward the broken machine. When he started tinkering with the mechanics, I lost interest.

Some workers drifted outside to the dock. The cool breeze was tempting, but I didn't want Pig or Ruby to see me. Instead, I searched for Leika, remembering her warning not to be alone.

After several minutes of searching, I saw her as I circled the last row of laundry vats. Partially hidden, she was conversing with the older man.

I didn't approach but she must have sensed my presence because she broke from her conversation and walked back to me. At the same time, the hunched man glanced up. I gasped as familiar green eyes scrutinized me.

"Stop looking at him. You'll give him away." Similar green eyes bored into mine as I looked down at Leika.

"He's got your eyes. Who is he?"

"Not here. I'll tell you later," she promised. "Here comes Ruby."

Ruby pointed at Leika. "Go help with the dryers. Bokk, you clean the toilets."

Leika hesitated. "I'll show her what to do. She's never done bathroom detail before."

"No, you won't." Ruby grimaced and threatened her with a clenched fist. "Bokk can do it. Alone."

19

THE TATTOOED TRIO

I knew it was a setup.

My heart battered my ribcage as I headed into the bunker toward the bathrooms. I wedged open the door. There was comfort in the steady din of the laundry.

In the bathroom, I searched for anything I could use to protect myself. A scrubber, a broom and a bucket were my only defenses.

Nerves pushed my muscles into frenzied action as I scoured the first toilet in less than a minute. I hummed an island song, trying to relax, knowing I'd be useless in an attack otherwise. As I moved to the second toilet, my humming sounded louder. The ambient noise had diminished. A door lock clicked.

I stopped humming and waited inside the cubicle. Footsteps approached. Several.

"Where are you, Bokk?" A voice demanded.

"She knows what's coming." A second one laughed. "She's hiding."

But there was nowhere to hide.

I propped the broom between the door and the toilet, but it snapped when the door flung open.

Meaty hands wrenched my arms almost from the sockets as the two women dragged me into the empty bunker.

I didn't see the first punch coming but I knew it had cut my temple when I saw my blood dripping onto the floor. Locked in tattooed arms, facing the other attacker, I twisted my head to protect my eyes. The second blow smashed my cheek and the side of my nose. My neck snapped back then I slouched forward as the first assailant prepared a third strike. It didn't come.

Instead, my captor bellowed and sagged to the floor. A small knife sat hilt-deep in her beefy shoulder. The first striker let me go to tend to her comrade.

My knees buckled. I crumpled to the ground. Fearing a kick, I crawled out of striking distance. Barely conscious, I swiped blood from my eyes and looked toward the door. Leika and the twins approached. Fists clenched, arms raised, they were ready for battle.

I slumped, relieved that I wasn't alone.

"Now you're in trouble." The injured woman clutched her shoulder and laughed.

Beyond my friends, Ruby stood in the doorway. She slapped a thick club against her palm as she marched forward.

"Look out, Leika." I edged along the floor, but all I could do was watch.

Ruby's friends rose to their feet to join her. One passed close by. I reached for her ankle, hoping to trip her. I wanted to protect my friends.

A booted foot slammed into my chest.

"What's going on here?" Pig's voice drifted away as my consciousness dissolved.

∼

"Help me get her onto her bunk."

Gentle hands lifted my legs and I settled onto the hard pad as if it was feathers.

"They've done some serious damage," said Leika as she cleaned my cuts and scrapes. "You'd better get humming," she whispered.

I wanted to grin at her comment, but my face was too painful to make the effort worthwhile.

"I'm not kidding. Start humming," she commanded. Her hands staunched the blood that still oozed from my cuts, but she carefully avoided my swollen nose.

"Where are the others?" I mumbled.

"Ruby's goons have gone. Pig made them leave, but the twins are keeping watch by the door. The washers are still down. You're safe for now."

"Thank you, Leika." She and the twins had saved my life.

She shrugged then started to hum off key. I got the hint.

Humming was challenging, but eventually my body responded to the healing vibrations.

"Feeling better already?" Leika asked when I pushed my legs over the side of my bed an hour later.

I cradled my nose and nodded. The bleeding had stopped.

"Healing is a good skill to have."

"So is your skill with a knife." I managed a lopsided grin.

"You need to be able to defend yourself. We'll have to figure out something. Next time I might not be nearby."

"Next time I might not survive."

THE LAST SINGER

We sat silently for several moments then I looked at her and remembered the other pair of green eyes.

"Now tell me about the repairman."

She hesitated but finally admitted their connection. "He's my brother, Kaaluk."

"I gathered he was a relation, but what's he doing dressed as an old man?"

Leika laughed. "It's one of his better disguises. Fools them every time."

"I don't understand. Why is he disguised?"

I understood her hesitation. We didn't know each other very well. She looked deeply into my eyes but after a minute, I sensed a shift in her—an acceptance of friendship.

"Because otherwise he'd be recognized as a member of Delio's guard. Prince visits his uncle, that's Pig, and my brother is usually with him."

"That's where I know him from." I told Leika the story of Calia and Prince, leaving out my reaction to the second guard. "I remember the green eyes. But I don't get why he's here."

"We use the machine breakdowns to communicate. I break them. He fixes them. While he's here, he can pass me information about what's going on outside this place. He's working on a plan to get me out."

"Why? How long are you in for? I'm only here for three months."

Leika's sad expression filled my heart with dread. "Haven't you figured out yet that laundry is a euphemism for prison? Pig will find a reason to keep us here. There's no other way out but to escape."

Did Father know this? He couldn't have or he wouldn't have agreed. But perhaps he had no choice—the alternative was worse. "Escape from here seems impossible. I can't even imagine how it could be accomplished. It would certainly take extensive planning and considerable resources."

"Kaal has the skills." Pride filled Leika's voice. She leaned in and whispered "He's one of the rebels."

I immediately thought of Jarryd.

I hesitated, then trusted our newfound connection.

"My brother is working with them as well. We've been trying to get information about Premier Delio's plans, but haven't been successful so far."

"We're attempting to do the same thing," said Leika. "Sometimes at night, I search Pig's desk to see if there is anything incriminating. So far, there's been nothing, but I keep trying."

"What else have you heard from the outside?"

"Kaal is concerned about the military force that Prince is building, but lately he's uneasy about the number of people being transported. Men to Haven, some women to Prima Feminary and some who are old or weak are just disappearing. He doesn't know what's happening, but suspects that Premier Delio is culling the population of Hypor for some reason."

"My roommate disappeared just before I was sent here. And my brother's fiancée said that several people from the market had been absent for over a week. One was an elderly janitor. I thought it was just coincidence." Grub from the foodpod came to mind.

"We think that Delio is trying to get rid of anyone who opposes him."

"But that doesn't explain the others."

"There must be some reason that we haven't discovered yet."

My stomach clenched. "Oh, no. My mother. She could be a target."

"Why?"

"She's almost blind and all alone on our island. My father is Delio's biggest opposition on council. Perhaps that's why the drones have been surveying our island. They might try to take Mother. I have to warn my brother. Do you think Kaaluk would take a message to Jarryd?" I grabbed Leika's arm. "Can you ask him?"

"If your brother is working with the rebels, I'm sure my brother knows him."

"Can you get to Kaaluk before he leaves today?"

Leika pointed to the laundry where the machines were working again. "Too late. But I can arrange another breakdown in a few days."

Although it made sense not to have Kaaluk back too soon, I felt disappointed. The delay only heightened my fear.

"Leave her and get back to work." Ruby stood at the bunker entrance.

"Keep humming and healing." Leika mouthed the words before obeying the command.

Ruby glared at Leika as they passed one another, then Ruby sneered at me and shook her fist before leaving the bunker. I knew that problem wasn't going away.

I needed a plan.

THE POWER WENT OUT AS WE ENTERED THE BUNKER THAT night. The food was barely warm and with only two emergency lights, it was impossible to attempt to read the diary. There was no news video so, like the others, I went to bed, but my thoughts churned over ideas about Pig and Ruby and Steepchase.

Next morning, I got light duty, sitting, plying a needle at the sewing table. Not one of my skills, but I was glad for the diversion.

Another argument erupted between Pig and Ruby. There was no need to move closer when the altercation started. The combatants left the confines of the office and their strident voices boomed throughout the laundry.

"You better make sure I win—" A slight pause followed Ruby's angry words.

"I can't fix Steepchase." Pig sounded frustrated. I also detected apprehension in his tone. "You need to get clean and start training."

"I'd better win." Her voice was cold. This time she didn't leave any doubt. "Or else."

They must have parted because the voices went quiet and the women returned to their workstations.

Or else what? What did Ruby have on Pig that made him vulnerable? If I found out, perhaps I could use it against him as well.

20

A DEAL WITH THE DEVIL

Another attack was imminent.

As we filed from the bunker next morning, sneers from Ruby's tattooed entourage left me in no doubt. My only option was to make a deal with Pig.

When he finally arrived and sauntered into his office, I followed him inside and slammed the door behind me.

He turned in surprise. His face broke into a lascivious grin but was quickly followed by a fearful frown as he peered around me.

"Well, Bokk." Confident I was alone, he continued, "If you've changed your mind, I'm not sure I'm interested in you anymore, particularly looking like you do." His eyes raked my body, his lip curled as if he'd tasted something nasty.

With two black eyes and swollen cheeks I wasn't at my best but I knew I had to make an effort. "I want to make a deal."

His eyelids drooped, his lips pursed and his head tilted, sending his earlobes wobbling. "Deal? You think you can make deals with me? I'm the podmaster, you're nothing here."

Was my brash approach a mistake? I'd counted on his licentious nature and was reassured when his glance fell to my chest. "What deal?"

"I know that you need Ruby to win Steepchase."

His eyes narrowed suspiciously. Most of the laundry had overheard his argument with Ruby. Surely he knew that. If he didn't comply with her demands, his secret might soon surface. Gossip was a valuable commodity in the laundry and Pig knew it. He had power and connections, but would still be subject to the laws of Hypor.

"I can help her win." I kept my tone positive. I was betting my future on my gut sense that whatever Ruby had on Pig was huge.

He rubbed his damaged earlobe then winced. "How?" He snarled.

"I'll get her off drugs." Mother had helped addicts, but I wasn't sure I could. Pig didn't know that. This time I didn't worry about the lie. "I know herbs that will help her."

"It's not only the drugs. She needs intensive training. What do you know about Steepchase?"

His curiosity lent me confidence.

"Before coming here, my goal was to meet the time requirement to enter Steepchase. I watched the premier's guards train. They're the fastest. I learned the best methods for improving performance on the circuit. I know I can work with Ruby to get her ready to compete and win." My heart battered my ribs. I swallowed the bile that rose in my throat. Would my bluff work?

"What do you want in return?"

I stiffened my legs as they threatened to buckle with relief. "My freedom. If she wins, you grant me a pardon."

"And if she loses? What do I get?" He licked his lips, anticipating my answer.

"If Ruby loses Steepchase, I'll return here, under your control." I didn't allow my imagination free rein to consider the possibility. One way or another, I had to find out about my family and help fight the Delios.

He didn't answer immediately. Pulling on his good lobe, he walked to a window and stared out.

Seconds ticked by. I broke into a cold sweat.

What if he refused my deal? He was the podmaster and could force me to do his will despite Ruby's protests. My only advantage was that he needed to have her win.

"Agreed," he said. "If Ruby wins, you are free. But if she loses, you'll never leave the laundry. You'll be mine."

I suppressed a shudder. "Agreed." I thrust out my hand, wanting to confirm the deal.

As his clammy hand clasped mine, the door banged open.

"Get away from him!"

Dropping his hand, I turned to see my nemesis lunging toward me. As she neared, Pig stepped between us, placing his considerable bulk in her path.

Ruby's eyes were wild, frenzied. Much to my surprise, he slapped her face. She lifted a hand to her cheek and took a step back.

"What's going on?" Her teeth clamped tight, her fists curled at her sides.

"Bokk and I have made a deal." Pig stepped from between us.

Suspicion replaced jealousy and Ruby's eyes narrowed. "What kind of deal?"

Pig explained my offer, but only part of it.

Ruby's mouth hung open in disbelief. "Her? That scrawny bitch? How can she help me?"

"She'll get you off the drugs for a start. That will help you win Steepchase. That's what you want isn't it?"

I could see the conflict on Ruby's face. She hated me, but she desperately wanted to be a winner.

"What's in it for her?"

"If you win, she will be free to leave the laundry." Pig didn't mention the alternative. "Well, do you agree to let her help you?"

Her eyes narrowed. Her nod was barely discernible.

"Good. That's settled then. You'll start training next week at the recpod when Bokk's recovered." He opened the door and motioned to us to leave, but grasped Ruby's arm as she passed by. "And warn your goons to leave her alone."

I followed Ruby out.

She stopped and joined her friends who waited nearby. They glowered as I passed, but I knew that for the time being at least, I had a reprieve.

"You won't make it out alive," said Leika when I told her the deal I'd made. "Ruby will make sure you'll never stay here with Pig if you lose."

"I don't intend to fail." I was feeling confident and a little cocky now that I'd found a possible way out.

"I wish you'd told me what you were planning."

"Why? What difference does it make?"

"Kaal is planning to break us out during the games. We could both be free without you having to make a pact with the devil."

"I had no option. The games are still a ways off. I might not survive another attack by Ruby's cronies."

Leika pondered my answer then nodded. "Do you really think you can wean Ruby off the drugs?"

"I'll find a way. I can't afford to fail."

THE LAST SINGER

∽

THERE WAS NO TUBE CONNECTING THE LAUNDRY WITH THE dome network. The recpod dome was a boat ride away. It was almost dark when we made the first crossing. Focusing on the destination, I managed to control my fears of the open water.

Inside, the familiar beige hallways felt oppressive. It was late and only the guards would be training at the recpod. I'd miss the camaraderie of training with Jarryd and the others. Was he still training to compete in Steepchase? Or spending most of his time plotting with the rebels? I could only guess.

The stark reality of my situation weighed on my soul and slowed my pace.

"Hurry up!" Ruby pulled at my arm. No extra guards accompanied us. She was more than capable of subduing me if necessary.

The empty halls reflected the enforced curfew, but I heard the hum of voices as we got closer. Once inside, we changed in silence then I followed Ruby into the workout area. The recpod was crowded with the premier's guards.

Hostile glances followed our progress to the track. Ruby started to run. Nerves made me clumsy and I stumbled behind her. Laughter followed as I raced to catch up.

Ruby had kicked her drug habit without my intervention. She'd missed several days in the laundry then reappeared looking haggard but sober. She'd spurned my assistance when offered, saying she'd rather suffer than take help from me.

I discovered that the only way I could help Ruby was to compete with her. The drugs had taken their toll on her body and she had to push herself in order to keep up with me in most activities. Competition suited me as well. I timed our runs and made sure that I was always in her sight, but slightly ahead. Often, I'd hear her growl with exertion and I'd see the dagger of fire in her eyes if I caught her gaze. She despised me but we were tied to a singular goal—to win Steepchase.

As we circled the track and settled into a rhythm, my mind wandered to other times with Jarryd, Marta and Weyland. Their absence was like a physical ache. Were they safe? Were my parents? My father had always been so strong, but my mother's vulnerability terrified me.

Distracted by my thoughts, Ruby had passed me and was out of sight. Picking up speed, I curved past the climbing walls toward the aquatic compound where I spotted a group of guards and Ruby. They laughed at something she said, then glanced in my direction as if watching for my arrival. At my approach, they lined up. Ruby ran on.

I slowed but continued forward. I looked for any opening that I could speed through, but more bodies arrived until there was a solid streak of black slashing across the red lanes of the track.

Nine strides from the human barrier I froze.

Perhaps I'd been too sure of my safety. Perhaps Ruby had planned this to be my end. My pulse throbbed at my temples. Should I turn and run? I hummed quietly. The vibrations soothed my fear and brought clarity. Perhaps there was a better way to deal with this threat.

The fear returned with my first step, but I forged ahead —each step as difficult as walking through a muddy bog— until I was two feet from the lineup.

"I am Brynna Bokk and my father is a member of the ruling council. I demand that you move aside." The words sounded strong, but I bit into my bottom lip to stop it trembling.

The men exchanged glances, grinned, and then laughed loudly. One burly guard stepped forward; his brawny arms crossed his chest.

"Your father has no power over us. We only report to Prince Delio."

"The council has power over everyone on Hypor. Stand aside or I'll report you." I stood my ground, trying to keep my legs from trembling.

"I guess we'll have to show her who's in charge here." The man nodded to his comrades.

The men surged forward. The air went stale as they surrounded me. My limbs went rigid, expecting an attack—but it never came. No one touched me.

A thunderous voice sounded from beyond my ring of captors. "What's going on?"

Bulky shoulders impeded my view.

"Just having a little fun," replied one of the men.

"Clear off. Back to your training," the new voice commanded.

There were grumblings as the men drifted away.

"Who does he think he is?" one of them asked.

"Prince Delio's pet," another answered.

"Are you all right?" The tall figure dripped with water and wore swimming goggles but his voice had a particular cadence that was comforting and familiar.

"I'll be okay. Thanks." Was it Kaaluk behind the goggles?

"Only guards and Steepchase contestants are allowed to train in Hypor's recpod. What are you doing here?" he demanded, hands on hips.

"I'm with Ruby, from the laundry. Pi...the podmaster gave us permission to train."

His brows furrowed, but the goggles made his eyes impossible to read.

"I'll make sure the men don't bother you again, but Ruby is your concern."

"I can deal with her," I replied confidently.

"I hope so." His head lifted, his attention focused over my right shoulder.

I turned and spied Ruby leaning against a boulder. She smirked before drifting away.

I hoped so too.

That night when I returned to the laundry, I told Leika what had transpired.

"Might have been Kaal. Just as well you didn't say anything. Who knows what cameras and audio devices are in the recpod. Kaal says Prince is so paranoid he doesn't trust his own guards."

"Paranoid is good. We want him to panic and make a mistake so we'll finally uncover the truth behind the solar threat."

"Perhaps, but your immediate concern is Ruby."

During the days that followed the confrontation, Ruby continued to treat me with disdain. Despite my assurances, she remained unconvinced of my disinterest in Pig, but grudgingly accepted my presence at the recpod. There were no further incidents and the guards kept their distance.

As our speeds increased, the goal of Ruby winning Steepchase became more realistic. But I started to wonder if my deal with Pig was the best alternative. Perhaps winning Steepchase would improve my prospect of freedom, but there was no guarantee.

21

DELIO'S DECEPTION

A week later horizontal rain lashed the docking area. A wretched job at the best of times, two barges arrived at once for unloading. The soiled clothes were more pungent than usual. We worked in silence, each coping with our own wet misery. We were issued mesh slings so we could carry larger loads. With the sling hoisted high up my back, I walked close to the wall to avoid the punishing storm. I kept my head bowed to hide from Pig who watched from his office windows overlooking the docks.

Anticipating the welcome warmth of the laundry, I rushed toward the entrance to complete my final run but my load slipped. The weight pulled me sideways. I scraped my shoulder against the rough wall and the sopping garments tumbled to the dock as the sling fell open. Clutching my bleeding arm, I hummed quietly to relieve the pain. The others trudged by, ignoring me.

I crouched near the wall until the abrasions started to heal then gathered the smelly clothes and piled them back into the sling. I was alone on the dock when I heard a window open. I flattened against the wall and held my breath.

"Ciao." The booming timbre was Pig's.

My shoulders sagged with relief when I realized he wasn't calling to me. He had a visitor. But who? It was impossible to climb the wall. Fortunately, my acute hearing gave me an advantage.

"You're soft and more accustomed to sniffing wine. A soldier wouldn't cringe at the stench." Pig laughed. "Perhaps the sea air will help."

"Nothing could improve the laundry. It always reeks," a younger male responded.

I strained to hear the conversation. It took me several seconds to realize that the men were speaking Italian.

"I was expecting your father," said Pig.

"He's busy beating the council members into submission."

It was Prince Delio. I hardly dared to breathe as I listened.

"Is that what he told you to say?"

Prince laughed. "You know him too well. He's busy—with his new mistress."

Pig chuckled. "Sadly, the men in our family have a weakness for women."

"No woman will ever control me," said Prince. "Father's an old fool ruled by prophecies and the stars. He treats me like a slave and has me running his errands while he satiates himself. He controls the council, but not for long. I'm done being treated like a failure."

"Does he suspect your ambitions?"

"It's no secret that the guards answer only to me. I'll be the one to take the lead when we leave Hypor City."

"What news of the rebels?"

"They've been sabotaging the power generating stations and water purification equipment so we've doubled the guards. Those actions are probably diversions. I think they're trying to access our computer files to find our plans to deal with the solar threat. Two nights ago, we caught a woman searching the administrative offices. Last night, the cameras recorded a man trying to hack the computer system in the sci-labs."

"Are you going to make an example of them?"

"We don't want martyrs. The woman is a cripple and would get too much sympathy. We've sent her to Prima Feminary. The man's been transported to Haven. Tarvek can decide what to do with him."

My roommate Rebecca sprung to mind. It was difficult to picture her working with the rebels, but she had disappeared. Then I thought about Weyland and my stomach knotted. Was he the man in the sci-lab?

"Any changes to the plan to escape the solar threat?" asked Pig.

"No, we're still waiting for the new spaceships."

Pig laughed. "Won't the council be surprised when they realize the ships are only for those loyal to the premier?"

I gasped at the boldness of the statement. His intention was to escape with his cronies and leave the populace of Hypor City to die.

"Quiet, the window is open. Someone might hear," said Prince.

"No one can understand us," Pig responded.

The rest of the conversation, however, was quieter and more difficult to follow. Scraping of chairs and booted footsteps accompanied more laughter then all went silent.

I hurriedly pulled the sling over my uninjured shoulder and moved away from the wall.

"What are you doing, Bokk?" Ruby stood in the arch of the laundry entrance.

I froze, wondering if she'd seen me listening, waiting for her to expose me.

"Get that load to the washers," she commanded as she walked away.

~

EXHAUSTED FROM MY LABORS AND WORKOUTS WITH RUBY, AND hampered by the blackouts, I'd had no opportunity to sneak to the bathroom and read the diary. Curiosity fueled my imagination as I wondered what Mother's translation might reveal.

Next morning, we'd barely started work when metal screeched and gears protested as the machines came to a halt. The overhead dryers clanked in a final tumble. The sound of sloshing water in the washing vats diminished to gentle laps then the dome became eerily silent.

I gave Leika a discreet thumbs-up. I'd told her what I'd overheard the day before and she'd promised to arrange a machine breakdown so we could get a message to Kaaluk.

She shook her head and shrugged.

"Power outage," Ruby yelled from the doorway of Pig's office. The women hooted and clapped then dispersed to their favorite spots to wait out the interruption.

I forced myself to saunter to Leika's side. "Will Kaaluk come?"

"Not for this. It's probably citywide. We'll have to wait for another day."

"This information is too important to wait. My father needs to know about Delio's plans."

"Yes, and so does Kaal, but too many interruptions will

be suspicious. I'm not prepared to risk Kaal's life. If he's caught, the rebellion might falter and we'll have no means of defeating Delio even if he is exposed."

I felt frustrated but understood her concern for her brother. "You're right, but there must be something we can do."

"Perhaps there is another way to contact Kaal."

Metallic squeals drowned her voice as the equipment lurched into action.

"Back to work." Ruby stalked around the machines as the women scrambled to their workstations. "That means you, Bokk."

"I'll tell you later," Leika mouthed the words and hurried away.

That evening I pulled her aside. She didn't look happy to lose her place in the dinner line.

"What's your plan?" I asked when we were a safe distance from the others.

"It's hard to think on an empty stomach," she grumbled then grinned unexpectedly. "You better smile too or someone might think we're plotting."

I curled up the edges of my mouth and even forced a laugh.

"So what's your idea?"

"You'll have to find Kaal at the recpod. He's there most evenings. It's the only way to get a message to him quickly."

"*If* I can find him among all the guards." The recpod was getting busier every night. Guards not only trained there, they socialized at Swigs.

"And you'll have to make sure no one sees you," warned Leika. "Especially Ruby. Can you find a way to ditch her while she's training?"

"I might have a way. Where's the best place to look for Kaaluk? It's a big place."

"I've never been in the recpod, but apart from swimming, I know that Kaal likes heights. He loves the challenge of the climb and being able to see everything."

Something we had in common. A flutter of anticipation whispered through my body. "So maybe I should start with the rock walls. Ruby avoids climbing. She hates heights and I usually go up alone."

"That would be the perfect opportunity to look for Kaal. You know what he looks like and you can recognize his eyes, can't you? He also has a faded scar here." She drew her finger across her high cheekbone and smiled. "It's where I caught him with a blade. I was eleven and he was teaching me to throw. He lied and told his friends he'd won a knife fight."

"Sounds like something my brother would say."

"They'll get along well then."

For a few seconds, fond memories left us silent, then I confirmed my task.

"Okay. I'll look for Kaaluk tonight."

SIX FEET TALL, BROAD SHOULDERS, ATHLETIC BUILD, GREEN eyes, scar. How hard could it be to find Leika's brother?

My confidence dropped when I entered the recpod behind Ruby. A mass of dark-clad bodies impeded my view. Cheering men blocked the entrance to the track. The noise level lessened when a countdown commenced.

"What's going on?" Ruby demanded of a man beside her.

"It's a race."

Ruby swore and pushed her way through the crowd. It was easy to follow in her broad wake. She crossed the track in front of runners, lifting a finger to the booing crowd. I kept going as well, fully aware that our disruption had stopped the countdown and probably made us some enemies.

"I'm going swimming." Ruby strode away, not waiting for my response.

She'd expect me to follow, but I decided to take a chance.

"I'll be climbing. Meet you later." Would she demand my company? I held my breath and waited.

She stopped and frowned. "Be back in the change room in one hour. Or else." Her raised fist punched the air as she turned to leave.

Could I complete my mission in an hour? I broke into a run and sped toward the rock walls.

Most of the men still watched the race so climbers were few. I quickly found a clear route to the summit. Adrenaline fueled my progress, but near the peak my muscles started to burn. After a twenty-minute ascent, I hooked one foot over the final edge and pulled my legs onto the uppermost plateau. Exhausted, I lay for several minutes before checking for somewhere to wait without being noticed.

There was no place to hide so I removed a boot and fiddled with it so as not to look conspicuous. As climbers arrived and left, I watched for distinguishing characteristics but none matched Kaaluk's description. I sensed my time was almost up and started to feel despondent. I'd been certain I'd find him tonight, but in reality, the odds were against me.

Another climber neared the top as I prepared to descend. Long fingers curled over the edge. A head thrust above the rim. The torso emerged. The build was right, the height too. I saw the faint white line on his cheek. It was Kaaluk.

Green eyes shot to my position. He approached as I slipped on my boot. A surge of warmth flooded my chest when his strong hands pulled me to my feet.

"What are you doing here?" he demanded then lowered his voice. "I know who you are. Pretend you're afraid while we speak. Cameras are everywhere."

I glanced around but saw nothing.

"Well, speak up," he ordered thunderously.

Even though he was acting, his tone alarmed me. I launched into a hurried explanation, remembering to whisper at the last minute. I have information about Premier Delio. I overheard Prince say that his spaceships won't take everyone, only those loyal to the premier. I think that's why people are disappearing."

He nodded but said nothing.

"Do you know my brother, Jarryd? Can you contact him? Can you give him the information so he can get it to my father on the council?"

Distracted by the noisy conversation of approaching climbers, Kaaluk ignored my questions. "Go now," he commanded as two men rolled onto the plateau. Seconds later, he strode to the rock rim and disappeared over the edge.

With agility and impressive speed, he was well down the rock face when I hooked my toes into the first foothold. When I reached the ground, I searched the milling crowd in vain. Kaaluk had disappeared.

If only I'd been able to speak with Kaaluk longer. The Delios weren't my only concern. I craved news about my family, but I understood his caution.

Certain my climb had taken longer than an hour, I clenched my fists and pumped my arms as I ran to meet Ruby, pushing past black bodies, not caring about the furious grunts.

"You're late!" Ruby exploded angrily as I entered the change room. "Where were you?"

"I told you I went climbing." I stripped off my workout gear and donned my prison garb.

"And I told you to be back here in an hour. If you disobey me like that again, I'll tell the podmaster. I don't need you anymore and I'll get your recpod privilege pulled."

My deal was with Pig so I suspected her threat was an empty one, but I didn't want to test that theory.

I mumbled a 'sorry' but she continued to rant and spent the entire boat ride grilling me about my whereabouts. She didn't touch me, but I still felt battered by the time we'd reached the laundry.

Only the emergency lights were on as I entered the bunker. I looked at Leika who pointed to the wedge. I pushed it under the door, then staggered toward my bed. As usual, no one else acknowledged my presence.

As I sat removing my boots, Leika's hand dropped from the bunk above and brushed my shoulder.

"Meet me in the bathroom in half an hour."

22
THE DIARY REVEALED

Despite a daily cleaning, the smell of urine persisted around the toilet cubicles.

I suspected that like me Leika was wrinkling her nose but I couldn't see since only a dim globe lit the area around the stalls.

"This is something I won't miss," she said.

"The smell or the secret meetings?"

"The smell, of course. Secret meetings can be fun. How did yours go? Did you find Kaal?"

"Yes. He showed up at the top of the climbing wall. I told him what I'd overheard Prince say. I tried to ask him about Jarryd, but other climbers arrived. It was too dangerous to continue the discussion."

"I'm sorry." Her gentle tone soothed my disappointment. "At least you were able to tell him what you overheard. That's important."

Shuffling footsteps approached. We crouched into a corner while a woman used a toilet. We were surprised when the cubicle light came on. The power was back. We remained hidden until we heard her leave.

"Maybe next time you can ask about your family." Leika's boots scraped the floor as she stood. "I've had enough of this cesspit. Time for bed."

I pushed open a cubicle door. "Toilet, then bed for me. Sleep well."

Leika yawned. "Same to you."

I didn't like to deceive Leika but I needed time alone. I'd shoved the diary into my boot before meeting her. With the power back on, I was determined to read the diary.

The first week in the laundry, I'd worn the diary, strapped to my leg. It was secure but my skin became raw from the irritation inside my sweaty boots. I had to find an alternative.

Since there were no bed checks or dorm searches, I surmised that Ruby and Pig had little interest in the bunker. Fashioning a headscarf into a small sling, I tied it to the metal grid that supported my bed and slipped the diary inside. Out of sight, it was the perfect hiding spot.

The power outages plus exhaustion from physical labor combined with evenings at the recpod had forced me to abandon my intentions to uncover the diary's secrets until now. More than ever, I needed to feel close to my family and the diary was a connection to my island life.

The light beamed as I opened the cubicle door. I closed the lock and pulled the book from my boot.

The ancient cover felt warm to my touch. My fingers stroked the faint impression. I'd forgotten to ask Mother about it because I'd been so upset that weekend. Memories flooded back. Mother's care. Hiking with Circe. Jarryd and Marta's engagement announcement. Weyland's victory over the drone. Even Father's disapproval didn't bother me. I missed them all. So much had changed in such a short time.

The dark gray cubicle walls were a reminder of my internment.

I closed my eyes for a moment. Images of the island filled my inner landscape. Being home again seemed an impossible dream where I couldn't afford to wallow.

When I opened the diary, a paper slipped out. A lump filled my throat when I recognized Mother's handwriting.

Darling Brynna,

The diary was difficult to understand, but I think my translation is accurate. I've added some instruction that will assist you in learning the old language as well.

As I thought, this diary belonged to the Genetrix who lived on our island many years ago. Most details are memories of daily life in her feminary, but in the final pages, she has recorded a prophecy. It foretells of the destruction of the sisterhood by a strange-eyed visitor. The last page of the diary is missing, so the source and the timing of the prophecy are unknown.

Prophecies are only predictions. During my time at the feminary, this foretelling was never mentioned. It was probably discarded or forgotten over the years. Still, it is important that you wear your lens at all times.

She mentions a second diary containing details about the secret rituals and ceremonies of feminary life known only to the Genetrix. It might hold some answers that could explain the unusual vocal experiences—both yours and Weyland's.

The impression on the front cover is an outline of the oracle stone worn by the Genetrix. It's a large circular crystal. A symbol of her rank and power. A falcon is etched onto the back cover. I expect that the second book will have the same cover markings.

The cave is the most likely place to look for the second diary.

My weak eyesight prevents me from searching for it, but I hope that once you are home again you will find it.
  Until you return,
  All my love,
  Mother

Be strong and safe. Your voice is your power.

My heart thumped in my chest as I gasped shallow breaths. My shaky hand flew to my necklace. It represented family and love and gave me strength.

I flipped to the end of the book. My fingers followed the foreign words, reading Mother's translation under each line.

Strange-eyed? Could they mean mismatched? Could it be me?

Logic dictated that the diary was from before the Rising. The old Genetrix was from a different feminary than the one that now survived. As Mother wrote, it might have been just a prediction that never came true. One long forgotten.

Momentary relief fled as the damning phrase replayed in my mind. Strange-eyed.

Then I remembered that my lens had belonged to my grandmother. She'd been a Genetrix but the sisterhood hadn't been destroyed. Perhaps mismatched eyes were a genetic variation that affected other Femin.

I couldn't be the only one.

Could I?

I turned to the first page of the diary and started to read.

"Brynna? Are you in here?" Leika knocked on my stall door.

"Yes. Not so loud. You'll wake the others."

Leika harrumphed. "It's morning, you idiot. If you don't hurry you'll miss breakfast."

My all-night venture proved unsuccessful. The writings offered insights into feminary life, but no additional information about the prophecy.

I shoved the diary down the side of my boot and opened the door. Fatigue made my head spin. I stifled a yawn but when I saw Leika's stern scrutiny, I doubled with laughter. "Your scowl makes you look like a mad ferret."

"Thanks a lot." She grinned but persisted. "Are you going to tell me what kept you in here all night?"

"Private business." My words weren't harsh, just direct. For the first time, I hadn't tried to soften my response to please someone else. Instead, I'd been true to myself.

She shrugged. "Okay then. Let's go."

Unlike Calia, she didn't push and prod. Instead, she respected my answer without question, as a real friend would.

Leika peeped cautiously into the bunker, but workers were gathered around the video screen and paid no attention as we joined the group.

"What's happening?" she asked.

"Special announcement," said one of the women.

From the door came a clack of heeled boots. The crowd parted for Ruby and her entourage as they headed to the front. Moments later, the screen went live and Premier Delio's face appeared. He uttered the usual comments about the rebels and security that we'd heard before but he added one final announcement.

"For security reasons, Steepchase will be canceled unless the rebels are apprehended. The council has offered a reward for information leading to the arrest of the rebel leaders. Their

capture will ensure the continuation of our annual games. Once again, loyal citizens are asked to come forward with any information."

Delio's image flickered out.

"He can't do that," growled Ruby as she strode to the door, her acolytes on her heels.

"Pig's in trouble," said Leika.

"So are we if Steepchase is canceled," I added.

"Steepchase will go on."Leika nodded.

"How can you be so sure?"

"Delio's already got enough trouble on his hands without canceling the games. My bet is the Premier is getting desperate and looking for any leverage."

"I hope you're right." I wasn't as confident.

As far as I knew, there was no Ruby-Pig confrontation. Later that afternoon Ruby appeared again, Pig beside her. Her arms draped around his neck. His hands stroked the sides of her breasts. They shared a smile of satisfaction.

I felt nauseated when I guessed at the reason, but also some relief that she might have managed to persuade him to push for the games to continue.

Getting out of the laundry was my route to freedom.

My future depended on Steepchase.

CHANGING THE WATER IN THE LAUNDRY VATS WAS A disgusting job. It involved scraping out several inches of black sludge that lined the bottom of the washers. The only positive was that Leika and I were both assigned to the task so we were able to talk.

"Can you sabotage the machines today?" I was on edge after a second sleepless night.

It was obvious from the morning video that Delio was still in charge. Perhaps Kaaluk hadn't yet passed the information to my brother, or Jarryd to Father. I was desperate to know what was happening on the rest of Hypor.

Leika shook her head. "It's too soon. Kaal will need time. He knows we're anxious but he has to be careful. He'll contact me when he can. You have to trust him."

Trust was difficult with so much at stake, but stuck in the laundry all I could do was wait. With luck, I'd soon be free to join the rebellion and help expose Delio's plans if it wasn't too late.

I leaned over to scrub the last section of dirt that ringed the tub when Leika jabbed me with the toe of her boot.

"That hurt." I rubbed my calf and scowled but quickly forgot the injury when I looked in the direction she nodded.

Prince Delio and two guards had entered the bunker and were walking toward Pig's office. Prince went inside. One guard proceeded onto the dock while the other leaned against the wall beside the office door and surveyed the room. His piercing green eyes hesitated slightly when he spotted Leika.

It was Kaaluk.

My heart quickened as Leika started forward.

"Don't watch, just keep scrubbing," she whispered before gathering an armful of dirty clothes from a nearby pile.

I couldn't stop myself. From the corner of my eye, I saw her stumble and tip her load of garments onto the floor. The operation must have been one they'd executed before. Kaaluk kicked at the offending pile and walked away, but not before dropping something. Leika quickly picked up the item, then the clothes, and returned to our task.

She grabbed a scrub brush but said nothing. Her slight smile gave me hope.

A short while later Ruby appeared and sent Leika to clean the toilets. It wasn't until dinner that I was able to ask her about her brother's exchange.

"Meet me in the toilets." She had news, but she didn't look happy.

I arrived before her.

"There's no one here. I already checked." Impatience strained my words as I watched her give each stall door a push. "I know you got a message from Kaaluk. What did it say? Did he give my father the information about Delio?"

"Yes. But he said it's only hearsay and without hard evidence, it won't be enough to convince the council."

"So we're stuck unless we can find something in Pig's office that might incriminate Delio." The futility of our situation left me discouraged and I slumped against the wall. "Did Kaaluk mention anything about your escape?"

"It's going to happen during Steepchase." Leika hesitated and glanced away.

"Something wrong?"

She reached out and touched my shoulder. I was puzzled by her concerned expression. "What is it?"

"Your father is missing."

I slid down the wall indifferent to the hard cold floor. Leika crouched beside me.

"Did Kaaluk have any details?" I had difficulty choking out the words.

"Premier Delio is blaming the rebels, saying they sabotaged your father's lander. There were propulsion problems and it went down over the ocean. They're searching for debris. Kaal blames Delio." Leika's voice softened. "I'm sorry, Brynna."

I remembered the lander faltering on my initial trip to Hypor. I hoped it was an accident. The idea that someone had planned to kill my father was too frightening to imagine.

"When did it happen?" I asked with a choked whisper.

"Late yesterday. There's still a chance they'll find him."

Rescue was possible but I dreaded the thought of my father struggling to stay alive in the cold ocean.

"If they don't find him, Mother will be vulnerable. I have to go to her." I surged to my feet, only to sink down again as I struggled to pull air into my lungs. I searched Leika's face. "Delio's won, hasn't he?"

"No he hasn't." Leika's tone was firm. "You have to trust, Brynna."

"Trust who?" I fought to make sense of her words.

"Trust Kaal and Jarryd and the others who are fighting to save our city and our planet." Her hand squeezed mine. "There's nothing more we can do now but wait. We have to put our faith in them."

Leika led me back to the bunker. I stumbled and doubled over several times so it wasn't hard to convince Ruby that I was unwell. I fell gratefully onto my bunk, happy for once not to go to the recpod.

I curled my hand around my necklace and rubbed my thumb over the curved beak of the falcon before tears pushed me into an exhausted sleep.

23

STEEPCHASE CONFIRMED

Leika's sharp elbow prodded my side as we sat with the other women clustered around the video screen watching the government report.

"See?" Steepchase wasn't canceled as threatened. The evening broadcast declared a date two weeks away. "Nothing to worry about."

Maybe not for her, but I hadn't expected the games to be held so soon. I'd have to train harder on my swimming, which I'd neglected or perhaps subconsciously avoided.

Stick's replacement continued his presentation.

"The Premier is pleased to announce that the rebel opposition has been dealt a fatal blow and is on the verge of collapsing. It is believed that one of the leaders has been killed."

Groans and curses reverberated through the bunker.

Dizziness obscured my thinking. "Are they talking about my father?"

"He isn't a rebel leader." She leaned forward. Her white-knuckled hands gripped her knees. "I'm more worried about Kaal."

"Or maybe Jarryd." I stared at Leika but she was focused on the screen.

"Listen, there's more."

"Finally, we regret to report that two esteemed members of the council are missing. Councilors Bokk and Vasch were over the ocean when their lander experienced difficulties. Premier Delio suspects that the rebel force is responsible. Rescue teams are searching the site of the accident."

Despite knowing about the crash beforehand, the official announcement was a like a body blow. I wrapped my arms around my waist and hunched slightly, taking several deep breaths. It took a moment to process Councilor Vasch's involvement.

"If Marta's father is also missing, it means that Delio has full control of the council," I murmured, thinking of the possible consequences.

"What did you say?" Leika turned to me. "Who's Marta?"

"Jarryd's girlfriend—fiancée. Her father and mine opposed Delio on Council. They were working to expose his true plans."

"I hope she's gone into hiding. With her father missing, she'll be vulnerable if she's still on Hypor—just as you are."

"I'm no threat to Delio in here. I'm more concerned about Mother. And Jarryd."

"You'll still have to be careful. If Delio is responsible for your father's disappearance, he'll want to ensure that there's no one to raise suspicion, or seek revenge."

"I hope he's forgotten I'm here."

"I doubt it. Certainly, Pig hasn't."

NEXT MORNING, WHILE I WAS EATING, RUBY MADE A NOISY

entrance. Instead of her regular outfit, she was dressed in padded clothing, wore thick-soled boots and carried a rucksack.

"Bokk, get over here. Fast."

The news about Father had kept me awake most of the night. I was slow to respond, but her scowl got me moving. I gulped down one last mouthful of breakfast, then hurried to her.

"Steepchase participants are being moved to a special area near the recpod. Grab your gear. You've got five minutes."

Ruby's voice had been loud enough for Leika to hear. In fact, everyone had, but only Leika approached me.

"Now you'll really have to be careful." She spoke quietly as I gathered my few belongings. "Use this if you have to." She pressed a small knife against my palm.

I hugged her and was about to leave when I remembered the diary. It might be discovered if I took it to the recpod. There was only one choice.

"Hurry up, Bokk," Ruby yelled from the doorway.

Leika turned her back to Ruby and faced me. "What's wrong?" She mouthed.

"Remember that night in the toilet?" I whispered, continuing to fiddle with my gear.

"Your secret all-nighter?" Leika grinned.

"I was reading a diary. It's hidden under my bed. I can't take it with me. Will you hide it for me? It's important."

"Yes, of course. Better go. Ruby is starting to smolder."

"Thanks. Take care. I'll miss you." I hugged her tightly.

Her voice cracked when she spoke. "Remember what I said. Even though you have a pact with her, Ruby is still your enemy."

In the recpod, the men's sleeping quarters were cordoned off to the left of the aquatic area. As the only female competitors, Ruby and I slept on folding cots in the women's change room. She moved her bed as far from mine as possible, which I preferred as well. From a distance, I could still feel her enmity.

While she'd demanded my presence during training, now I rarely saw her until she returned at night. I always pretended to sleep through her noisy arrivals but my stomach tensed with her every move. We never spoke.

The first morning at the track, none of the competitors looked familiar so I steered clear of them. I headed for the aquatic area, but my intention to practice Weyland's breathing techniques died when I noticed several guards in the pool. Leika's warning rang loud in my head and I hadn't forgotten being restrained under water. I gravitated to the other areas with fewer contestants and where I felt less susceptible to attack.

The bright and airy recpod didn't alleviate the depression that came with my loneliness. I missed my family, Marta, Weyland and now Leika. A tiny bathroom mirror confirmed my red-rimmed eyes, swollen from tears I'd shed for my father.

During the day, I channeled my sorrow into my workouts. At night, dark images pestered my thoughts until exhaustion granted me blessed sleep. The same question loomed. Would I ever see my family again?

On the fourth day of training, as I slipped into my exercise gear, I felt an abrasion on the back of my right shoulder. That morning, I'd awoken with my necklace trapped under my shoulder. I'd felt a sharp poke as I arose. Now, my skin felt hot to the touch.

I traced the swollen patch with my finger. It was awkward to see so I pulled the skin and my shoulder forward to examine the area in the small mirror. It was my birthmark, the falcon, reddened with irritation.

I started to hum and pressed my hand over the area to ease the inflammation. Something stirred in me and I felt the warmth sear my palm. My spirit strengthened with resolve. I promised myself that I would gain my freedom and somehow return to my island to protect my mother.

The morning of Steepchase, I dressed alone as usual in my exercise gear and used a scarf to tie back my hair. I noticed that Ruby's bag and clothes were gone. We'd been instructed by the officials to meet near Swigs, so I headed out to join the other competitors. At the last minute, I extracted Leika's knife from its hiding place under my bed and pushed it down the side of my right boot.

Barely through the door into the practice area, I heard a rumble of laughter from the group of contestants. The men were dressed in thick trousers and belted tunics. Some, like Ruby, had also donned padded vests. All wore thick-soled boots and carried helmets and gloves. Various tools hung from their belts. They looked ready for more than just an athletic competition. They looked ready for combat.

With only my thin exercise clothes and a small knife, I wasn't prepared for what I was about to face.

"Hurry up, Bokk or the hydrofoil will leave without you," yelled Ruby.

For a moment, staying behind sounded like the best option.

24

THE GAMES BEGIN

The hydrofoil ripped across the water.

The ride to the Steepchase dome was over before I had time to decide if my knotted stomach was from my fear of water or because of the upcoming competition, but I suspected both were involved in my discomfort.

From the outside, the Steepchase dome and dock resembled the one at the laundry. We disembarked and I followed the other competitors through a rock-like tunnel toward a bright prick of light. As we progressed, the dot of light opened. A steady chant penetrated the walls, eventually swelling to a deafening pitch. A frenzied crescendo of voices greeted the first contestants as they exited the dark tube, and it continued until I emerged.

A thousand pairs of eyes peered from tiers of seats that ringed an arena. Above the crowds, gigantic video screens relayed our every move. Gold, black and red flags and banners flapped in the open air. On another occasion, the spectacle might have been exciting and entertaining, but today it only increased my trepidation of what was to come.

I didn't realize I'd stopped moving until a smiling female

attendant in a red juba walked alongside and threaded her arm with mine. She whispered "good luck" as we headed toward an area thick with officials in ceremonial robes. Premier Delio sat on an elevated platform draped with red garlands.

Three rows back, Prince sat with Calia at his side. Sunshine glistened on her silver juba. As she turned her head, jewels flashed from her hood. The vivid memory of her betrayal rushed back and I forced down the sour bile that flooded my mouth. I couldn't allow anything to distract me from my purpose, not even Calia.

Delio lifted his hands and the crowd went silent. "Today is a momentous day. The rebel faction has been routed and Hypor City is once again under council control."

The premier paused and waited for a reaction, but there were no cheers, just low murmurs. He scowled for a moment, but his smarmy smile returned as he continued addressing the crowd. "Once again, we are gathered to watch the best contestants..."

As he spoke, I turned my focus to the Steepchase course.

Positioned at the edge of a sandy track with the other contestants, I saw only a plane of small undulating dunes. An impenetrable wall of dark green foliage framed each side. In several places, heavy branches from the larger trees dipped to touch the sand, but otherwise the area was desert bare. At the far end of the golden expanse, through an opening in the trees, massive rock walls stood silhouetted against the sky. Even at a distance, they appeared taller than any I'd attempted at the recpod.

I surveyed the line of competitors in their battle dress. Feeling exposed and vulnerable in comparison, I forced myself to remember that the extra clothing meant extra weight. I clung to the idea that I might have an advantage.

My courage wavered. I fought shallow breaths, trying for calm. Then an itch on my right shoulder reminded me of the promise I'd made to myself. I straightened; more determined than ever that Ruby must win Steepchase.

"Let the games begin." Delio flapped one arm and took his seat.

The crowd roared with approval.

An official presented each opponent with a quiver holding two arrows. I'd expected an archery challenge but why just two arrows? And where was the bow?

The others seemed unconcerned, so I followed their lead and slung the strap across my chest, pushing the quiver onto my back.

A pair of gloves landed at my feet. I tried to locate the benefactor but there were too many faces. I'd never needed gloves in the recpod, but except for the little information Jarryd had given me, Steepchase was an unknown. I pushed the gift into the quiver along with the swim goggles I'd slung around my neck.

A gold-sashed official climbed onto a platform at the side of the track and raised his hand. The reverberation of a thousand voices pulsed around the arena as the spectators waited for the red starting flag to be tossed into the air. Suddenly, it floated free.

Ruby surged ahead and I followed. She zigzagged diagonally. I looked across the field and noticed that the others were running in lines of three using the same motion. Only one was on his own and running straight for the far opening.

My strategy was to gain an advantage at this early stage. I was lighter and easily drew alongside Ruby. She looked surprised. Suddenly she veered and swung her leg across my path. I leaped sideways to avoid her thrust, but was

THE LAST SINGER

horrified when the ground gave way. Something sucked at my right foot, then my ankle, then started to swallow my leg.

I had landed in quicksand.

I glanced toward Ruby but she didn't look back. She'd known what to watch for and to follow specific paths. So had the other experienced challengers. Only one other ran alone. He now flailed hopelessly as the fine dry sand pulled him down, his weight working against him. I heard his frantic screams. Then he was silent.

The cheering swelled.

The other contestants opened their lead as I struggled.

Sharp granules sucked on my left leg. I wasn't sure what to do. I'd heard the myths—lie flat, or use a swimming motion—so I tried both. When the sand reached my hips, I panicked and shouted for help, but no one responded. I looked for a branch, but there was nothing nearby. The crowd roared again when I sunk deeper.

Engulfed to my elbows, I clawed the sand, desperate to free myself. My nails raked something hard. A tree root, thin but strong, provided a lifeline.

My muscles screamed as I pulled myself hand over hand along its rough length. I kicked my legs free then rolled. Exhausted, I collapsed onto firm warm sand. After a few deep breaths, I scrambled to my feet. There was no one in sight, just several trails of footprints. I followed one, desperate to make up time and locate Ruby. I hadn't expected her early attack and would be more cautious next time. For the sake of my deal with Pig, she had to win. I knew she hated me, but my freedom was at stake.

At the far end of the dunes, the trees opened onto an obstacle course that fronted the climbing walls. Not far ahead, competitors scaled a series of rocks. I quickened my pace and raced across the hard ground.

The first challenge was an incline of staggered boulders. Much like my mountain path at home, I was able to sprint and jump from one to another at the lower levels. The sand trap, however, had tapped my energy and the higher leaps were tougher than expected. Several times, I had to backtrack and find an easier route.

One search for a better trail brought me close to a precipitous edge. Fifty feet below, a body lay awkwardly splayed on the ground. I peered over the edge, searching for movement. There was none.

Had he lost his footing? Taken an unnecessary risk? Or been the target of another competitor? I shuddered at the thought.

From a higher rock ledge, a noise drew my attention. I looked up into a scowling face. The helmet was gone and the man's unkempt hair gave him the look of a wild beast.

A large curled fist swung toward my head, but I ducked and his thrust went wide. The man growled and looked around. He was barring my way but unless he climbed down, he couldn't reach me. I crouched and waited. Eventually, he pulled back. Several seconds passed before I heard retreating footsteps crunching across the rock. I sucked in a deep breath. I'd been luckier than the dead man.

My legs shook with fatigue as I resumed climbing. Finally cresting the highest boulder, I was relieved to see the descent was a staircase of spiraling plateaus.

I set off at a steady pace following the line of the inside curve. My breathing slowed and my speed increased. Twenty feet from the ground, angry voices erupted from below.

My heart battered my ribs as I flattened against the granite. For several minutes, scuffling and grunting sounded beneath me. My cheek pressed cold stone as my pounding pulse thrummed a deafening beat in my ears. Rapid footsteps were followed by angry shouts. Finally there was silence.

I edged forward until the combatants came into view.

One man was fleeing toward the rock walls. Another lay on the ground, his hands and feet tied. Blood trickled from a cut on his cheek, but otherwise he seemed unhurt. He spat curses as he struggled with his bonds.

He held up his bound hands when he saw me descend. His foul language resumed when I ignored his pleas for help. I ran past him to follow the other man.

I hoped to see Ruby, but there was still no sign of her. I feared for her safety. She had to stay alive in order to win. She was a tough competitor, but that wouldn't stop her from facing a bad end. This was more than a competition. It was not only dangerous but lethal.

AT THE ROCK WALLS, WATER CASCADED FROM SMALL FISSURES made the climbing surfaces slick. I hoped that my thin boots would provide adequate traction. I scanned overhead, noting black specks scurrying like beetles across the vertical surfaces. When I counted eight remaining competitors, I felt relieved. Ruby had to be among them. I was getting close.

With renewed energy, I gripped the niches. The first fifty feet flew by. Hands and feet found their holds. My confidence grew that I'd catch the others.

Nearer the top, the handholds became less frequent. I stretched to curl my fingers over a higher lip. Instead of smooth stone, sharp points pierced my skin. I jerked my hand back and noticed blood dripping down my arm from a deep gash in my index finger. I sucked it a minute then bound it with my scarf. Remembering my gloves, I retrieved them from my quiver and pulled them on. I suspected that the other handholds might be trouble. I was right.

By the time I reached the top of the wall, my gloves were tattered slivers, the soles of my boots slightly less so, but more importantly I'd gained on my competitors. I ignored the painful throbbing of the cuts and sprinted across the sloping plateau.

Deep chasms sliced the surface. Some were easily traversed, but occasionally the landings were obscured on the far side. Jumping across one gap, I narrowly avoided landing on a body. The man lay strewn on the rock, his head haloed in blood. I jolted at the sight and fought a strong instinct to stop. But he was dead and those ahead were dropping from sight.

I pushed harder, lengthening my strides, halting at the edge of a canyon. The only way across was a precarious rope bridge. A sign hung haphazardly from a post that anchored the near side of the structure. I quickly scanned the words.

More than one will be your downfall.

It sounded like a riddle, but I understood its meaning.

The woven rope swung sideways as it took my weight. My next step plunged through the grid but my quiver snagged on the weave, saving me from a fatal fall. After a few ragged breaths, I untangled myself. My damaged hands stung as I gripped the rough twine, but I clung and crawled like a spider across a web.

Halfway across the void, I heard the fall of heavy footsteps behind me. A quick glance over my shoulder sent the bridge rocking. A man ran toward the ropes, heedless of the sign.

I quickened my pace. I was still ten feet from the far side

when I felt the bridge sway. His first step tensed the ropes; his second loosened them. He grunted then screamed.

Instinctively, I glanced back at the terrifying sound. His face twisted in terror as the knots behind him began to slip and his body started to drop.

I wrapped my arms and legs through the mesh and held tight, hoping the rope at my end would hold. Suddenly, I was flying through the air toward the canyon wall. I tucked my head and shifted my shoulders, hoping my quiver would take the brunt of the impact.

My body slammed into the rock wall. Pain shot along my collarbone and down my arm, but my hands and legs held tight. The impact made my head swim. I took quick breaths, trying to force back the acidic taste in my mouth. A glance upwards confirmed my end of the bridge was intact. Suddenly the ropes below were banging against the rock. The man hadn't fallen as I suspected. He hung below me, attempting to climb.

Our combined weight snapped one of the bindings above me trapping my left foot. I slid my knife from my other boot, freed my ankle and cautiously climbed the remaining feet to the top of the canyon. Breathing deeply, I rolled onto my back and splayed my arms and hands. For several minutes, I enjoyed the solid feel of the granite until a scream echoed from below. I crawled to the edge of the canyon and looked down.

I recognized my pursuer. The man, who had berated me for leaving him tied up, now hung upside down, one leg snarled in a knotty tangle.

Struggling to free himself, he tugged frantically on the twisted fibers causing them to fray. He looked up. "Help me! Pull me up!"

I backed away from the edge of the crevasse until he was

out of sight. Terrified shouts continued to echo from the canyon. Everything I'd learned as a healer and preserver of life pulled at my conscience. Leaving him to die was impossible. As I approached the edge, a scream tore at my soul then all went silent. I was too late.

The sound of his anguish echoed in my ears. Tears streamed across my cheeks as I left the broken bridge behind. I poured my torment into action. Ignoring spent muscles, I ran flat out, entering a wooded area, slowing only when I heard male voices ahead. From behind an ancient oak, I spied four men sitting at the base of a chestnut tree. The group's attention was on two other men up in the boughs.

One of those aloft grabbed a thin tree limb. He descended to the ground then pulled an arrow from his quiver. What I thought was a branch was a bow. Aiming high toward a target atop a granite pillar, his first shot went wide. The men on the ground heckled and laughed. The second arrow was true and as the target tumbled backward, a rope unfurled. The man raced toward it and climbed. Two other men ran toward the rope, hoping to grab another chance to advance. As they fought and pulled, the rope fell to the ground.

The second man descended from the tree with a bow but both his shots failed to reach a target. Swearing, he joined the other competitors on the ground. Since there was no sign of Ruby I assumed she had completed this task and moved on.

Getting by the men was a problem. I was sure I wouldn't be allowed to pass unchallenged. Confronting them on the ground was too risky, overhead might work. I jumped and clung to the lowest branch of the oak tree, stealthily threading my way up through the branches. Finding a thick bough, I squirmed along it toward the chestnut tree. Within arms-reach of a bow, I snapped a small twig. A chestnut fell free and landed among the men. Five pairs of eyes turned skyward.

"It's Ruby's friend! Get her."

Within seconds, they were climbing toward me.

My slim weight allowed me safety at the end of the thin limb. I grabbed the bow and drew an arrow from my quiver. Spotting the target, I took my shot. My hands shook and the first arrow missed. I notched the second arrow. Ignoring the taunts of the climbing men, I held my breath and released the arrow. It was a bull's-eye. The rope unfolded.

My delight quickly disappeared when my perch shook under the weight of an assailant. I threw my bow at him and clutched an overhead branch. The rope to safety dangled several feet away. My only option was to jump.

Taking a deep breath, I lunged for the impossibly tiny thread of escape. My hand gripped the slender twine with one hand. The other slipped, but I quickly wrapped my feet around the rope and steadied my position. Behind me, a branch cracked loudly as two men tried to follow. I didn't wait to watch but shimmied upwards.

At the top, I heard the steady thrum of the crowd as it roared with approval. Had someone other than Ruby already won the game? I pushed on, not wanting to consider that I might have lost my bid for freedom.

Scrambling across another series of granite boulders left me breathless. I finally reached the summit. In the distance I spotted Ruby and two men stripping off their gear. I'd caught up but my heart filled with dread when I heard rushing water.

As I moved forward, the view opened. I could see the crowd and another horrifying challenge—a waterfall.

Panic blackened my vision. I squeezed my eyes and fought back my terror. I couldn't allow my fear to triumph. I started to hum. With renewed focus, I threw off my quiver and gloves and donned my goggles. Seconds behind the others, I plunged over the edge toward the watery abyss.

25

A DEAD DEAL

The descent to the water was terrifying.

Instinct pushed my arms and legs into action when I felt the water engulf me. Thankful for Weyland's lessons, I quickly surfaced in a large pool.

Ignoring the deafening crowd noise, I scanned for the three other competitors. Ruby was a slow swimmer. Her red hair was easy to spot. The two others were farther ahead.

Pulling my hands through the water, I kicked my legs with renewed energy. I was gaining on Ruby. When I eventually pulled alongside, she stroked harder. Her competitive nature quickened her pace. I raced ahead with Ruby close behind. Two dark heads were seconds in front. As they approached an arch over the water, a red light flashed. Seconds later, the swimmers vanished.

Puzzled, my momentum slowed and Ruby surged past me. Her meaty fist connected with my sore shoulder. Thankfully, her kick missed my hips by inches. I cradled my shoulder and pulled out of reach. Suddenly, the red light flashed again. Ruby was gone.

Another flash followed. Unsure of what to do, I paddled aimlessly until an amplified voice commanded, "*Submerge.*"

No. No. No. I fought my paralyzing thoughts.

"*Submerge.*" The repeated instruction penetrated the fog of fear. I had no option but to follow. It was part of the course.

Remembering Weyland's instructions, I took several deep breaths. With the final one, I descended into the deep water. It was pristine clear but there was no sign of the others. Was I too far behind to help Ruby win? The only way was through a narrow tunnel.

The serpentine nature of the passage only allowed a limited view. At the second turn, I was shocked to see Ruby writhing frantically. From behind, a thick black arm wrapped her throat and two legs enclosed her body. Beside the struggling duo, another dark figure pulled a blade from a leg sheath.

Why were they attacking Ruby instead of heading to the finish line?

The explanation shot through my brain. It was Pig.

Ruby had threatened the podmaster. She wasn't meant to survive Steepchase, let alone win. I was certain he wouldn't honor our deal. I'd been a fool to think that anyone named Delio would keep his word.

I kicked wildly and pulled my hands through the water, determined to help Ruby. Her survival might still ensure my freedom, despite Pig's intentions.

As I neared, her assailant cupped her chin and twisted her neck. Ruby's body twitched wildly, then went limp. He shoved her lifeless corpse aside as if discarding garbage. Her body drifted slowly in the current.

Signaling his partner, the man then pointed at me. They lunged forward. Two sets of powerful arms whirled through the water like wind turbines through air. I knew I couldn't escape them.

My lungs strained, craving oxygen as I stroked through the water. My progress slowed and I straddled consciousness. In the murk of semi-awareness, I heard Mother's words.

Your voice is your power.

Clarity focused my actions. I forced valuable air over my vocal chords and started a high-pitched hum. The swimmers lifted their hands to their ears and hesitated as if disoriented. Moments later, they surged toward me again.

Remembering Weyland's negative reaction to my high-pitched tones, I opened my mouth and pushed the remaining air from my lungs. The intensified sounds penetrated the underwater tunnel. The men held their ears, writhing under the invisible onslaught. My breath dwindled. As I sustained the piercing pitch, I lifted my arms. As if by a rogue wave, the men were propelled backward, smashing into the tunnel wall. Two red plumes flowed from their inert bodies.

Panicked, I clawed the water like a caged animal with no thought except the certainty that I would drown. Someone seized my flailing arm. I struggled for freedom, but the pull upwards was persistent. A bellow of cheers assaulted my ears as my head broke the surface of the water. I greedily sucked in precious air.

Eyes closed and exhausted, I lay motionless on the hard deck, unable to protest the hands that dried my aching arms and legs. When the pummeling finally stopped, I opened my eyes. As if on signal, two guards hoisted me into the air and carried me to a dais adorned with gold banners and exotic flowers.

"Champion. Champion. Champion."

Energy waves stunned my senses as the pounding of the chanting crowd crisscrossed the stadium. Dignitaries closed around me, offering congratulations. The scene felt surreal until I saw the Delio contingent approaching: the Premier, Prince, and Calia.

My legs buckled when I was set down, but a hand grabbed my arm and kept me standing. Moments later, a gold juba dropped over my head and swimsuit. A crown of flowers held my hood in place.

Premier Delio grasped my arm and lifted it into the air.

"This year's Steepchase winner is Brynna Bokk." He spat my surname as if to rid his mouth of a distasteful morsel, then dropped my arm.

The crowd roared in response, but the premier had already exited the winner's area. Prince followed his father, completely ignoring me, but Calia threw me a furious look. Despite her malicious manipulations, I'd managed to score a triumph.

The noise and energy of the throng were euphoric. The reality of what I'd achieved seeped into my consciousness, rejuvenating my spirit and exhausted muscles. As winner, I was a celebrity and untouchable, at least for the moment. I hadn't seen Pig.

I frantically scanned the stands for Jarryd then saw my actions reflected on the giant overhead video screens. Like an actor, I forced a smile and waved, but continued my search. The jubilant crowd acknowledged my gesture, the volume swelled before suddenly dropping like a curtain at the closing act. The throng went silent.

The cameras found a new focus. Gasps and shouts replaced rhythmic chanting. Attendees around me pointed to the pool. I watched in horror as Ruby's body surfaced from its watery tomb.

"You killed her." Pig's hot breath brushed my ear.

I jerked back to escape his foul breath, but couldn't tear my gaze from Ruby's inert form. "I didn't. Your goons attacked her."

I cringed as her corpse was dragged from the water and carted unceremoniously from the arena. As the target of Ruby's malevolence, I couldn't dismiss her deeds, but she'd also been a victim. Pig had played her just as he had played me. And now she was dead.

"We had a deal. You broke it." His leer promised further bondage. "Now you are mine."

My stomach clenched in a sick churn at the crushing truth of his words. Ruby was dead and I'd gained nothing.

"Take her." Pig motioned to two of his guards, but a crowd of well-wishers surged toward me.

They shook my hand and clapped me on the back. A tall woman in a black juba approached. Hard arms crushed my battered body. "Don't react, Bryn."

My heart jumped when I heard Jarryd's voice. I returned his hug.

"I said don't react," he repeated with big brother annoyance. "We've planned a diversion. When you hear a blast, run behind the change room on my right. In the alley, take the gate to the landing pad. The alarm is off. We'll be waiting."

I had to fight my instinct to follow him. Instead, I trembled as his cloaked figure disappeared into the crowd.

The guards cleared away the remaining visitors. Pig motioned his men toward me.

I stalled, pretending to be sick. Doubling over, I moaned. The guards took my arms, but quickly released me when I rolled my eyes and allowed saliva to dribble down my chin. My antics drew a concerned crowd.

"She needs a doctor," cried one spectator.

"No. Toilet," I wailed. "I need to go to the toilet."

"Take her to the exit tunnel," Pig commanded. "The boat's waiting. We'll get her to a doctor later."

"I need the toilet," I wrapped my arms tightly over my stomach.

As Steepchase winner, I had the support of the crowd, who turned on Pig, yelling at him to let me go to the toilets. An outraged mob wasn't something he had bargained for. He withstood heckles and jeers for a few moments, then gave in.

"Escort her to the women's change room and wait outside the door."

Clasping my stomach, I ran to my left. The guards followed me until I disappeared into the change room. I hoped Pig's confidence in my reappearance would give me the time I needed to escape.

I splashed my face with cold water, took a few steadying breaths. Inside a cubicle, I removed the gold juba. My black swimsuit would attract some attention but far less than the sparkly dress.

Outside the facility, a series of explosion shook the ground. A crack appeared on the wall beside me. Screams intensified as additional blasts detonated. Dust billowed around me. If I waited, I could be buried alive. I had to go.

A glance outside confirmed that all was chaos. The guards were overrun by terrified hordes.

I crouched as I exited the entryway, then sped left along one wall of the squat building to a corner. After another left turn, I ran along a shorter wall. Turning the final corner, I stopped in a dead-end alley. A cloud of dust obscured my vision. My heart thumped in my chest as I waited for it to clear. Finally the metal gate became visible. Through the fence, I could see the lander waiting on the pad, silhouetted against an azure sky. Its engines hummed quietly. My escape was so close.

I thrust my hands and weight against the door. It didn't yield. Dread at the thought of recapture pushed adrenaline through my body. Frustrated, I pounded the door with both fists then pulled at the bars. The door opened a foot. Relief almost buckled my knees. I squirmed through the gap and ran.

The lander's near door opened. Tears coursed down my cheeks when I saw Jarryd waving me onward. As he pulled me into the lander, further explosions shook the ground. I glanced back to see dense smoke billowing into the air above the Steepchase arena.

I wondered what had happened, but there was no time to linger. I closed my eyes, thankful to be free.

26

ESCAPE FROM HYPOR CITY

Jarryd yanked me into the lander as it started to ascend. Two people sat forward and two behind us. All were dressed alike in dark clothes and helmets. It was impossible to tell who they were. A tense silence persisted while the pilot steered the craft skyward. After what seemed like forever, the pilot announced, "We've left the city airspace."

Several audible breaths confirmed I wasn't the only anxious passenger.

"How are you feeling, Bryn?" Jarryd's skin was pale and his eyes were ringed in dark shadows. He dropped his helmet between his feet.

"Better now that I'm away from Hypor." I squirmed in my damp swimsuit. "Where are we headed? I'm cold and wet." I kept my tone light, trying to hide the fear and uncertainty that hovered near the surface.

"The rebel hideout. We'll soon be there. It's not far from our island."

"If we're that close to home, tell the pilot to drop us off."

Our beautiful island. My heart yearned for its peaceful shelter and Mother's loving care.

"We can't do that. If there are drones watching the island, we'll attract their attention and draw them to her. Mother will be safe with old Joe and the villagers. For now, we'll rest and plan. There's a lot we need to discuss," he added solemnly.

Father's fate filled the stillness between us. I dropped my head and sniffed back tears when Jarryd's hand squeezed my shoulder.

"Prepare to land." The pilot turned his head. The voice was muffled, but the resonant undertone was familiar. "We're almost home."

"Good. I need a pee," yelled one of men behind us.

"I need a good meal," added the other.

Their laughter was a balm to my soul, but I wasn't ready to join in. The day's events plagued my mind. The image of Ruby's dead body wasn't easy to erase. Neither was the memory of the other two swimmers. What had I done?

From the lander window, my unfocused gaze surfed the expanse of turquoise ocean until a scattering of tiny black dots caught my attention. As we flew closer, the dots took the shapes of four-legged insects with rusty metal carapaces. What were they?

"They're derelict oil rigs." Jarryd read my mind. "From before the Rising. They're off the main trade routes and under Hypor's radar."

The closest one had a landing platform floating at sea level. The body of the structure soared fifty feet or more skyward. Up one side ran a corroded ladder, its rungs decayed by the unrelenting lapping of seawater.

"If we have to climb up that ladder, I'm staying in the

lander." Cranky and tired, I didn't bother to lower my voice as the airship dropped lightly onto the platform.

The engine went quiet. The pilot swiveled in his seat, removed his headgear and fixed me with an emerald stare. "A little gratitude would be nice."

"Kaal?" I ignored his sarcastic tone. "Where's Leika? Did she escape?"

"She sure did." Kaaluk's seatmate yanked off her helmet and glasses revealing another pair of piercing green eyes.

I reached over the seat and hugged Leika. I had a million questions, but they'd have to wait.

Last to exit the lander, I stepped onto the platform and eyed the ladder with hostility. Jarryd laughed and pointed to heavy chain that held a makeshift elevator cage. Clanging and creaking, it slowly descended alongside the rig. It appeared only slightly sturdier than the ladder, but I'd done my share of climbing and was prepared to take my chances.

It thudded to a halt. I entered the cage behind Leika and Jarryd.

"Hold on tight to the rail." Kaaluk stood behind me as we rose into the air. "I don't want to have to rescue you from the water a third time." His warm breath brushed my cheek.

What did he mean 'a third time'? Had he been my rescuer in the pool during the blackout? Was it possible he was the guard who saved me while I was free diving?

I twisted to look at him. "You?"

"Keep still, Bryn." Jarryd steadied Leika when the lift started to swing. "This thing isn't anchored."

Kaaluk grabbed the cage on either side of me.

His closeness set my pulse racing. "I guess I owe you."

"I don't expect repayment, but life has a way of balancing things."

My face went hot when he smiled. "I guess so." I tore my

gaze from his and tried to ignore the tingles shooting through my body.

~

THE SQUEAL AND SHUDDER OF THE SLOWING LIFT WAS A SWIFT reminder of our situation.

Inside, the hideout proved to be more comfortable than I expected. One large space had been split into four. Two rooms housed the men. A third was for the women. In the fourth, a rustic kitchen shared space with a long metal table and chairs. Two women stirred steaming pots of aromatic food that set my stomach gurgling. Leaning against the opposite wall was a collection of weapons that quickly brought home the seriousness of our situation, but even that didn't squelch my appetite.

Leika and I headed to the room farthest from the entry, where three other women sat talking. As I changed into the dry tunic, tights and boots she provided, a loud clanging tensed my nerves and I shot her a glance.

"Dinner." She smiled and rubbed her stomach. "Hurry or there won't be much left."

We weren't the first at the table, which was covered with plates of appetizing food. I sat beside Jarryd. Kaaluk sat at one end of the long table, Leika opposite him. Other men and women filled the dozen seats on either side.

Hoping for anonymity, I kept my eyes on my plate.

We started eating and a man voiced his curiosity. "So you're the Champion of Steepchase. How'd you win it?" His tone was teasing, but his question set my hands shaking. My fork clattered onto the table.

"Leave my sister alone." Jarryd surged from his chair, anger tightening his lips.

"It's okay." I grabbed his fisted hand. "I'm sure he meant no harm."

The other man was equally red-faced and tense. "Like she said, I was just curious," he muttered.

My brother's response was out of character. Usually difficult to rile, I wondered if something else had provoked his strong protective instinct.

"Jarryd, sit down. No more talk about Steepchase." Kaaluk's calm tone had a settling effect on both men. "There is still work to do. We don't need to be squabbling among ourselves."

My brother nodded and sat.

A comment about the food started a light banter, but an undercurrent of tension remained. Several times during the hour, Kaaluk left the table. Silence followed until he returned. He shook his head when someone asked if there was any news from Hypor City.

I finished my meal and stood to leave. Exhausted from the grueling day, I needed sleep.

"Don't leave yet, Brynna," Kaaluk said, returning to the table after a brief absence. "You'll want to hear this."

"Good news?" one of the men asked.

"Good and bad. Our plan to expose Delio worked."

"Whose plan? What happened?" I was anxious to know the details.

"Kaal planned the revolt, including the final ploy that brought Delio down," said Leika.

"Was it something to do with the explosions?"

"Yes, and a woman." Leika grinned. "His mistress in fact. She sold Kaal a video of Delio bragging about his scheme to get off the planet. We hacked into the video feed in the Steepchase arena. It was rigged to start once you were outside the gate."

"I heard explosions."

"A little theatrics to get the crowd's attention," added Kaaluk.

"What did Delio say exactly?" I asked.

"He admitted that the starships he'd ordered were only for his family and friends. He also gloated about the stupidity of the council and how he'd manipulated them. His stupidity was neglecting to include his mistress in his getaway plans. It gave her the incentive to betray him. She wanted revenge."

My stomach wrenched as I forced my words. "Did he confess to causing my father's crash?"

"Not directly, but one of the technicians admitted that Delio ordered the disabling of the lander." Jarryd's face flushed in rage then his eyes blinked away tears and he took a deep breath.

Leika put her arm around my shoulder. "The man is a psychopath."

"The guards have rallied in support of the council," continued Kaaluk. "The bad news is that Delio has escaped, along with Prince and his private army."

Where was Calia? Had she fled with her boyfriend?

"I bet they'll leave Hypor," someone commented.

"I promise you they won't get far." Kaaluk's confidence infused the room. The men started to clap and hoot with excitement.

"Let's go get them." One rebel stood, followed by others. They grabbed weapons from the stack opposite then waited for their leader's command.

Kaaluk simply nodded and reached for a long bladed knife and sheath that hung on the wall. "No women." He stopped beside Leika. "You stay here."

"I agree," said Jarryd.

I didn't like the idea of being left behind, but I was too tired to argue.

Leika's face was stony. Weapon in hand, her green eyes challenged the men. "Why do I have to stay?"

"Brynna is exhausted," said Kaaluk. "The other women are vulnerable. I need you here in case anything goes wrong." He gripped his sister's shoulder gently. "Please."

Her lips tightened as she struggled with his request but she finally nodded and propped her weapon by the door. When the men had left, she joined me. "Damn, Kaal. He's always right."

"Everyone seems to respect him." During dinner, I'd been surprised by Kaaluk's democratic approach to sharing information. No one else had left the table. They'd all waited for him to report the unfolding events.

"My brother is used to giving orders and having them obeyed," said Leika. "No one ever opposes him. Somehow he convinces you that doing what he says is the best option. Generally, I think he's a good leader, but I don't like to be discounted because I'm a woman."

"I agree. I haven't got your fighting skills, but I can still contribute."

Leika sighed. "Let's hope they catch them all. It's good to have Delio's deception exposed, but we still have to find an answer for the solar threat."

"Hopefully, the council and the scientists will find a solution." I put up my hand to cover a yawn.

"It's outside my area of expertise." Leika gave me a gentle push toward our sleeping quarters when I yawned again. "You'd better get some rest. We have a lot to talk about, including Steepchase."

She wasn't going to let me off easy. She'd want the truth

about my win, which was something I wasn't sure of myself. Had I really killed the swimmers with my voice?

Oblivious to the rusted walls and broken windows, I fell onto layers of soft blankets. They folded around me like a welcoming cocoon.

"Enjoy it while it lasts," Leika said from the doorway.

"Don't go yet." I rose on an elbow. "I want to hear about your escape from the laundry."

"I guess we both have stories to tell," she replied. "Get some sleep. We'll talk later."

∼

"Wake up, sleepy head." Leika whipped back my warm cover, exposing me to cold briny air.

"Some friend you are." I tugged at my blanket but she held firm. "I didn't sleep well."

"I know. I heard you moaning. Nightmares?"

I nodded. "About Steepchase."

"Might help to talk about it later. But now, you'll miss all the news if you don't get up."

"What news?" I shivered then quickly donned the tunic and tights I'd thrown off the night before.

"Kaal and Jarryd are back." Her voice teased. "That's all I'll say for now."

I straightened my wrinkled clothes as best I could and ran my fingers through my hair. The knots would need some time to comb out, but they'd have to wait for later. The news was more important. I hopped on one foot, tugging on my boot as I followed Leika to the kitchen area.

Weaving my way through the crowd of people wasn't easy, but the happy rumble of voices was a tonic. Hearty hugs and back slapping accompanied jubilant cheers. I scanned the jubilant throng, finally locating my brother. Kaaluk stood beside him, smiling with the other men, but his eyes looked weary. When he saw me he nudged Jarryd. The next moment I was wrapped in my brother's arms.

He smirked when we separated. "Are you okay? You look like you've been dragged through a hedge."

I glanced at Kaaluk when he joined us. Had he noticed my ragged appearance?

I flushed, but stood straight and regally—I hoped. "Never mind what I look like, what's happened?"

"Premier Delio is dead," said Jarryd.

"That's good news." Leika pumped her fists in the air, threw her arms around her brother then Jarryd.

My relief at the death of the premier was short lived when I saw Jarryd and Kaaluk exchange concerned glances.

"There's more, isn't there?" I squinted at Jarryd. "What aren't you telling us?"

Leika backed away from the men. "What is it, Kaal? What's the bad news?"

"Premier Delio was killed by his son." Kaaluk appeared as puzzled as the rest of us.

"Killed by his son?" Leika echoed incredulously.

"How?" I knew the Little Prince could be cruel, but to kill his own father was pure evil.

"I couldn't believe my eyes," said Jarryd. "We found them loading into landers at an outlying Hypor dome. We exchanged fire, but their guns were bigger so we hovered behind the curve of the dome, waiting until they took to the air. When the first one alighted, our landers engaged. Their final lander remained on the ground." He nodded to Kaaluk, who continued the story.

"I recognized Prince's uniform and saw him dive into the vehicle. A man emerged from the dome. Older, wearing a red robe. It was the premier. He ran toward his son. As his father reached the lander, Prince lifted his gun and fired. The older man crumpled to the ground. Prince's lander took off. We gave chase, but it was too quick for us."

"He escaped." Jarryd shook his head.

Kaaluk sighed heavily. "I knew his father was abusive when Prince was a kid. He let it slip one night after a few drinks at Swigs. The situation must have been worse than I imagined. Prince Delio is a more ruthless adversary than his father ever was. We have to find him before he gets reinforcements and returns to attack Hypor City."

"Why Hypor City? Won't he make for Tarvek and try to get off-planet?" asked Leika.

"If we're lucky," said Kaaluk. "Unfortunately, he boasted that his destiny was to rule Hypor. Now that his father is dead, we can't discount his desire to control the city." Kaaluk's eyes hardened, his cheekbones sharpened as his mouth tightened. "We're taking a force to find him before that happens."

"I want to go as well." I moved to get ready but Jarryd grasped my hand.

"There's more I have to tell you." He dragged two chairs to a corner of the kitchen. As we faced one another, his eyes clouded. Sadness dragged down the corners of his mouth.

Others around us maintained their distance as if sensing that we needed privacy.

"I know that Father is dead." My acknowledgment left an emptiness in my chest. So much had happened that I'd had little time to mourn his passing. But I knew that he'd want us to attend to the living, namely Mother.

Jarryd drew a long, staggered breath and closed his eyes as if trying to block out an unwelcome vision.

"What else?" I watched uncertainty and pain wrinkle his brow.

"Weyland is missing. He was transported a few weeks after you were betrayed by Calia." He wiped one eye with a shaky hand and dropped his head to his chest. "And Marta..."

"What about her?" I leaned forward, clasping his trembling hands in mine.

"After the lander incident, she was abducted from her home, along with her mother. We think they were sent to Prima Feminary."

His words dropped like stones in my heart. First Father dead, now Weyland and Marta missing.

My stomach twisted in fear. "What about Mother?" I couldn't bear the thought of losing her too. "If Marta's mother has been transported, they might search our island. Mother isn't safe there."

"If what Kaaluk said is true, Prince will be preparing to attack Hypor City. Tarvek is his ally. I think he'll make for Nuvega to regroup. There's no reason for him to go to our island."

The logic of his words didn't quell my fear. "I'd feel better knowing she's okay."

"Knowing who is okay?" Leika squatted beside me and glanced from me to Jarryd. "I'm sorry about your friends. Kaaluk just told me." She laid her hand on Jarryd's. He nodded and returned a weak smile.

"I'm worried about my mother. Prince might go after her."

Kaaluk approached us. His gaze skimmed Jarryd and Leika before settling on me. His head tilted slightly, his green eyes questioning.

Challenged by his attention, I lifted my chin and locked

my gaze with his. I hesitated, anchored for a moment by a wave of pleasure that coursed through my body. Did he feel it too?

"Did you want to ask me something?" His soft words unlocked my silence.

I tried to break eye contact, but couldn't. "I want...I want to take a lander to our island tomorrow, to find my mother."

When he didn't answer immediately, my resolve stiffened. I broke the connection, prepared for an argument, but then he spoke, "Can you fly a lander?"

I gulped. "N...No." I rapidly thought of an alternative. "Jarryd can take me."

All eyes focused on Jarryd. He stared at me as if to gauge my earnestness.

"If Kaal agrees, I'll check the island. Once we're sure Mother is safe, I'll rejoin the search for Prince."

Emboldened by Jarryd's suggestion, I stared defiantly at Kaaluk.

His eyes crinkled, then softened. "I know what it's like to lose loved ones but I can't spare a lander. You can take the cat."

"What's that?" I wasn't going to be distracted from my mission.

"It's a twin hulled boat. Very fast and quiet." Jarryd looked excited at the prospect.

I didn't relish the idea of another boat ride, but we had to get to the island.

"Thank you," I mumbled.

"What was that?" One corner of Kaaluk's mouth lifted slightly.

"I said thank you."

"You're welcome, little one." His finger stroked my flushed cheek.

Jarryd's eyes narrowed and he glanced at me. I lifted my chin in challenge until he shrugged. With a bemused grin, he joined Kaaluk and the revelers.

Leika slid onto Jarryd's seat. "Kaal senses something special in you." She grinned and I looked away. "Don't be embarrassed. I noticed only because I'm his sister. You're special to him. Please don't hurt him."

"How could I hurt him? I hardly know him." Her remark puzzled me. It seemed improbable that someone like Kaaluk would be affected by anything I did.

"Forget I said anything."

How could I forget her remark and ignore the tiny tingles playing over my skin.

"I wish I could go with you to your island tomorrow," she continued, genuinely concerned.

She'd become like a sister. I'd miss her, but she was a warrior with responsibilities and priorities. I knew she was determined to join the attack force against Prince.

"I'll be fine with Jarryd."

"Yes, he's like Kaal in a way. A strong leader." Admiration filled her voice and her gaze drifted to the two men. "He's more than a friend. We'll miss him." There was a wistful tone to her voice that suggested a deep connection.

"I hope you'll come and visit me on the island when all this is over."

"Of course I will. You and Jarryd are special to me and I'd like to meet your mother."

"Where will you and Kaaluk go?" I dreaded her answer, hoping she'd remain nearby.

"Definitely not Hypor City," she replied. "Our home is in the Windlands northwest of Nuvega City. Our people, the ones who survived the Rising, settled there. We're only a small group, so we have to stick together and try to rebuild our community."

"I thought you were from Hypor. How is it that you ended up here and part of the rebel group?"

"Premier Delio's father betrayed our people. In exchange for valuable minerals, he promised them safety during the flooding. When the oceans swelled, most were unable to escape. He broke his word and let them die." Her sad eyes reflected ancestral pain. "Sound familiar?"

"I'm sorry." I remember reading about the horrific number of deaths during the Rising and what followed. "Is that why you came to live in Hypor City—to find Delio?"

She nodded. "My father was the leader of our tribe. Upon his death, Kaal took his place and continued the promise of revenge for our people. Delio is dead, but Prince stills lives." Her nostrils flared and fierce pride flashed across her face.

Sadness filled my heart. Revenge and death. There was a weight to carry when you took a life. It was something I now understood.

"Enough about Delio." I shook my head to shed my heavy mood. "You haven't told me how you escaped from the laundry."

"And you haven't told me how you won Steepchase."

I laughed when Leika's eyebrows almost reached her hairline. "You first. I insist."

"Okay." She took a breath. "Once Steepchase started, Kaal led a group of rebels and invaded the laundry. Pig had only assigned three security guards to watch the laundry. They were easily overpowered. I left with Kaal, but our men stayed to protect the women in case things went sideways."

"An easy escape then."

"Yes, but not for Pig. Once Delio's intentions were exposed in the video at the Steepchase arena, Pig rushed back to the laundry. I guess he thought he'd be safe in his office. But the twins were waiting for him. One of our men told me that four women pitched Pig into a washing vat and started it up."

I winced, imagining what the metal agitators would do to a human body.

"A fitting end, but I'm glad I didn't see it. I prefer simpler methods." She patted the side of her boot where she kept her knife. "Now your turn." She stretched her legs and crossed her arms. "Tell me how you won Steepchase."

The aroma of hot food hit my nostrils. "Let's eat first. I promise to tell you in private after dinner."

"I'll make sure you do," she promised as we followed our noses.

An hour later, we left the kitchen and headed back to the women's section.

Leika sprawled across one end of my bedding while I sat cross-legged at the other. "Don't leave anything out."

As I regaled her with each Steepchase challenge, she probed for details, but went silent when I described the guard's attack on Ruby. She agreed that Pig probably ordered the men to kill her, then she looked puzzled. "How did you escape the guards? Why didn't they attack you?"

Her final question was the only one that mattered and the most difficult to answer. How could I explain what I didn't fully understand?

"I think I killed the guards with my voice."

She didn't look surprised, just curious. "Our elders said that singers were healers."

"That's true, but somehow my voice is different. My high notes have an unusual effect."

The rest came out fast. I told her about the drone in the

forest. I was certain now that my voice had something to do with it veering away. Also, Weyland's reaction to my high notes. "Using my voice underwater against the swimmers was an act of desperation. Self-protection."

"But it worked." Leika sat up. "Is that why you're having nightmares?"

"Yes, I keep seeing their bodies." I wiped my hand over my eyes.

"Your voice is a weapon, a powerful one."

Leika's words troubled me. I'd been trained as a healer yet the truth was that I'd used my voice to defend myself and my actions had resulted in two deaths.

Heavy footsteps approached along the hall. Jarryd appeared in the doorway. "You'd better get some rest, Bryn. We have to be up in a few hours."

"Okay." My answer was automatic.

"Does Jarryd know about your voice?" she asked when we were alone again. "It's a good advantage to have."

"He's worried about Marta and Weyland. We haven't had an opportunity to discuss Steepchase." I scraped my lower lip with my teeth. "Honestly, I'm not sure how to tell him about my voice. It's been a secret for so long."

Leika nodded, then stood and strode to her bed. From a leather satchel, she removed the diary and tossed it into my lap.

"You'd better have this back; you might need it." She gave me a final hug. "Look after yourself tomorrow."

27

THE SECOND DIARY

As the night progressed, the glow of a full moon filled the metal-walled room with eerie light.

The soft rhythmic breathing of the other women didn't dispel my unease. I dreaded the dream that might come but sleep eluded me. Instead, the underwater scenario replayed incessantly in my brain, always culminating in the image of Ruby's inert body.

I was still awake when morning light brightened the hideout. Pushing aside the images that had plagued me during the night, I focused on my purpose.

Leika had placed some clean clothes and a comb by my bed. After dressing, I pushed the diary into my boot and joined Jarryd in the kitchen. I expected we'd be alone, given the early hour, and was surprised when Kaaluk strolled into the room.

"You look better today. More rested than yesterday." He grinned as he spoke and Jarryd laughed.

I felt the blush and decided not to reply. When he sat beside me, my body grew hot and tense.

"Do you have a safe docking area on your island?" he asked Jarryd.

"There's a beach near an abandoned mill. It's a short walk to our house. Bryn can do a quick check of the house and meet me in the village. I'm sure that's where Mother will be."

"No." Kaaluk shook his head. "Stay together. We still don't know where Prince has gone."

"I doubt he'd come near here," insisted Jarryd. "He's probably hundreds of miles away by now."

"Some of his guards might be nearby." Kaaluk grasped Jarryd's arm. "We've all lost family members. You mustn't take chances with Brynna's life."

Jarryd stood abruptly, bristling at the warning. "Don't worry. I can take care of my own." He stowed his breakfast dishes in the sink and moved to retrieve a weapon.

Kaaluk remained at my side. His soft breath caressed my neck as he leaned toward me. "Don't let your brother's confidence overwhelm your feminine instincts. I trust Leika's and you should trust yours."

Heat rushed to my cheeks when I heard the concern in his voice. I looked up into warm green eyes.

"Take care of yourself, little one." He rose from the table, leaving behind a cold emptiness.

My throat clogged with sadness. Would I ever see him again?

∽

"ALL ABOARD," JARRYD JOKED AS I STEPPED ONTO THE swaying deck of the cat, having braved a creaky descent in the outside lift.

"How long will it take to get home?"

"About half an hour, then we'll be on home turf."

Our progress was smooth on the still ocean. The boat's speed was impressive and I made the journey without feeling queasy. My heart swelled when the verdant profile of my beloved forest rose in the distance. Jarryd pulled alongside an old dock near the deserted beach on the far side of the island, in the shade of a flank of tall oaks.

Jumping onto familiar soil, I felt a surge of strength and courage. I jogged into the forest and inhaled the clean comforting air.

"Maybe Kaal is right. Maybe we should stick together," said Jarryd.

I wondered about my brother's change of mind until I saw him searching the sky.

"There might be drones nearby. We can check the house together then go to the village."

Being on home turf, I was feeling bold. "It will be faster if we split up. I'll check the house and meet you in the village. It shouldn't take long." I didn't wait for his reply but set off along the path to the greenhouse.

The familiar trail gave me confidence and I quickened my pace, but when the structure came into view I stopped. Shielding behind a tree, I noticed a broken window pane, then another. From my vantage point, it appeared that most of the glass was either cracked or broken, whereas they'd been previously intact.

My pulse quickened as I crouched and ran through the vegetable garden toward Mother's sanctuary. I squatted along one wall, hoping to hear her hum or her voice as she spoke to her plants, but there was only silence. A searching peek through broken spears of glass confirmed that the greenhouse was empty.

Fear for Mother urged me on toward home. I froze when I spied the charred remains of my childhood home.

The back door, usually familiar and welcoming, hung haphazardly on its hinges, splintered and open. Again, there was only silence as I crept over the kitchen threshold carefully avoiding broken shards of pottery. Anger filled my chest when I recognized shattered pieces of Mother's favorite stewing pot.

The fire had consumed the walls and roof. The acrid odor of destruction tainted every breath. Bits of furniture poked blackened fingers among the ashes. Nothing had survived the brutal assault. I prodded piles of ashes, thankful to find no human remains, all the time praying that Mother had found refuge in the village.

I left the deserted house. Where was Mother? Was she dead? Then I thought of Circe. Panicked, I headed for the mews, terrified of what I'd find.

A weak squawk filled me with hope. Inside the dim shed, I was horrified by the sight of Father's bird who hung headless and broken from the wire mesh. Frantic, I searched for Circe.

Wild eyes watched me from a wooden crossbeam at the peak of the enclosure. Thankfully, she was alive. I retrieved the old water bottle that hung on the wall, pleased to hear a swish. I hummed and pulled on a gauntlet. Circe hesitated then fluttered from her perch and landed unsteadily on my arm. She meekly accepted the water I dribbled into her beak. Her trust filled me with joy that our bond was still strong and with relief that my falcon had survived.

Leaving the mews, I took one final glance at my past, wondering if I would ever return, then sped toward the forest. There was one last stop I had to make before rejoining Jarryd.

I settled Circe on a low rocky point then bounded up the familiar path toward my favorite perch. I didn't stop at the top but shimmied along the tiny ledge toward the cave opening. Inside, nothing had changed except perhaps for added layer of dust.

I had to find the second diary, but without Weyland's help, I wasn't sure I could. Experience told me to concentrate on the area around the bed where he'd located the first diary. Time was precious, but I moved my hands slowly over the pile of books, hoping I'd feel something. I was about to give up when my knee nudged the side of the bed. The thin mattress slid sideways, revealing a faded red corner. I gently tugged the diary from its hiding place.

This time, the impression on the cover was more distinct. I ran my fingers around the outline, identifying the same circular pattern. I flipped the book over. On the back cover was a clearly defined falcon.

I stiffened when a faint shriek penetrated the cave entrance. I recognized Circe's danger warning. I thrust the diary into my right boot, then crept toward to the cave entrance. I now had both diaries, one in each boot, but they were only of use if I could avoid detection. There was only way out—and in.

In cautious silence I approached the bright opening, sliding my body along the cool stone wall. I leaned forward to view the ledge. From a crevice on my right, a gloved hand thrust from the darkness and covered my mouth, while the other grabbed my hands.

I was trapped.

Fighting against the vice-like grip was futile. I twisted in an attempt to identify my captor but all I could see was his helmet. He dragged me from the cave onto the thin ledge. I struggled but froze when he stopped and thrust my body over the cliff edge. All I could see was the terrifying drop below. I stopped writhing. He pulled me back and we continued down the path.

At forest level, I continued to fight my captor, kicking his shins relentlessly. He wasn't fazed so I tried a different tactic. At the first opportunity, I bit hard into his hand. That got his attention.

"You hell-born babe," he yelped in pain and shoved me away from him.

Another one of Delio's guards grabbed my arms and bound them.

"Let me go." My predictable demand yielded predictable results. The man held me tighter.

"Bring her over here," a bald man ordered. "Commander Delio will want this one." His leer resembled one I'd seen on Pig. "If he doesn't, I know what to do with her."

A harsh squeal ripped the air.

Claws extended, Circe swooped down and raked his scalp.

"Kill that bird," he screamed, mopping at the blood that trickled into his eyebrow.

I forced a whistle through dry lips and watched my falcon soar in response. She was quickly out of range of their blasters.

"Gag her," Baldy commanded.

I lunged sideways, avoiding the hands that reached for my head.

Another guard threw off his helmet and surged forward. "Leave Princess Bokk to me." It was the malevolent one I'd encountered with Calia on the seventh floor.

"You—"

"Yes," he sneered. "Your Father's dead. We burned your

house and we've got your Mother. She's on her way to Prima Feminary. Now it's your turn."

Weakened by the truths he uttered, I stumbled back. Mother's words resounded in my brain. 'Your voice is your power' triggered an impulse I couldn't ignore. I dreaded using my voice again. I didn't want to kill, but it was my only weapon. I inhaled deeply and let my voice soar. The tone was high and clear.

One by one, the men stumbled, dropped their weapons and lifted their hands to their ears. Six pairs of eye rolled back in anguished faces as they screamed. Like dominos, they crumbled and fell, their bodies splayed awkwardly on the ground. The nearest one had a red halo starting to form as blood seeped from his ears and eyes.

I slowly surveyed the bodies scattered on the ground. There was no movement. The face closest to me was twisted in grotesque agony. Clenched fists hung from contorted limbs. His skin was spotted with red dots as if blood had penetrated every pore

Farther back, the other men's faces appeared less tormented, but their limbs jutted unnaturally from their sides as if reaching for ears now caked in blood.

Retrieving a knife from the nearest body, I freed my hands. I turned away from the carnage. Sick with horror, I doubled over and emptied my stomach. When the retching stopped, I wiped my mouth.

Exhausted, I closed my eyes and inhaled deeply, trying to rebuild my energy. I knew I had to go, run, find Jarryd and Mother and get off the island, but I was paralyzed by the enormity of what I'd done.

The first time underwater had been an instinctive defensive reflex. I hadn't anticipated killing two men. This time, my actions had been intentional, fueled by fear and revenge. I'd killed six men.

My stomach roiled again. Had they deserved to die?

Compassion left me conflicted until I remembered my father's fate and the burned-out shell of our beloved family home. My back stiffened as I accepted responsibility for what I'd done.

Circe's cry alerted me to danger.

"This way," a man yelled from the woods on my right. "Check over there near the rocks."

The harsh male voice sent blood pounding in my head. How many more guards were there? I crouched and headed into the forest toward a hollowed oak tree. Hiding inside, I waited trying to determine my best escape route.

"Bodies over here," one guard's voice cut through the trees behind me. "Looks like they're all dead."

"Certainly this ugly-faced brute," called another man. "Never liked him."

"This guy has a pulse. And this one."

They were checking all the bodies.

"Except for the nasty brute, they're all alive."

I gasped. Except for the one who had been closest to me, my voice hadn't killed the men, just stunned them. I stored that fact away for later examination.

"No signs of any wounds. I wonder what killed him?"

The men were clustered around the awakening bodies, now was the time to escape.

"Split up and search for the attacker. He can't be far away."

I could hear shouts behind me, but my feet had wings. I darted from my hideout and dodged through the underbrush. Finding Jarryd and the boat was uppermost in my mind. Mother's life might depend on it—if she was still alive.

I swiped away the tears that blurred my view.

Two hundred feet beyond, I spied another guard and flattened to the ground. With toes and elbows, I inched to the edge of the forest and rolled into a small meadow of tall grass.

The dewy vegetation turned my clothing into a cold sodden blanket as I lay motionless on my belly. In the surrounding forest, the crackle of twigs and the crunch of feet on decaying underbrush warned of men approaching.

"This way," a guard nearby yelled. "They've found them."

I held my breath as footsteps pounded across the terrain fifty feet from where I hid. I curled into a ball, expecting at any moment to feel the angry prod of a weapon, but the boots passed my location. Finally, there was silence.

I rose to my knees and glanced ahead. The way was clear.

Scrambling to my feet, I hunched as I ran. The island was home ground and I knew the best route to get to the dock where Jarryd had hidden the boat. Strong and fast from my Steepchase training, I was confident that I could outpace the guards.

As I neared the water, I tried to ignore thoughts of Mother and Jarryd that lingered at the edge of my mind, but it was hard to contend with the trepidation and sadness. There was no time for reflection, only survival and freedom mattered. Without them, I couldn't find Jarryd and save Mother.

My acute hearing detected a soft whoosh to my left.

Too late. I felt a prick in the side of my neck. What was happening?

Circe cried out overhead as my hand swiped at the stinging invader.

My legs buckled. Flaccid muscles refused to respond.

As I fell to the ground, a shadowy outline approached. Who was he?

Lethargy staged the world in bizarre slow motion as I watched the figure through blurry eyes. Questions scrambled my dulled senses.

What about Mother and Jarryd?

Would I ever see my family and friends again? Or Circe?

As my senses dimmed, a gravelly voice commanded. "Take her to the ship."

THIS IS THE END OF BRYNNA'S JOURNEY SO FAR...

HER ADVENTURE CONTINUES IN *THE LOST PROPHECY*, THE FALCON CHRONICLES BOOK 2.

Don't forget to sign up for The Falcon Chronicles newsletter. See details on the next page.

Here's what Amazon reviewers are saying...

"...lots of plot twists and turns to keep you reading."

"Adventure and intrigue abound...Love this author's voice!"

Reviews are important to authors and much appreciated. If you enjoyed this book, please consider leaving a **review** on Amazon or Goodreads.

THE FALCON CHRONICLES NEWS

Please visit my website (marjorielindsey.com) to sign up for the latest news about special book offers and for details about *THE LOST PROPHECY* - **The Falcon Chronicles Book 2.**

Copyright © 2017 by Marjorie Lindsey

All rights reserved.

No part of this book may be reproduced in any form or by any electronic or mechanical means, including information storage and retrieval systems, without written permission from the author, except for the use of brief quotations in a book review.

The Last Singer is a work of fiction. Names, characters, places and incidents are the product of the author's imagination or are used fictitiously, and any resemblance to actual persons, living or dead, events or locales is entirely coincidental.

Book cover copyright Marjorie Lindsey

ISBN 978-1-988787-00-8 (ebook)

ISBN 978-1-988787-01-5 (print)

This book is dedicated to my husband for all his love and support.

Thanks to my friend/author Jacqui for her encouragement and generosity from the beginning.

Thank you also to Joan, Alan, Therese and other friends/readers for their valuable feedback.

Finally, thank you to my editor Laura for her professional insights and guidance.

Marjorie's new book *The Last Singer* is the first in her teen/young adult series *The Falcon Chronicles*.

For further information:
www.marjorielindsey.com
marjorie@marjorielindsey.com

Made in the USA
Middletown, DE
07 December 2017